DRAGON'S FIN SOUP

DRAGON'S FIN SOUP

Eight Modern Siamese Fables

S.P. Somtow

DIPLODOCUS PRESS • BANGKOK • LOS ANGELES

This is a work of fiction. All of the characters and events portrayed are either products of the author's imagination or are used fictitiously.

Copyright © 1998, © 2013 by Somtow Sucharitkul

All rights reserved, including the right to reproduce this book,
or portions thereof, in any form, except for review.

First edition: 2000, Babbage Press
Second Edition: Asia Books, 2007
Third Edition: Diplodocus Press, November 2013

ISBN 978-0-9860533-4-4

*Dedicated to my mother,
who has refused to translate some of
them into Thai on the grounds that Thais
would consider them too mundane.*

Contents

In the House of the Spirits
An introduction by S. P. Somtow   9

Dragon's Fin Soup   15

Lottery Night   54

The Steel American   89

Chui Chai   113

The Bird Catcher   133

Diamonds Aren't Forever   174

Fiddling for Water Buffaloes   208

The Last Time I Died in Venice   245

Glossary   265

S. P. Somtow: A Brief Biography   269

The stories in this book are set in a Bangkok that doesn't exist. They are fiction. Locations of streets, addresses and so on have all been jumbled up so you could never find any of these places even if you wanted to. All personages, events, and places are either the creation of this author, or uses fictitiously. That is to say, nothing in this book is true. Nothing at all. I made it up. Similarities between anything here and anything in the real world are incredibly unlikely, and nevertheless entirely coincidental. Sorry. I wish I could live in a fiction, too, but I don't.

In the House of the Spirits

In my semi-autobiographical novel, *Jasmine Nights*, a young boy is growing up in a huge, baroquely-fantastical family estate in Bangkok, surrounded by eccentric relatives and weird architecture. There are servants, a polygamous patriarch, dangerous liaisons galore, and the odd supernatural event.

The fictional estate is actually a conflation of two different estates of my grandfather's in the city of Thonburi, where he actually did live, surrounded by wives, concubines, and mistresses, much as described in my novel. The other estate was part of my mother's inheritance. It was there that I actually lived. There was a huge mango orchard, a small artificial lake with a pavilion, a ruined house where I played, and the main house, also known as the Blue House, one of those rambling, wooden structures that are often seen in historical movies about the British Raj.

Thailand is a country with more ghosts than people. The belief in the omnipresence of spirits comes from animism, the dominant tribal religion in the region in the days before the inhabitants of the peninsula were converted to Buddhism by the missionary zeal of King Ashoka. Today, the house I grew up in is a multi-storey condominium, and across the street is a high-tech techno-rave establishment frequented by teenagers. But the spirit population hasn't gone down.

Recently, for instance, a woman threw herself off the top floor of my aunt's office building. My aunt immediately engaged an exorcist to appease the *phii tai hong*. That is, the vengeful ghost of someone who has died violently. It was as normal a thing to do as hiring a new secretary or putting in new filing cabinets.

I wrote a short story—which you will read in this collection–about a Thai boy and American boy who spend the night in a cemetery in order to get a winning lottery number from the spirits. Since it's the night before the results are announced, there's a whole convention's worth of people in the graveyard all camped out. The boys encounter a *phii krasue*, which is a monster consisting of a decapitated head with trailing guts, slithering around using its tongue as a pseudopod. They are briefly transported into heaven for an encounter with the Thai boy's dead great-aunt.

Now, here's the point I'm making. A friend of mine was teaching a course in modern-fantastic literature in Arizona, and he had a Thai student in the

Dragon's Fin Soup

class. This is one of the stories he had the students read. The young man from Thailand couldn't figure out why he had to read my story. "There is," he said to my friend, "no fantasy element in it." This, you must understand, is the prevailing atmosphere in the land where I grew up, so any real-life incidents I relate here must be understood in that context. Everybody knew that the Blue House was haunted. That it was a magical place where the rules were somewhat fuzzier than elsewhere. Ghosts were common. Everyone sees ghosts all the time in Thailand anyway, but they loved to congregate at the Blue House, especially on the veranda which overlooked the garden and which was always permeated with the sickly-sweet odor of *phuttachat*, a night-blooming jasmine.

My bedroom looked out over this veranda, and shortly after my great-grandmother's death (the servants having gossiped for days about a black cat having leapt out of her funeral pyre) I did have occasion to see her, hovering in mid-air, at the window, gibbering about her will. I was always terrified of my great-grandmother when I was little. She had a skeletal face, and her teeth were completely black from chewing betelnut. Her hair was wispy and white. In death, she was even more frightening. I woke up the maid (Thai children of upper class families tend to have a maid sleeping at the foot of their beds) and I screamed, pointed, and shouted; she saw nothing.

The will was never found, and to this day the finances of my late grandparents and step-grandparents are a matter of controversy and conjecture.

Most of the events were less terrifying, though. For instance, I woke up one night to see a winged horse in my room. Not a full-sized one, this one was about the size of my palm. It fluttered about. The night was all softly backlit, and blue and hazy, very Spielbergian in fact; and I was not at all afraid. I got out of bed and followed the mini-Pegasus all over the house until it reached the bedroom of my little sister.

The horse hovered over her pillow, pointing with a front hoof, waiting for something; I don't know. Well, I looked under the pillow and discovered, to my delight, a bright red 100-baht note. (About five dollars in those days). I was amazed at this supernatural largesse. I took the money to school (a British school, mind you) and showed it to all my friends. Around lunchtime, one of the maids came marching into the schoolyard. Everyone had been accused of stealing, and the house was in an uproar. I gave the money back, but my explanation of how I had obtained it never seemed to convince anyone. But how else could I have known that it was there?

All right, here's another event. Back at the British school, the kids a year ahead of me were putting on a production of *A Midsummer Night's Dream*. For a couple of weeks, I had dreams that impelled me to memorize the part of Bottom, even though I had nothing to do with this production. That day, my friend Kwonping Ho, now a big Singapore tycoon, mysteriously fell ill, and I just happened to know the part. And did it, too. Rather badly, as I recall. It's this childhood incident that compelled me, thirty years later, to make a film of *A Midsummer Night's Dream*, so obviously it has haunted me.

The Blue House, indeed, has haunted me all my life. Shortly after my tenth birthday, we moved away to a modern, split-level, American-style home. Since then, I have never experienced any supernatural events whatsoever. Oh, perhaps a slight *frisson* now and then, but never the real thing.

What you are about to read, then, are stories produced by someone crushed between the Scylla and Charybdis of conflicting cultures. It took me years before I started to write stories about Thailand; my initial forays into the field of fiction were all quite white bread in their own way. I was afraid to be identified as an "ethnic" writer, and for years I got away with being culturally uncommitted.

It was Frederik Pohl who convinced me to try it, and my story *Fiddling for Water Buffaloes* was the first of eight stories that deal, in different ways, with my cultural schizophrenia.

It's an ongoing adventure.

Dragon's Fin Soup

At the heart of Bangkok's Chinatown, in the district known as Yaowaraj, there is a restaurant called the Rainbow Café which, every Wednesday, features a blue plate special they call dragon's fin soup. Though little known through most of its hundredyear existence, the café enjoyed a brief flirtation with fame during the early 1990s because of an article in the *Bangkok Post* extolling the virtues of the *specialité de la maison*. The article was written by the enigmatic UengAng Thalay, whose true identity few had ever guessed. It was only I and a few close friends who knew that UengAng was actually a Chestertonian American named Bob Halliday, exconcert pianist and *Washington Post* book critic, who had fled the mundane madness of the western world for the more fantastical, cuttingedge madness of the Orient. It was only in Bangkok, the bastard daughter of feudalism and futurism, that Bob had finally been able to be himself, though what himself was, he alone seemed to know.

But we were speaking of the dragon's fin soup.

Perhaps I should quote the relevant section of Ueng Ang's article:

> *Succulent! Aromatic! Subtle! Profound! Transcendental! These are but a few of the adjectives your skeptical food columnist has been hearing from the clients of the Rainbow Café in Yaowaraj as they rhapsodize about the mysterious dish known as dragon's fin soup, served only on Wednesdays. Last Wednesday your humble columnist was forced to try it out. The restaurant is exceedingly hard to find, being on the third floor of the only building still extant from before the Chinatown riots of 1945. There is no sign, either in English or Thai, and as I cannot read Chinese, I cannot say whether there is one in that language either. On Wednesday afternoons, however, there are a large number of official-looking Mercedes and BMWs double-parked all the way down the narrow soi, and dozens of uniformed chauffeurs leaning warily against their cars; so, unable to figure out the restaurant's location from the hastily scrawled fax I had received from a friend of mine who works at the Ministry of Education, I decided to follow the luxury cars ... and my nose ... instead. The alley became narrower and shabbier. Then, all of a sudden, I turned a corner, and found myself joining a line of people, all dressed to the teeth, snaking singlefile up the rickety wooden steps into the small, un-airconditioned, and decidedly unassuming restaurant. It was a kind of timetravel. This was not the Bangkok we all know, the Bangkok of insane traffic jams, of smörgåsbord sexuality, of iridescent skyscrapers and stagnant canals. The people in line all waited patiently; when I was finally ushered inside, I*

found the restaurant to be as quiet and as numinous as a Buddhist temple. Old men with floorlength beards played mah jongg; a woman in a cheongsam directed me to a table beneath the solitary ceiling fan; the menu contained not a word of Thai or English. Nevertheless, without my having to ask, a steaming bowl of the notorious soup was soon served to me, along with a cup of pipinghot chrysanthemum tea.

At first I was conscious only of the dish's bitterness, and I wondered whether its fame was a hoax or I, as the only pale-faced rube in the room, was actually being proffered a bowl full of microwaved Robitussin. Then, suddenly, it seemed to me that the bitterness of the soup was a kind of veil or filter through which its true taste, too overwhelming to be perceived directly, might be enjoyed ... rather as the dark glasses one must wear in order to gaze directly at the sun. But as for the taste itself, it cannot truly be described at all. At first I thought it must be a variant of the familiar shark's fin, perhaps marinated in some geriatric wine. But it also seemed to partake somewhat of the subtle tang of bird's nest soup, which draws its flavor from the coagulated saliva of cave-dwelling swallows. I also felt a kind of coldness in my joints and extremities, the tingling sensation familiar to those who have tasted fugu, *the elusive and expensive Japanese puffer fish, which, improperly prepared, causes paralysis and death within minutes. The dish tasted like all these things and none of them, and I found, for the first time in my life, my jaundiced tongue confounded and bewildered. I asked the beautiful longhaired waitress in the* cheongsam *whether she could answer a few questions about the dish; she said, "Certainly, as long as I don't have to divulge any of the ingredients, for they are an ancient family secret." She spoke an antique and grammatically quaint sort of Thai, as though she had never watched television, listened to pop songs, or hung out in the myriad coffee shops of the city. She saw my surprise and went on in English, "It's not my first language, you see; I'm a lot more comfortable in English."*

"Berkeley?" I asked her, suspecting a hint of Northern California in her speech.

She smiled broadly then, and said, "Santa Cruz, actually. It's a relief to meet another American around here; they don't let me out much since I came home from college."

"American?"

"Well, I'm a dual national. But my great-grandparents were forty-niners. Gold rush Chinks. My name's Janice Lim. Or Lam or Lin, take your pick."

"Tell me then," I inquired, "since you can't tell me what's in the soup … why is it that you only serve it on Wednesdays?"

"Wednesday, in Thai, is Wan Phutth … *the day of Buddha. My parents feel that dragon's flesh should only be served on that day of the week that is sacred to the Lord Buddha, when we can reflect on the transitory nature of our existence."*

* * *

At this point it should be pointed out that I, your narrator, am the woman with the long hair and the *cheongsam*, and that Bob Halliday has, in his article, somewhat exaggerated my personal charms. I shall not

Dragon's Fin Soup

exaggerate his. Bob is a large man; his girth has earned him the sobriquet of "Elephant" among his Thai friends. He is an intellectual; he speaks such languages as Hungarian and Cambodian as well as he does Thai, and he listens to Lulu and *Wozzeck* before breakfast. For relaxation, he curls up with Umberto Eco, and I don't mean Eco's novels, I mean his academic papers on semiotics. Bob is a rabid agoraphobe, and flees as soon as there are more than about ten people at a party. His friends speculate endlessly about his sex life, but in fact he seems to have none at all.

Because he was the only American to have found his way to the Rainbow Café since I returned to Thailand from California, and because he seemed to my father (my mother having passed away in childbirth) to be somehow unthreatening, I found myself spending a great deal of time with him when I wasn't working at the restaurant. My Aunt Lingling, who doesn't speak a word of Thai or English, was the official chaperone; if we went for a quiet cup of coffee at the Regent, for example, she was to be found a couple of tables away, sipping a glass of chrysanthemum tea.

It was Bob who taught me what kind of a place Bangkok really was. You see, I had lived until the age of 18 without ever setting foot outside our family compound. I had had a tutor to help me with my English. We had one hour of television a day, the news; that was how I had learned Thai. My father was obsessed with our family's purity; he never used our dearly bought, royally granted Thai surname of Suntharapornsunthornpanich, but insisted on signing all documents Sae Lim, as though the Great Integration of the Chinese had never occurred and our people were still a nation within a nation, still loyal to the vast and distant Middle Kingdom. My brave new world had been California, and it remained for Bob to show me that an even braver one had lain at my doorstep all my life.

Bangkoks within Bangkoks. Yes, that charmingly hackneyed metaphor of the Chinese boxes comes to mind. Quiet palaces with pavilions that overlooked reflecting ponds. Galleries hung with postmodern art. Japanesestyle coffee houses with melonflavored ice cream floats and individual shrimp pizzas. Grungy noodle stands beneath flimsy awnings over open sewers; stratospherically upscale French *patisseries* and Italian *gelaterias*. Bob knew where they all were, and he was willing to share all his secrets, even though Aunt Lingling was always along for the ride. After a time, it seemed to me that perhaps it was my turn to reveal some secret, and so one Sunday afternoon, in one of the coffee lounges overlooking the atrium of the Sogo shopping mall, I decided to tell him the biggest of all secrets. "Do you really want to know," I said, "why we only serve the dragon fin soup on Wednesdays?"

"Yes," he said, "and I promise I won't print it."

"Well you see," I said, "it takes about a week for the tissue to regenerate."

* * *

That was about as much as I could safely say without spilling the whole can of soup. The dragon had been in our family since the late Ming Dynasty, when a multi-multi-great-uncle of mine, a eunuch who was the Emperor's trade representative between Peking and the Siamese Kingdom of Ayuthaya, had tricked him into following his junk all the way down the Chao Phraya

Dragon's Fin Soup

River, had imprisoned him beneath the canals of the little village that was later to become Bangkok, City of Angels, Dwelling Place of Vishnu, Residence of the Nine Jewels, and so on so forth (read the *Guinness Book of Records* to obtain the full name of the city) known affectionately to its residents as City of Angels Etc. This was because the dragon had revealed to my multigreatuncle that the seemingly invincible Kingdom of Ayuthaya would one day be sacked by the King of Pegu and that the capital of Siam would be moved down to this unpretentious village in the Chao Phraya delta. The dragon had told him this because, as everyone knows, a mortally wounded dragon, when properly constrained, is obliged to answer three questions truthfully. MultiGreatUncle wasted his other question on trying to find out whether he would ever regain his manhood and be able to experience an orgasm; the dragon had merely laughed at this, and his laughter had caused a minor earthquake which destroyed the summer palace of Lord Kuykendaal, a Dutchman who had married into the lowest echelon of the Siamese aristocracy, which earthquake in turn precipitated the Opium War of 1677, which, as it is not in the history books, remains alive only in our family tradition.

Our family tradition also states that each member of the family may only tell one outsider about the dragon's existence. If he chooses the right outsider, he will have a happy life; if he chooses unwisely, and the outsider turns out to be untrustworthy, then misfortune will dog both the revealer and his confidant.

I wasn't completely sure about Bob yet, and I didn't want to blow my one opportunity. But that evening, as I supervised the ritual slicing of the dragon's fin, my father dropped a bombshell.

The dragon could not, of course, be seen all in one piece. There was, in the kitchen of the Rainbow Café, a hole in one wall, about nine feet in diameter. One coil of the dragon came through this wall and curved upward toward a similar opening in the ceiling. I did not know where the dragon ended or began. One assumed this was a tail section because it was so narrow. I had seen a dragon whole only in my dreams, or in pictures. Rumor had it that this dragon stretched all the way to Nonthaburi, his slender body twisting through ancient sewer pipes and under the foundations of century-old buildings. He was bound to my family by an ancient spell in a scroll that sat on the altar of the household gods, just above the cash register inside the restaurant proper. He was unimaginably old and unimaginably jaded, stunned rigid by three thousands years of human magic, his scales so lusterless that I had to buff them with furniture polish to give them some semblance of draconian majesty. He was, of course, still mortally wounded from the battle he had endured with Multi-Great-Uncle; nevertheless, it takes them a long, long time to die, especially when held captive by a scroll such as the one we possessed.

You could tell the dragon was still alive, though. Once in a very long while, he breathed. Or rather, a kind of rippling welled up him, and you could hear a distant wheeze, like an old house settling on its foundations. And of course, he regenerated. If it wasn't for that, the restaurant would never have stayed in business all these years.

The fin we harvested was a ventral fin and hung down over the main charcoal stove of the restaurant

Dragon's Fin Soup

kitchen. It took some slicing to get it off. We had a new chef, Ah Quoc, just up from Penang, and he was having a lot of trouble. "You'd better heat up the carving knife some more," I was telling him. "Make sure it's red hot."

He stuck the knife back in the embers. Today, the dragon was remarkably sluggish; I had not detected a breath in hours; and the flesh was hard as stone. I wondered whether the event our family dreaded most, the dragon's death, was finally going to come upon us.

"*Muoi, muoi,*" he said, "the flesh just won't give."

"Don't call me *muoi,*" I said. "I'm not your little sister, I'm the boss's daughter. In fact, don't speak Chiuchow at all. English is a lot simpler."

"Okeydoke, Miss Janice. But Chinese or English, meat just no slice, *la.*"

He was hacking away at the fin. The flesh was stony, recalcitrant. I didn't want to use the spell of binding, but I had to. I ran into the restaurant—it was closed and there were only a few old men playing mah jongg—grabbed the scroll from the altar, stormed back into the kitchen and tapped the scaly skin, whispering the word of power that only members of our family can speak. I felt a shudder deep within the dragon's bowels. I put my ear up to the clammy hide. I thought I could hear, from infinitely far away, the hollow clanging of the dragon's heart, the glacial oozing of his blood through kilometer after kilometer of leaden veins and arteries. "Run, blood, run," I shouted, and I started whipping him with the brittle paper.

Aunt Lingling came scurrying in at that moment, a tiny creature in a widow's dress, shouting, "You'll rip the scroll, don't hit so hard!"

But then, indeed, the blood began to roar. "Now you can slice him," I said to Ah Quoc. "Quickly. It has to soak in the marinade for at least twentyfour hours, and we're running late as it is."

"Okay! Knife hot enough now, *la*." Ah Quoc slashed through the whole fin in a single motion, like an imperial headsman. I could see now why my father had hired him to replace Ah Chen, who had become distracted, gone native—even gone so far as to march in the 1992 democracy riots–as if the politics of the Thais were any of our business.

Aunt Lingling had the vat of marinade all ready. Ah Quoc sliced quickly and methodically, tossing the pieces of dragon's fin into the bubbling liquid. With shark's fin, you have to soak it in water for a long time to soften it up for eating. Bob Halliday had speculated about the nature of the marinade. He was right about the garlic and the chilies, but it would perhaps have been unwise to tell him about the sulfuric acid.

It was at that point that my father came in. "The scroll, the scroll," he said distractedly. Then he saw it and snatched it from me.

"We're safe for another week," I said, following him out of the kitchen into the restaurant. Another of my aunts, the emaciated Jasmine, was counting a pile of money, doing calculations with an abacus and making entries into a leatherbound ledger.

My father put the scroll back. Then he looked directly into my eyes—something he had done only once or twice in my adult life—and, scratching his beard, said, "I've found you a husband."

That was the bombshell.

* * *

Dragon's Fin Soup

I didn't feel it was my place to respond right away ... in fact, I was so flustered by his announcement that I had absolutely nothing to say. In a way, I had been expecting it, of course, but for some reason ... perhaps it was because of my time at Santa Cruz ... it just hadn't occurred to me that my father would be so ... so ... old-fashioned about it. I mean, my God, it was like being stuck in an Amy Tan novel or something.

That's how I ended up in Bob Halliday's office at the *Bangkok Post*, sobbing my guts out without any regard for propriety or good manners. Bob, who is a natural empath, allowed me to yammer on and on; he sent a boy down to the market to fetch some steaming noodles wrapped in banana leaves and iced coffee in little PVC bags. I daresay I didn't make too much sense. "My father's living in the nineteenth century ... or worse," I said. "He should never have let me set foot outside the house ... outside the restaurant. I mean, Santa Cruz, for God's sake! Wait till I tell him I'm not even a virgin anymore. The price is going to plummet, he's going to take a bath on whatever deal it is he's drawn up. I'm so mad at him. And even though he did send me to America, he never let me so much as set foot in the Silom Complex, two miles from our house, without a chaperone. I've never had a life! Or rather, I've had two half-lives—half American co-ed, half Chinese dragon lady—I'm like two halfpeople that don't make a whole. And this is Thailand, it's not America and it's not China. It's the most alien landscape of them all."

Later, because I didn't want to go home to face the grisly details of my impending marriage contract, I rode back to Bob's apartment with him in a *tuktuk*. The motorized rickshaw darted skillfully through jammed streets and minuscule alleys and once again—as so often with Bob—I found myself in an area of Bangkok I had never seen before, a district overgrown with weeds and wild banana trees; the *soi* came to an abrupt end and there was a lone elephant, swaying back and forth, being hosed down by a country boy wearing nothing but a *phakomaah*. "You must be used to slumming by now," Bob said, "with all the places I've taken you."

In his apartment, a grizzled cook served up a screamingly piquant *kaeng khieu waan*, and I must confess that though I usually can't stand Thai food, the heat of this sweet green curry blew me away. We listened to Wagner. Bob has the most amazing collection of CDs known to man. He has 12 recordings of *The Magic Flute*, but only three of Wagner's *Ring* cycle—three more than most people I know. "Just listen to that!" he said. I'm not a big fan of opera, but the kind of singing that issued from Bob's stereo sounded hauntingly familiar ... it had the hollow echo of a sound I'd heard that very afternoon, the low and distant pounding of the dragon's heart.

"What is it?" I said.

"Oh, it's the scene where Siegfried slays the dragon," Bob said. "You know, this is the Solti recording, where the dragon's voice is electronically enhanced. I'm not sure I like it."

It sent chills down my spine.

"Funny story," Bob said. "For the original production, you know, in the 1860s ... they had a special dragon built ... in England ... in little segments. They were supposed to ship the sections to Bayreuth for the première, but the neck was accidentally sent to Beirut instead. That dragon never did have a neck.

Imagine those people in Beirut when they opened that crate! What do you do with a disembodied segment of dragon anyway?"

"I could think of a few uses," I said.

"It sets me to thinking about dragon's fin soup."

"No can divulge, *la*," I said, laughing, in my best Singapore English.

The dragon gave out a roar and fell, mortally wounded, in a spectacular orchestral climax. He crashed to the floor of the primeval forest. I had seen this scene once in the Fritz Lang silent film *Siegfried*, which we'd watched in our History of Cinema class at Santa Cruz. After the crash there came more singing.

"This is the fun part, now," Bob told me. "If you approach a dying dragon, it *has* to answer your questions … three questions usually … and it has to answer them truthfully."

"Even if he's been dying for a thousand years?" I said.

"Never thought of that, Janice," said Bob. "You think the dragon's truth-seeing abilities might become a little clouded?"

Despite my long and tearful outpouring in his office, Bob had not once mentioned the subject of my Damoclean doom. Perhaps he was about to raise it now; there was one of those long pregnant pauses that tend to portend portentousness. I wanted to put it off a little longer, so I asked him, "If you had access to a dragon … and the dragon were dying, and you came upon him in just the right circumstances … what *would* you ask him?"

Bob laughed. "So many questions … so much I want to know … so many arcane truths that the cosmos hangs on! ... I think I'd have a lot to ask. Why? You have a dragon for me?"

I didn't get back to Yaowaraj until very late that night. I had hoped that everyone would have gone to bed, but when I reached the restaurant (the family compound itself is reached through a back stairwell beyond the kitchen) I found my father still awake, sitting at the carving table, and Aunt Lingling and Aunt Jasmine stirring the vat of softening dragon's fin. The sulfuric acid had now been emptied and replaced with a pungent brew of vinegar, ginseng, garlic, soy sauce, and the ejaculate of a young boy, obtainable in Patpong for about 100 baht. The whole place stank, but I knew that it would whittle down to the subtlest, sweetest, bitterest, most nostalgic of aromas.

My father said to me, "Perhaps you're upset with me, Janice; I know it was a little sudden."

"Sudden!" I said. "Give me a break, Papa, this was more than sudden. You're so oldfashioned suddenly ... and you're not even that old. Marrying me off like you're cashing in your blue chip stocks or something."

"There's a worldwide recession, in case you haven't noticed. We need an infusion of cash. I don't know how much longer the dragon will hold out. Look, this contract ..." He pushed it across the table. It was in Chinese, of course, and full of flowery and legalistic terms. "He's not the youngest I could have found, but his blood runs pure; he's from the village." The village being, of course, the village of my ancestors, on whose soil my family has not set foot in 700 years.

"What do you mean, not the youngest, Papa?"

"To be honest, he's somewhat elderly. But that's for the best, isn't it? I mean, he'll soon be past, as it were, the age of lovemaking …"

"Papa, I'm not a virgin."

"Oh, not to worry, dear; I had a feeling something like that might happen over there in Californ'… we'll send you to Tokyo for the operation. Their hymen implants are as good as new, I'm told."

My hymen was not the problem. This was probably not the time to tell my father that the deflowerer of my maidenhead had been a young, fast-talking, vigorous, muscular specimen of corn-fed Americana by the name of Linda Horovitz.

"You don't seem very excited, my dear."

"Well, what do you expect me to say?" I had never raised my voice to my father, and I really didn't quite know how to do it.

"Look, I've really worked very hard on this match, trying to find the least offensive person who could meet the minimum criteria for bailing us out of this financial mess—this one, he has a condominium in Vancouver, owns a computer franchise, would probably not demand of you, you know, too terribly degrading a sexual performance—"

Sullenly, I looked at the floor.

He stared at me for a long time. Then he said, "You're in love, aren't you?"

I didn't answer.

My father slammed his fists down on the table. "Those damned lascivious Thai men with their honeyed words and their backstabbing habits … it's one of them, isn't it? My only daughter … and my wife dead in her grave these 22 years … it kills me."

"And what if it *had* been a Thai man?" I said. "Don't we have Thai passports? Don't we have one of those 15syllable Thai names which *your* grandfather purchased from the King? Aren't we living on Thai soil, stewing up our birthright for Thai citizens to eat, depositing our hard-earned Thai 1000-baht bills in a Thai bank?"

He slapped my face.

He had never done that before. I was more stunned than hurt. I was not to feel the hurt until much later.

"Let me tell you, for the four hundredth time, how your grandmother died," he said, so softly I could hardly hear him above the bubbling of the dragon's fin. "My father had come to Bangkok to fetch his new wife and bring her back to Californ'. It was his cousin, my uncle, who managed the Rainbow Café in those days. It was the twenties and the city was cool and quiet and serenely beautiful. There were only a few motorcars in the whole city; one of them, a Ford, belonged to Uncle Shenghua. My father was in love with the City of Angels Etc. and he loved your grandmother even before he set eyes on her. And he never went back to Californ', but moved into this family compound, flouting the law that a woman should move into her husband's home. Oh, he was so much in love! And he believed that here, in a land where men did not look so different from himself, there would be no prejudice—no bars with signs that said *No Dogs or Chinamen*—no parts of town forbidden to him—no forced assimilation of an alien tongue. After all, hadn't King Chulalongkorn himself taken Chinese concubines to ensure the cultural diversity of the highest ranks of the aristocracy?"

Dragon's Fin Soup

My cheek still burned; I knew the story almost by heart; I hated my father for using his past to ruin my life. Angrily I looked at the floor, at the walls, at the taut curve of the dragon's body as it hung cold, glittering and motionless.

"But then, you see, there was the revolution, the coming of what they called democracy. No more the many ancient cultures of Siam existing side by side. The closing of the Chineselanguage schools. Laws restricting those of ethnic Chinese descent from certain occupations … true, there were no concentration camps, but in some ways the Jews had it easier than we did … someone *noticed*. Now listen! You're not listening!"

"Yes, Papa," I said, but in fact my mind was racing, trying to find a way out of this intolerable situation. My Chinese self calling out to my American self, though she was stranded in another country, and perhaps near death, like the dragon whose flesh sustained my family's coffers.

"It was 1945," my father said. "The war was over, and Chiang Kai Shek was demanding that Siam be ceded to China. There was singing and dancing in the streets of Yaowaraj! Our civil rights were finally going to be restored to us … and the Thais were going to get their comeuppance! We marched with joy in our hearts … and then the soldiers came … and then we too had rifles in our hands … as though by magic. Uncle Shenghua's car was smashed. They smeared the seats with shit and painted the windshield with the words: *Go home, you slantyeyed scum*. Do you know why the restaurant wasn't torched? One of the soldiers was raping a woman against the doorway and his friends wanted to give him time to finish. The woman was your grandmother. It broke my father's heart."

I had never had the nerve to say it before, but today I was so enraged that I spat it out, threw it in his face. "You don't know that he *was* your father, Papa. Don't think I haven't done the math. You were born in 1946. So much for your obsession with racial purity."

He acted as though he hadn't heard me, just went on with his pre-set lecture: "And that's why I don't want you to consort with any of them. They're lazy, self-indulgent people who think only of sex. I just know that one of them's got his tentacles wrapped around your heart."

"Papa, you're consumed by this bullshit. You're a slave to this ancient curse … just like the damn dragon." Suddenly, dimly, I had begun to see a way out. "But it's not a Thai I'm in love with. It's an American."

"A *white* person!" he was screaming at the top of his lungs. My two aunts looked up from their stirring. "Is he at least rich?"

"No. He's a poor journalist."

"Some blond young thing batting his long eyelashes at you—"

"Oh, no, he's almost fifty. And he's fat." I was starting to enjoy this.

"I forbid you to see him! It's that man from the *Post*, isn't it? That bloated thing who tricked me with his talk of music and literature into thinking him harmless. Was it he who violated you? I'll have him killed, I swear."

"No, you won't," I said, as another piece of my plan fell into place, "I have the right to choose one human being on this earth to whom I shall reveal the secret of the family's dragon. My maidenhead is yours to give away, but not this. This right is the only thing I can truly call my own, and I'm going to give it to Bob Halliday."

* * *

It was because he could do nothing about my choice that my father agreed to the match between Bob Halliday and me; he knew that, once told of the secret, Bob's fate would necessarily be intertwined with the fate of the Clan of Lim no matter what, for a man who knew of the dragon could not be allowed to escape from the family's clutches. Unfortunately, I had taken Bob's name in vain. He was not the marrying kind. But perhaps, I reasoned, I could get him to go along with the charade for a while, until old Mr. Hong from the Old Country stopped pressing his suit. Especially if I gave him the option of questioning the dragon. After all, I had heard him wax poetic about all the questions he could ask ... questions about the meaning of existence, of the creation and destruction of the universe, profound conundrums about love and death.

Thus it was that Bob Halliday came to the Rainbow Café one more time—it was Thursday—and dined on such mundane delicacies as beggar chicken, braised sea cucumbers stuffed with pork, cold jellyfish tentacles, and suckling pig. As a kind of *coup de grâce*, my father even trotted out a small dish of dragon's fin which he had managed to keep refrigerated from the day before (It won't keep past 24 hours) which Bob consumed with gusto. He also impressed my father no end by speaking a Mandarin of such consonant-grinding purity that my father, whose groveling deference to those of superior accent was millennially etched within his genes, could not help addressing him in terms of deepest and most cringing respect. He discoursed learnedly on the dragon lore of many cultures, from the salubrious, fertility-bestowing water dragons of China to the fire-breathing, maidenravishing monsters of the West; lectured on the theory that the racial memory of dinosaurs might have contributed to the draconian mythos, although he allowed as how humans never co-existed with dinosaurs, so the racial memory must go back as far as marmosets and shrews and such creatures; he lauded the soup in high astounding terms, using terminology so poetic and ancient that he was forced to draw the calligraphy in the air with a stubby finger before my father was able vaguely to grasp his metaphors; and finally—the clincher—alluded to a great-great-great-great-aunt of his in San Francisco who had once had a brief, illicit, and wildly romantic interlude with a Chinese opium smuggler who might *just possibly* have been one of the very Lims who had come from *that* village in Southern Yunnan, you know the village I'm talking about, that very village ... at which point my father, whisking away all the *haute cuisine* dishes and replacing them with an enormous blueberry cheesecake flown in, he said, from Leo Lindy's of New York, said, "All right, all right, I'm sold. You have no money, but I daresay someone of your intellectual brilliance can conjure up some money somehow. My son, it is with great pleasure that I bestow upon you the hand of my wayward, worthless, and hideous daughter."

I hadn't forewarned Bob about this. Well, I had meant to, but words had failed me at the last moment. Papa had moved in for the kill a lot more quickly than I

Dragon's Fin Soup

had thought he would. Before Bob could say anything at all, therefore, I decided to pop a revelation of my own. "I think, Papa," I said, "that it's time for me to show him the dragon."

We all trooped into the kitchen.

The dragon was even more inanimate than usual. Bob put his ear up to the scales; he knocked his knuckles raw. When I listened, I could hear nothing at all at first; the whisper of the sea was my own blood surging through my brain's capillaries, constricted as they were with worry. Bob said, "This is what I've been eating, Janice?"

I directed him over to where Ah Quoc was now seasoning the vat, chopping the herbs with one hand and sprinkling with the other, while my two aunts stirred, prodded, and gossiped like the witches from *Macbeth*. "Look, look," I said, and I pointed out the mass of still unpulped fin that protruded from the glop, "see how its texture matches that of the two dorsal fins."

"It hardly seems alive," Bob said, trying to pry a scale loose so he could peer at the quick.

"You'll need a redhot paring knife to do that," I said, then, when Papa wasn't listening, I whispered in his ear, "Please, just go along with all this. It really looks like 'fate worse than death' time for me if you don't. I know that marriage is the farthest thing from your mind right now, but I'll make it up to you somehow. You can get concubines. I'll even help pick them out. Papa won't mind that, it'll only make him think you're a stud."

Bob said, and it was the thing I'd hoped he'd say, "Well, there *are* certain questions that have always nagged at me … certain questions which, if only I knew the answers to them, well ... let's just say I'd die happy."

My father positively beamed at this. "My son," he said, clapping

Bob resoundingly on the back, I *already* know that I shall die happy. At least my daughter won't be marrying a Thai. I just couldn't stand the thought of one of those loathsome creatures dirtying the blood of the House of Lim."

I looked at my father full in the face. Could he have already forgotten that only last night I had called him a bastard? Could he be that deeply in denial? "Bob," I said softly, "I'm going to take you to confront the dragon. "Which was more than my father had ever done, or I myself.

* * *

Confronting the dragon was, indeed, a rather tall order, for no one had done so since the 1930s, and Bangkok had grown from a sleepy backwater town into a monster of a metropolis; we knew only that the dragon's coils reached deep into the city's foundations, crossed the river at several points, and, well, we weren't sure if he did extend all the way to Nonthaburi; luckily, there is a new expressway now, and once out of the crazy traffic of the old part of the city it did not take long, riding the sleek air-conditioned Nissan taxicab my father had chartered for us, to reach the outskirts of the city. On the way, I caught glimpses of many more Bangkoks that my father's blindness had denied me; I saw the *Blade Runneresque* towers threaded with mist and smog, saw the buildings shaped like giant robots and computer circuit boards designed by that eccentric

Dragon's Fin Soup

genius, Dr. Sumet; saw the not-very-ancient and very-very-multicolored temples that dotted the cityscape like rhinestones in a cowboy's boot; saw the slums and the palaces, cheek by jowl, and the squamous rooftops that could perhaps have also been little segments of the dragon poking up from the miasmal collage; we zoomed down the road at breakneck speed to the strains of Natalie Cole, who, our driver opined, is "even better than Mai and Christina."

How to find the dragon? Simple. I had the scroll. Now and then, there was a faint vibration of the parchment. It was a kind of dousing.

"This offramp," I said, "then left, I think." And to Bob I said, "Don't worry about a thing. Once we reach the dragon, you'll ask him how to get out of this whole mess. He can tell you, *has* to tell you actually; once that's all done, you'll be free of me, I'll be free of my father's craziness, *he'll* be free of his obsession."

Bob said, "You really shouldn't put too much stock in what the dragon has to tell you."

I said, "But he *always* tells the truth!"

"Well yes, but as a certain wily Roman politician once said, 'What is truth?' Or was that Ronald Reagan?"

"Oh, Bob," I said, "If push really came to shove, if there's no solution to this whole crisis ... could you actually bring yourself to marry me?"

"You're very beautiful," Bob said. He loves to be all things to all people. But I don't think there's enough of him to go round. I mean, basically, there are a couple of dozen Janice Lims waiting in line for the opportunity to sit at Bob's feet. But, you know, when you're alone with him, he has this ability to give you every scintilla of his attention, his concern, his love, even; it's just that there's this nagging concern that he'd feel the same way if he were alone with a Beethoven string quartet, say, or a plate of exquisitely spiced *naem sod*.

We were driving through young paddy fields now; the nascent rice has a neongreen color too garish to describe. The scroll was shaking continuously and I realized we must be rather close to our goal; I have to admit that I was scared of out of my wits.

The driver took us through the gates of a Buddhist temple. The scroll vibrated even more energetically. Past the main chapel, there were more gates; they led to a Brahmin sanctuary; past the Indian temple there was yet another set of gates, over which, in rusty wrought-iron, hung the character *Lim*, which is two trees standing next to one another. The taxi stopped. The scroll's shaking had quieted to an insistent purr. "It's around here *somewhere*," I said, getting out of the cab.

The courtyard we found ourselves in (the sun was setting at this point, and the shadows were long and gloomy, and the marble flagstones red as blood) was a mishmash of nineteenth-century *chinoiserie*. There were stone lions, statues of bearded men, twisted little trees peering up from crannies in the stone; and tall, obelisklike columns in front of a weathered stone building that resembled a ruined ziggurat. It took me a moment to realize that the building was, in fact, the dragon's head, so petrified by time and the slow process of dying that it had turned into an antique shrine. Someone still worshipped here at least. I could smell burning josssticks; in front of the pointed columns— which, I now could see, were actually the dragon's

Dragon's Fin Soup

teeth—somebody had left a silver tray containing a glass of wine, a pig's head, and a garland of decaying jasmine.

"Yes, Yes," said Bob, I see it too; I feel it even."

"How do you mean?"

"It's the air or something. It tastes of the same bitterness that's in the dragon's fin soup. Only when you've taken a few breaths of it can you smell the underlying sensations … the joy, the love, the infinite regret."

"Yes, Yes, all right," I said, "but don't forget to ask him for a way out of our dilemma."

"Why don't you ask him yourself?" Bob said.

I became all flustered at this. "Well, it's just that, I don't know, I'm too young, I don't want to use up all my questions, it's not the right time yet … you're a mature person, you don't—"

" … have that much longer to live, I suppose," Bob said wryly.

"Oh, you know I didn't mean it in quite that way."

"Ah, but, sucking in the dragon's breath the way we are, we too are forced to blurt out the truth, aren't we?" he said.

I didn't like that.

"Don't want to let the genie out of the bottle, do you?" Bob said. "Want to clutch it to your breast, don't want to let go …"

"That's my father you're describing, not me."

Bob smiled. "How do you work this thing?"

"You take the scroll and you tap the dragon's lips."

"Lips?"

I pointed at the long stucco frieze that extended all the way around the row of teeth. "And don't forget to ask him," I said yet again.

"All right. I will."

Bob went up to the steps that led into the dragon's mouth. On the second floor were two flared windows that were his nostrils; above them, two slitty windows seemed to be his eyes; the light from them was dim, and seemed to come from candlelight. I followed him two steps behind—it was almost as though we were already married!—and I was ready when he put out his hand for the scroll. Gingerly, he tapped the dragon's teeth.

This was how the dragon's voice sounded: it seemed at first to be the wind, or the tinkling of the temple bells, or the faroff lowing of the water buffalo that wallowed in the paddy; or, or, the distant cawing of a raven, the cry of a newborn child, the creak of a teak house on its stilts, the hiss of a slithering snake. Only gradually did these sounds coalesce into words, and once spoken the words seemed to hang in the air, to jangle and clatter like a loaded dishwasher.

The dragon said:

We seldom have visitors anymore.

I said, "Quick, Bob, ask."

"Okay, okay," said Bob. He got ready, I think, to ask the dragon what I wanted him to ask, but instead, he blurted out a completely different question. "How different," he said, "would the history of music be, if Mozart had managed to live another ten years?"

"Bob!" I said. "I thought you wanted to ask deep, cosmic questions about the nature of the universe—"

Dragon's Fin Soup

"Can't get much deeper than that," he said, and then the answer came, all at once, out of the twilight air. It was music of a kind. To me it sounded dissonant and disturbing; choirs singing out of tune, donkeys fiddling with their own tails. But you know, Bob stood there with his eyes closed, and his face was suffused with an ineffable serenity; and the music surged to a noisome clanging and a yowling and a caterwauling, and a slow smile broke out on his lips; and as it all began to die away he was whispering to himself, "Of course ... appoggiaturas piled on appogiaturas, bound to lead to integral serialism in the mid-romantic period instead, then minimalism, mating with impressionism, running full tilt into the Wagnerian *gesamtkunstwerk* and colliding with the pointillism of late Webern ..."

At last he opened his eyes, and it was as though he had seen the face of God. But what about me and my miserable life? It came to me now. These *were* Bob's idea of what constituted the really important questions of life. I couldn't begrudge him a few answers. He'd probably save the main course for last; then we'd be out of there and could get on with our lives. I settled back to suffer through another arcane question, and it was, indeed, arcane.

Bob said, "You know, I've always been troubled by one of the 100-letter words in *Finnegans Wake*. You know the words I mean, the supposed 'thunderclaps' that divide Joyce's novel into its main sections ... well, its the ninth one of those ... I can't seem to get it to split into its component parts. Maybe it seems trivial, but it's worried me for the last 29 years."

The sky grew very dark then. Dry lightning forked and unforked across gathering clouds. The dragon spoke once more, but this time it seemed to be a cacophony of broken words, disjointed phonemes, strings of frenetic fricatives and explosive plosives; once again it was mere noise to me, but to Bob Halliday it was the sweetest music. I saw that gazing-on-the-face-of-divinity expression steal across his features one more time as again he closed his eyes. The man was having an orgasm. No wonder he didn't need sex. I marveled at him. Ideas themselves were sensual things to him. But he didn't lust after knowledge, he wasn't greedy about it like Faust; too much knowledge could not damn Bob Halliday, it could only redeem him.

Once more, the madness died away. A monsoon shower had come and gone in the midst of the dragon's response, and we were drenched; but presently, in the hot breeze that sprang up, our clothes began to dry.

"You've had your fun now, Bob. Please, please," I said, "let's get to the business at hand."

Bob said, "All right." He tapped the dragon's lips again, and said, "Dragon, dragon, I want to know …"

The clouds parted and Bob was bathed in moonlight.

Bob said, "Is there a proof for Fermat's Theorem?"

Well, I had had it with him now. I could see my whole life swirling down the toilet bowl of lost opportunities. "Bob!" I screamed, and began pummeling his stomach with my fists … the flesh was not as soft as I'd imagined it must be … I think I sprained my wrist.

"What did I do wrong?"

"Bob, you idiot, what about *us*?"

"I'm sorry, Janice. Guess I got a little carried away."

Yes, said the dragon. Presumably, since Bob had not actually asked him to prove Fermat's Theorem, all he had to do was say yes or no.

What a waste. I couldn't believe that Bob had done that to me. I was going to have to ask the dragon myself after all. I wrested the scroll from Bob's hands, and furiously marched up the steps toward that row of teeth, phosphorescent in the moonlight.

"Dragon," I screamed, "dragon, dragon, dragon, dragon, dragon."

So, Ah Muoi, you've come to me at last. So good of you. I am old; I have seen my beginning and my end; it is in your eyes. You've come to set me free.

Our family tradition states clearly that it is always good to give the dragon the impression that you are going to set him free. He's usually a lot more cooperative. Of course, you never do set him free. You would think that, being almost omniscient, the dragon would be wise to this, but mythical beasts always seem to have their fatal flaws. I was too angry for casuistric foreplay.

"You've got to tell me what I need to know." Furiously, I whipped the crumbling stone with the old scroll.

I'm dying, you are my mistress; what else is new?

"How can I free myself from all this baggage that my family has laid on me?"

The dragon said:

There is a sleek swift segment of my soul

That whips against the waters of renewal;
You too have such a portion of yourself;
Divide it in a thousand pieces.
Make soup;

Then shall we all be free.

"That doesn't make sense!" I said. The dragon must be trying to cheat me somehow. I slammed the scroll against the nearest tooth. The stucco loosened; I heard a distant rumbling. "Give me a straight answer, will you? How can I rid my father of the past that torments him and won't let him face who he is, who I am, what we're not?"

The dragon responded:

There is a sly secretion from my scales
That drives a man through madness into joy;
You too have such a portion of yourself;
Divide it in a thousand pieces;
Make soup;
Then shall we all be free.

This was making me really mad. I started kicking the tooth. I screamed, "Bob was right … you're too senile, you're mind is too clouded to see anything that's important … all you're good for is Bob's great big esoteric enigmas … but I'm just a human being here, and I'm in bondage, and I want out … what's it going to take to get a straight answer out of you?" Too late, I realized that I had phrased my last words in the form of a question. And the answer came on the jasmine-scented breeze even before I had finished asking:

> *There is a locked door deep inside my flesh*
> *A dam against bewilderment and fear;*
> *You too have such a portion of yourself;*
> *Divide it in a thousand pieces;*
> *Make soup;*
> *Then shall we all be free.*

But I wasn't even listening, so sure was I that all was lost. For all my life I had been defined by others—my father, now Bob, now the dragon, even, briefly, by Linda Horovitz. I was a series of half-women, never a whole. Frustrated beyond repair, I flagellated the dragon's lips with that scroll, shrieking like a pre-menstrual fishwife: "Why can't I have a life like other people?" I'd seen the American girls with their casual ways, their cars, speaking of men as though they were hunks of meat; and the Thai girls, arrogant, plotting lovers' trysts on their cellular phones as they breezed through the spanking-new shopping mall of their lives. Why was I the one who was trapped, chained up, enslaved? But I had used up the three questions.

I slammed the scroll so hard against the stucco that it began to tear.

"Watch out!" Bob cried. "You'll lose your power over him!"

"Don't speak to me of empowerment," I shouted bitterly, and the parchment ripped all at once, split into a million itty-bitty pieces that danced like shooting stars in the brilliant moonlight.

That was it, then. I had cut off the family's only source of income, too. I was going to have to marry Mr. Hong after all.

Then the dragon's eyes lit up, and his jaws began slowly to open, and his breath, heady, bitter, and pungent, poured into the humid night air.

"My God," Bob said, "there is some life to him after all."

My life, the dragon whispered, is but a few brief bittersweet moments of imagined freedom; for is not life itself enslavement to the wheel of sansara*? Yet you, man and woman, base clay though you are, have been the means of my deliverance.*

I thank you.

The dragon's mouth gaped wide. Within, an abyss of thickest blackness; but when I stared long and hard at it, I could see flashes of oh, such wondrous things … far planets, twisted forests, chaotic cities …

"Shall we go in?" said Bob.

"Do you want to?"

"Yes," Bob said, "but I can't, not without you; dying, he's still *your* dragon, no one else's; you know how it is; you kill your dragon, I kill mine."

"Okay," I said, realizing that now, finally, had come the moment for me to seize my personhood in my hands, "but come with me, for old times' sake; after all, you did give me a pretty thorough tour of *your* dying dragon …"

"Ah yes; the City of Angels Etc. But that's not dying for a few millennia yet."

I took Bob by the hand and ran up the steps into the dragon's mouth. He followed me. Inside the antechamber, the dragon's palate glistened with crystallized drool. Strings of baroque pearls hung from the ceiling, and the dragon's tongue was coated with

Dragon's Fin Soup

clusters of calcite. Further down, the abyss of many colors yawned

"Come on," I said.

"What do you think he meant," Bob said, "when he said you should slice off little pieces of yourself, make them into soup, and *that* would set us all free?"

"I think," I said, "that its the centuries of being nibbled away by little parasites ..." But I was no longer that interested in the dragon's oracular pronouncements. I mean, for the first time in my life, since my long imprisonment in my family compound and the confines of the Rainbow Café's kitchen, since my three years of rollercoastering through the alien wharves of Santa Cruz, I was in territory that I instinctively recognized as my own. Past the bronze uvula that depended from the cavern ceiling like a soundless bell, we came to a motherofpearl staircase that led ever downward. "This must be the way to the esophagus," I said. "Yeah." There came a gurgling sound. A dull, foul water sloshed about our ankles. "Maybe there's a boat," I said. We turned and saw it moored to the banister, a golden barque with a silken sail blazoned with the ideograph *Lim*.

Bob laughed. "You're a sort of goddess in this kingdom, a creatrix, an earthmother. But I'm the one with the waistline for earthmothering."

"Perhaps we could somehow meld together and be one." After all, his mothering instinct was a lot stronger than mine.

"Cosmic!" he said, and laughed again.

"Like the character *Lim* itself," I told him, "two trees straining to be one."

"Erotic!"

And I too laughed as we set sail down the gullet of the dying dragon. The waters were sluggish at first. But they started to deepen. Soon we were having the flume ride of our lives, careening down the bronzelined walls that boomed with the echo of our laughter ... the bronze was dark for a long long time till it started to shine with a light that rose from the heat of our bodies, the first warmth to invade the dragon's innards in a thousand years ... and then, in the mirror surface of the walls, we began to see visions. Yes! there was the dragon himself, youthful, pissing the monsoon as he soared above the South China Sea. Look, look, my multi-great-great-uncle bearing the urn of his severed genitals as he marched from the gates of the Forbidden City, setting sail for Siam! Look, look, now Multi-Great-Uncle in the Chinese Quarter of the great metropolis of Ayutthaya, constraining the dragon as it breached the raging waters of the Chao Phraya! Look, look, another great-great-uncle panning for gold, his queue bobbing up and down in the California sun! Look, look, another uncle, marching alongside the great Chinese General Taksin, who wrested Siam back from the Burmese and was in turn put to an ignominious death! And look, look closer now, the soldier raping my grandmother in the doorway of the family compound ... look, look, my grandfather standing by, his anger curbed by an intolerable terror ... look, look, even that was there ... and me ... yielding to the stately Linda Horovitz in the back seat of rusty Toyota ... me, stirring the vat of dragon's fin soup ... me, talking back to my father for the first time, getting slapped in the face, me, smashing the scroll of power into smithereens.

Dragon's Fin Soup

And Bob? Bob saw other things. He heard the music of the spheres. He saw the Sistine Chapel in its pristine beauty. He speed-read his way through Joyce and Proust and Tolstoy, unexpurgated and unedited. And you know, it was turning him on. And me, too. I don't know quite when we started making love. Perhaps it was when we hit what felt like terminal velocity, and I could feel the friction and the body heat begin to ignite his shirt and my *cheongsam*. Blue flame embraced our bodies, fire that was water, heat that was cold. The flame was burning up my past, racing through the dirt roads of the ancestral village; the fire was engulfing Chinatown, the roller coasters of Santa Cruz were blazing gold and ruddy against the setting sun, and even the Forbidden City was on fire, even the great portrait of Chairman Mao and the Great Wall and the Great Inextinguishable Middle Kingdom itself, all burning, burning, burning, all cold, all turned to stone, and all because I was discovering new continents of pleasure in the folds of Bob Halliday's flesh, so rich and convoluted that it was like making love to 300 pounds of brain; and you know, he was considerate in ways I'd never dreamed; that mothering instinct I supposed, that empathy; when I popped, he made me feel like the apple that received the arrowhead of William Tell and with it freedom from oppression; oh, God, I'm straining aren't I, but you know, those things are so so hard to describe; we're plummeting headlong through the mist and foam and flame and spray and surge and swell and brine and ice and hell and incandescence and then:

In the eye of the storm:
A deep gash opening and:

Naked, we're falling into the vat beneath the dragon's flanks as the *ginsu*-wielding Ah Quoc is hacking away at the disintegrating flesh and:

"No!" my father shouted. "Hold the sulfuric acid!"

We were bobbing up and down in a tub of bile and semen and lubricious fluids, and Aunt Lingling was frantically snatching away the flask of concentrated H_2SO_4 from the kvetching Jasmine.

"Mr. Elephant, *la*!" cried Ah Quoc. "What you do Miss Janice? No can! No can!"

"You've gone and killed the dragon!" shrieked my father. "Now what are we going to do for a living?"

And he was right. Once harder than titanium carbide, the coil of flesh was dissipating into the kitchen's musty air; the scales were becoming circlets of rainbow light in the steam from the bamboo *cha shu bao* containers; as archetypes are wont to do, the dragon was returning to the realm of myth.

"Oh, Papa, don't make such a fuss," I said, and was surprised to see him back off right away. "We're still going to make soup today."

"Well, I'd like to know how. Do you know you were gone for three weeks? It's Wednesday again, and the line for dragon's fin soup is stretching all the way to Chicken Alley! There's some kind of weird rumor going around that the soup today is especially *heng*, and I'm not about to go back out there and tell them I'm going to be handing out rain checks."

"Speaking of rain—" said Aunt Ling-ling.

Rain indeed. We could hear it, cascading across the corrugated iron rooftops, sluicing down the awnings, splashing the deadend canals, running in the streets.

Dragon's Fin Soup

"Papa," I said, "we *shall* make soup. It will be the last and finest soup-making of the Clan of Lim."

And then—for Bob Halliday and I were still entwined in each other's arms, and his flesh was still throbbing inside my flesh, bursting with pleasure as the thunderclouds above—we rose up, he and I, he with his left arm stretched to one side, I with my right arm to the other, and together we spelled out *the two trees melding into one* in the calligraphy of carnal desire— and, basically, what happened next was that I released into the effervescing soup stock *the swift sleek segment of my soul, the sly secretion from my scales*, and, last but not least, *the locked door deep inside my flesh;* and these things (as the two trees broke apart) did indeed divide into a thousand pieces, and so we made our soup; not from a concrete dragon, time-frozen in its moment of dying, but from an insubstantial spirit-dragon that was woman, me, alive.

"Well, well," said Bob Halliday, "I'm not sure I'll be able to write this up for the *Post*."

* * *

Now this is what transpired next, in the heart of Bangkok's Chinatown, in the district known as Yaowaraj, in a restaurant called the Rainbow Café, on a Wednesday lunchtime in the mid-monsoon season:

There wasn't very much soup, but the more we ladled out, the more there seemed to be left. We had thought to eke it out with black mushrooms and *bok choi* and a little sliced chicken, but even those extra ingredients multiplied miraculously. It wasn't quite the feeding of the 5,000, but, unlike the evangelist, we didn't find it necessary to count.

After a few moments, the effects were clearly visible. At one table, a group of politicians began removing their clothes. They leaped up onto the Lazy Susan and began to spin around, chanting "Freedom! Freedom!" at the top of their lungs. At the next table, three transvestites from the drag show down the street began to make mad passionate love to a platter of duck. A young man in a pinstripe suit draped himself in the printout from his cellular fax and danced the hula with a shrivelled crone. Children somersaulted from table to table like monkeys.

And Bob Halliday, my father and I?

My father, drinking deeply, said, "I really don't give a shit who you marry."

And I said, "I guess it's about time I told you this, but there's a strapping Jewish tomboy from Milwaukee that I want you to meet. Oh, but maybe I *will* marry Mr. Hong—why not?—some men aren't as selfcentered and domineering as you might think. If you'd stop sitting around trying to be Chinese all the time—"

"I guess it's about time I told you this," said my father, "but I stopped caring about this baggage from the past a long time ago. I was only keeping it up so you wouldn't think I was some kind of bloodless halfbreed."

"I guess its about time I told you this," I said, "but I *like* living in Thailand. It's wild, it's maddening, it's obscenely beautiful, and it's very, very, very unAmerican."

"I guess it's about time I told you this," my father said, "but I've bought me a oneway ticket to Californ', and I'm going to close up the restaurant and get a new wife and buy myself a little self-respect."

"I guess it's about time I told you this," I said, "I love you."

That stopped him cold. He whistled softly to himself, then sucked up the remaining dregs of soup with a slurp like a farting buffalo. Then he flung the bowl against the peeling wall and cried out, "And I love you too."

And that was the first and only time we were ever to exchange those words.

But you know, there were no such revelations from Bob Halliday. He drank deeply and reverently; he didn't slurp; he savored; of all the *dramatis personae* of this tale, it was he alone he seemed, for a moment, to have cut himself free from the wheel of *sansara* to gaze, however briefly, on nirvana.

As I have said, there was a limitless supply of soup. We gulped it down till our sides ached. We laughed so hard we were sitting ankle-deep in our tears.

* * *

But do you know what?

An hour later we were hungry again.

Lottery Night

"You've got everything you need now."
My grandmother was even more fidgety than usual; she didn't quite look me in the eye as she fanned herself continually with a folded-over fashion magazine. "Your sleeping bag ... don't forget that. And insect repellent."

"We've been through it a thousand times," I said, trying to conceal my trepidation at the adventure to come.

"Food—"

"A Snickers bar and a Big Mac," I said. "It's all here." I tapped the brown paper bag. I hoped it wouldn't rain. The air was humid; on the balcony of our highrise, my little sister Kaew was glued to a soap opera on the portable television—a courtroom scene—and my mother was pounding coconuts.

"I almost forgot ... the amulets! You mustn't forget the amulets!" My *khun yaa* scrambled up off the floor and hobbled into her room, muttering darkly to herself, just as my father let himself in, took off his shoes and began unbuttoning his khaki police uniform.

Dragon's Fin Soup

He glanced at me, squatting in the middle of the room, wishing I could eat the Big Mac now—that was a special treat my Aunt Joom bought for me down at the mall, you could have bought three bowls of noodles for the same price—and immediately began hectoring my mother.

"I really don't understand why we have to send the boy," he said. "Looks like another monsoon shower tonight. I could go myself."

"There's no need to baby him," my little sister piped up. "He's 14 years old and he 'polishes his rocket' every night."

"I do *not*!" I said. "Well, not every night."

"Where ever did you learn such filthy language, little girl?" my grandmother screeched from the inner room. My father couldn't stop himself from laughing.

My mother patiently pounded coconuts. On television, in the soap opera, the judge was declaring that the two-headed daughter of the peasant woman was the rightful heir to the Petchari millions, and the lawyer had just revealed that he was actually the god Indra in disguise.

"I mean, honored mother of my wife," my father went on, after he had recovered from laughing, "I *am* the patriarch of this family, and it's only proper if there's any favor to be sought from the venerable ancestors, I should be, the one to—"

"Don't be silly," my grandmother said, coming back in with a tray of amulets. My father quickly ducked so that his head would not be higher than hers. "In the first place, it's your doing that we're reduced to these present straits; in the second, he was her favorite greatgreatnephew; in the third, you know very well that your GreatAunt Snit hated your guts. She couldn't even stand to be in the same room as you when she was alive. Why on earth would she want to tell you a winning lottery number?"

"Even so," my father said, "the dead can be propitiated with the right gifts ... and ... and that was *years* ago, and it was because she was senile and kept mistaking me for the man who jilted her for an Indian woman."

My mother strained the pulped coconut through a cheesecloth and poured some of the juice into a *Batman* glass for my sister to drink. "We can't take any chances," she said. There was a sad finality in her voice, and my father sat down sulkily on a floor cushion.

"It's all superstition anyway," he said. "If everyone could win the lottery by sleeping in a cemetery and having some charitable ghost whisper the winning number in a dream ... why, everybody'd be a millionaire! Some of those graveyards get more crowded than the kickboxing stadium on Wednesday nights ... and speaking of *chok muai* ..." He stalked out to the balcony and started to twiddle the channel. The shrill snarl of the war oboe filled the air, punctuated by the pounding of drums. He turned the volume up so high it even drowned out the traffic.

"Oh, please, Khun Por! I wanna see what happens to the two-headed—" my sister started whining.

"Shut up! I've got a lot of money riding on the red tonight."

My mother and grandmother looked at each other and rolled their eyes. To me, it was just one more indication of our desperate plight. My father had faithfully gambled on the blue for ten years.

Dragon's Fin Soup

"The amulets," my grandmother said. She lifted each one in turn, held it in between her palms in an attitude of reverence. As my father farted and belched in the background, she enumerated their virtues: "Here's an old and very powerful *luangpoh* I acquired from a Chinaman who makes his living gambling on cockfights … here's an amethyst *pohngkham* that was dug up in Chiang Rai …" She put each one around my neck and ran through a couple of mantras appropriate to each. "Are you sure you'll be all right with all this American food?" she said. "I don't want you getting diarrhea in a graveyard in the middle of the night. You might attract a *phii krasue*."

I shuddered. For the first time it occurred to me that tonight's outing wasn't just another boyish lark—it was to be an encounter with the supernatural world that surrounds us all. No one wants to attract a *phii krasue*. Many *phii krasue* are seductively beautiful at first—until they lose their heads. We'd had one in the family once, my Great-Great-Great-Uncle Noi, whose bad karma had caused him to be reincarnated as one of these vile creatures. I had been raised on tales of how his head used to detach itself from his body, and, dragging the slimy guts behind it, would slither around the family compound using its tongue as a pseudopod. *Phii krasue* live entirely on shit, of course, and there was a practical side to having a malevolent spirit around in those olden days without indoor plumbing; but as soon as my family had been able to afford a toilet, back in the late fifties, my grandmother had an exorcist brought in to propel my multiuncle on to the next world.

This was long before I was born; I had never seen the much-vaunted village home, never even so much as set foot beyond the city limits of Bangkok except when we went to the beach; then again, everyone knows there is nothing worthwhile outside the Cityof-Angels-the-Divine-and-Great-Metropolis-Etc.-Etc.

My grandmother finished bedecking me with amulets and was now blessing me. My father was still absorbed in his boxing match; my mother was in the kitchen, praying to a plaster reproduction of the Emerald Buddha that sat in a niche above the refrigerator, next to the photographs of Their Divine Majesties. The smell of burning joss-sticks wafted through the living room. I closed my eyes, trying to achieve a state of *samadhi* before setting out on this pilgrimage that might mean the difference between the family retreating to the boondocks or moving to a more upscale condominium on Sukhumvit.

In the midst of my rêverie I heard my grandmother singing. It was an old lullaby from the village in a hick dialect, but it was strangely soothing. A mood of profound inner *shanti* swept over me, but it was soon disrupted by the sound of my elders arguing.

"I really should drive him down to the cemetery myself," my father was saying.

"Don't be a fool," said my grandmother. "That old Datsun pickup of yours won't make it past the edge of the *soi*."

"Yes, but I could take him in my police car," said my father, "and maybe get a couple of hundred baht in traffic bribes on my way home."

"How crass," said *khun yaa*.

"I'll take the bus," I said. "The *soi* is flooded anyway."

* * *

Dragon's Fin Soup 59

I didn't want a ride from my father because I had a secret errand or two to do on the way to the cemetery where Khun Chuad Snit's remains had lain since the time of the Divine King Chulalongkorn. I needed time to get in the right state of mind; I wanted to eat the Big Mac; and I had a mind to see if my American friend, Joey Friedberg, wanted to come along.

The *soi* was completely flooded from yesterday's monsoon outburst and I had to take a boat to the main road at a cost of two baht. I was dressed in my best—I didn't want to feel ashamed in front of my ancestors—a Ralph Lauren shirt from the best counterfeiter in town, a gold Rolex that would've fooled Mr. Rolex himself I didn't want to ruin my clothes, so instead of climbing up the drainage pipe to get into Joey's apartment, I actually rang at the front gate. My Aunt Joom, who worked for the Friedbergs as a maid or something, buzzed me in.

The first thing I heard was the television. Traditional *ranaat* music filled the living room. It was one of those cultural programs that are only watched by old people and American anthropologists. You see, the Friedbergs were a very unusual species of American. Like real people, they didn't wear shoes in the house, and instead of going to ISB, Joey actually went to a Thai school. Joey's mother made a living entirely by writing scholarly papers about our national peculiarities, for which the Ford Foundation supplied everything: the apartment, the servants, the chauffeur. (She had even done a fiftypage monograph analyzing all the Sanskrit components of the true name of the City of Angels the Divine Metropolis Etc. Etc., which is, of course, the only city whose name is so long it is always written with two etc's) She didn't appear to have a husband. At the moment, Mrs. Friedberg was having Aunt Joom walk back and forth across the living room striking various statuesque poses, and taking endless snapshots.

"Oh, Samraan," she called out to me, confusing me a bit, because I wasn't used to being called by my True Name, "Joey'll be right out ...

Joom, *undulate* a bit more, will ya? ... beautiful, beautiful."

Joey came out of his bedroom. He was loaded down with gear: compasses, Swiss army knives, canteens, dangling all over his gangly frame. We stood for a while, transfixed by Aunt Joom's virtuoso performance. She was wiggling her hips, fluttering her eyelids, and slithering sinuously across the room as the lanky Mrs. Friedberg snapped furiously away, leaping over sofas and climbing onto credenzas, to get the best possible angles.

"Rad!" said Joey.

"Totally," I said in English, impressed in spite of myself.

"The illusion is complete," Joey said, switching to Thai.

"I've known her all my life, and I *still* can hardly tell she isn't a woman," I said.

Aunt Joom paused for a breath. "Let me get you a Coke," she said to me.

"You really don't have to, Joom, dear," said Mrs. Friedberg. "You're not a servant, you know." Nonetheless, Joom minced off to the kitchen, every inch the proper serving maid, though the nuances of her servility were doubtless lost on her mistress. Mrs.

Dragon's Fin Soup

Friedberg sighed. "I can't wait to get these pictures developed."

"What're they for, Mom?"

"Oh, its a paper called '*Katoey*; transvestitism in the resonating contexts of contemporary Thai society.'" She shook her long red hair into place and noticed me at last. Joey and I stood side by side. My friend was, of course, much taller than me, and his height was further accentuated by his immaculately spiked blond hair. He limped a bit, and one arm was longer than the other; it was from a car accident he'd been in when he was five that had put him in a coma for a year. He wore a neon pink tee shirt that depicted a surfing triceratops. "Going camping, dears?" Mrs. Friedberg said to us.

"Aw, c'mon, Mom," said Joey. "I told you all about it, didn't I? Like, it's lottery night—tomorrow's the last day to buy lottery tickets—and we're spending the night at the tomb of Samraan's Khun Chuad Snit!"

"Oh, ah ... right! The business about sleeping in a graveyard and getting winning lottery numbers from ghosts, right? Interesting example of cultural syncretism ... gotta do a paper on it sometime ... well, be careful, dears," she said, "and Joey, maybe you can do some field notes or something." Absently, she handed him a fivehundredbaht note. White people never know the value of money.

I closed my eyes and thought of the ordeal to come. It was a bad idea to bring Joey, I thought. Even though I'd promised, even though he and his mother were almost like Thai people. I was going to end up as a footnote in Mrs. Friedberg's dissertation and even Joey wasn't going to take the spirits seriously ... maybe they'd be so angry at my bringing a *farang* that they wouldn't materialize at all. I found myself attempting to put myself back into a state of *samadhi* ... without thinking, I began to hum the lullaby my grandmother had sung to me earlier that day.

When I opened my eyes again, Mrs. Friedberg was staring at me, wideeyed. "Why, Samraan, that was such a curious, wonderful song ... what was it?"

"Just ... a song, Mrs. Friedberg. My grandmother's ..."

"From the provinces?"

I was suddenly embarrassed at having betrayed the hick origins of my family. I don't know why I was so sensitive about losing face; they wouldn't have understood anyway. I didn't know what to say, so I just stared at the floor.

"Does your grandmother know any more of those songs? Ya know, the Ford Foundation's shelling out megashekels for ethnomusicology these days—"

"Right, Mom, later," Joey said, rolling his eyes. He just couldn't wait to be out of there.

As we reached the door, we heard Mrs. Friedberg's final admonishment: "And don't get stoned!"

"Who's she fucking kidding?" Joey said to me, pulling a reefer out of his pocket just as we reached the corner of *Soi* Jintana and the main road. We were on higher ground and the water was only ankle deep. Banana trees lined the walls of the apartment complex. The sun was setting behind veils of smog; the odors of gasoline and nightblooming jasmine wafted across the skyline of highrises and silhouetted pagodas. Traffic screeched endlessly by and we had to wait ten minutes before we could safely jaywalk the intersection. At the corner, a withered Indian hawked lottery tickets.

"Not yet," I said. "Not until tomorrow."

Dragon's Fin Soup

"I can't wait," Joey said. A pretty young prostitute of indeterminate gender accosted him, and he yelled back, "*Hii men meuan turian kuan*!!"

"*Ai hia*! You can't say things like that!" The irate whore was coming after us, swinging her purse. She was making straight for me—of course, it hadn't occurred to her that it was the *farang* boy calling her names.

"Duck!" I grabbed Joey's arm and pushed him into an alley.

"Didn't I get it right?" he said as he lit up.

"Of course you got it right," I said, "but you can't just go around telling someone her pussy smells like a puréed durian fruit and hope to get away with—"

"Shit!" he said, laughing too loud. "She's fuckin' gaining on us!" Wielding the purse with deadly accuracy, the woman fetched me a hefty clout on the side of the head. Joey yanked me into the back doorway of a crowded noodle shop, and we dived under a table and scrambled through the forest of diners' legs to reach the front door.

A bus appeared and we ran wildly after it. About a dozen people were hanging on the door and the bus careened at a fortyfive degree angle as it rounded a corner. As we hopped on board, the prostitute tripped over a stray dog and sprawled into a sidewalk noodle vendor. We hung out of the side of the bus, clutching the doorpole with one hand, our legs trailing the traffic as we wove lurching through the ooze of jampacked cars, glinting in the sunset like the scales of a giant serpent.

"Why do I always have to rescue you, little brother?" Joey said.

"Fuck off," I said in English, "and don't call me 'little brother'." Joey might be my best friend, but that didn't give him the right to count me as his relative. Foreigners never know their place.

* * *

My great-great-aunt's tomb was in a pretty out-of-the-way *tambon* of the City of Etc. Etc. In the days when Great-Great-Aunt Snit had been cremated and her ashes interred there, there was this temple in the middle of nowhere, surrounded by paddy fields. Now there were a few signs of development; beside the temple was the skeleton of a shopping mallinprogress, and there was a halfbuilt overpass that was hulking over the cemetery. There was a palatial movie theater across the street from the cemetery. It was showing *Alien*; a thirty-foot-tall statue of the H. R. Giger monster welcomed the patrons, its mechanized jaws opening and closing to the strains of a Michael Jackson song. At its entrance, a bunch of kids hawked boxes of incense sticks and candles in case someone might want to make a quick offering at the shrine across the street.

"Hey, maybe we can go to the movie first," Joey said. "We've got all night."

"I don't know why I ever brought you along." He just wasn't taking this seriously enough. And my whole family's fate at stake! "You're only going to embarrass me."

"Embarrass you? How come you're so sure *you're* going to get a revelation from the spirits? How do you know they won't come to *me*?"

"They don't speak English."

"But they're supernatural beings, right? They probably all know English. They probably don't even speak real languages—they're probably all telepaths."

"They won't come to you, Joey, because ... because ... they don't have spirits in America. They don't have reincarnation and stuff. In America, people just die and turn to dust."

"The Friedbergs aren't like other Americans. We're liberals,"

"And how, pray, are the supernatural beings to know that? You all look alike to them."

"Fuckin' bigot," he said in English, and slapped a mosquito.

By now we had crossed the street and reached the gate of the cemetery, and I was experiencing real dread. It was all very well hearing all one's life that I was the favorite greatnephew of this longdead woman, but my only memory of her was that of a whitehaired, cadaverous figure with a face like a skeleton and teeth blackened from betel nut, sitting crosslegged in the shadows, screeching abuse at any family member who passed by without showing appropriate obeisance. I had been ushered into her presence perhaps three or four times; each time it was either my birthday or New Year's Day. I would prostrate myself at her feet, as was proper for such a momentous occasion, with such a venerable ancestor, and look up into her fierce sunken eyes, and she would hand me a little velvet bag containing a little spending money.

"Getting big," she would say. "Getting big, aren't you, tadpole! Can you talk yet?"

I could, of course, but she was too senile to realize it, and besides, I was too scared to utter a word in her exalted presence. Her house smelled of sandalwood and of the scented paste old women put on their faces to soften their skin.

She died before my fifth birthday; the funeral was a lot of fun, with all my favorite foods, including Mr. Donut, which had just opened in Siam Square and was the biggest craze of 1979 among the young.

It was a wrought-iron gate in a design of angelic *thephanoms* with folded palms. Joey leaped up and vaulted over; much to my annoyance, I had to have help from him to get over. It seemed to get dark the minute our feet touched the ground. The walls of the cemetery cut off the brash neon lights of the movie theaters and the noodle shops. The air was thick with mosquitoes. "Here," I said, breaking out the insect repellent, "use this." We stood in the shadow of the wall for a while, rubbing our arms and legs with the nastysmelling liquid from the British Dispensary. The last of the sunlight died.

Joey turned on his flashlight. "Well, we'd better find the tomb," he said. I started to walk toward where I thought the path was. I bumped into a gravestone. A temple dog howled in the distance, and I smelled incense. Joey found me, led me toward the gravel pathway. As our eyes got more used to the darkness, we could make out three low pagodas in the middle distance, bathed in moonlight and faint reflected neon. "C'mon, little brother," said Joey.

I started to cuss him out, but I remembered in time that I was in a sacred place. I murmured a quick prayer to the Lord Buddha, hoping it would compensate for my impiety. We walked on. The pagodas never seemed to get any nearer. The insects twittered and keened and made it hard to think. We walked on. Out of the insect voices came a persistent

Dragon's Fin Soup

rhythmic buzzing, and I suddenly realized that it came from Joey. He was listening to his Walkman. "Depêche Mode!" He was shouting, as those with earphones are wont to do. His voice echoed. I saw rows and rows of white marble tombs and I realized that I had become very frightened.

"Respect the dead," I said, yanking away his headphones.

We walked on.

The path turned. There was another kind of music now, high-pitched, tinkly. We must be getting close to our goal. I heard footsteps. Froze in my tracks. Soft, padding footsteps on gravel. Something was approaching! Someone ... in a long, white robe, with long white hair ... moving ineluctably in our direction ... humming weirdly ...

"C'mon," Joey said. "Maybe he knows the way."

"He's p-p-probably a—"

The figure stopped. "Please excuse me," he said in a thick Indian accent, "I am having lost my way. Are you not the two gentlemen who ordered an exorcism?"

"Awesome!" said Joey.

"No ... we're here for the lottery."

"Oh ... second fork on the left is where most of the lottery dream-seekers are, isn't it?" he said. "But where, oh where are those customers of mine?"

"What kind of exorcism are you doing?" Joey said.

"Oh ... no major thing," said the Brahmin, priest, just a little matter of a *phii krasue* that has gotten out of hand ... in her former life, my client's sisterinlaw, Khun Mayurii, doomed to wander the earth in this hideous shape because of some unflattering remarks she once made concerning a minor functionary of His Divine Majesty's Ministry of the Interior."

"What terrible karma," I said, shaking my head in rueful sympathy.

"Well, sirs, if you should ever need any help along those lines …" he solemnly removed a card from his robes and handed it to me. I read: *Shri Narayan Dass: houses blessed, exorcisms, scrying, love potions, and general astrology; reasonable rates.*

"Quite a racket," Joey said.

"Don't be disrespectful!" I said. "Don't you see he's a spirit doctor, a *mor phii*?"

"No, the young *farang* boy is being quite correct," said Shri Narayan Dass. "It is something of a racket, but it beats selling polyester in Paburat to the nouveau riche." He fished something else out of his capacious robes—it was a length of cotton rope. "Take this *saisin*," he said. "That should stave off the more egregious evil spirits."

I thanked him humbly and watched him leave the path and shamble, muttering incantations, into the darkness.

"Jesus," Joey said, "that dude could really clean up on the Beverly Hills guru circuit. Why are exorcists always Indians, anyways?"

"They must have ancient secrets which the Thais, people of a modern kingdom, have lost," I said, wondering about this for the first time.

We followed the exorcist's instructions, and presently we reached the oldest part of the cemetery, where my greatgreataunt's ashes were. As my father had predicted, it was a madhouse. There was a Porsche parked on the grass beside one ostentatious monument, and a woman in black was praying hysterically beside it, weeping and shrieking imprecations in Chinese. There was hardly a tomb without a straw mat laid out next to it with someone desperately trying to sleep or slapping mosquitoes. There was a woman hawking meatballs on skewers with chili sauce as well as lottery tickets. A man in a pair of silk pajamas was watching a "Twilight Zone" episode on a portable television set. The fragrance of incense melded with the stagnant odor of a nearby canal.

Where was my greatgreataunt's tomb? Every New Year I had paid my respects there with the rest of my family. In daylight I could have found it in my sleep, but now everything looked different. I wandered around in circles while Joey went off to buy food.

It was maddening. The place was getting more and more crowded by the minute. Suddenly I heard Joey cry out, "This way!"

"You've never been here before." Angrily, I stalked toward him.

His eyes were glazed over. "Something awesome's happening ... like, déjà vu, dude! I've been here before! I remember ... Jesus, I remember—"

"Control yourself!" He must have smoked that entire joint while I was looking the other way.

"I know the way, I'm telling you!" he said, jumping up and down. He dragged me past the food vendor toward—

"Tadpole!" A familiar voice. It was Aunt Joom. "How nice to see you!"

She was wearing an embroidered silk sarong, gold bracelets, necklaces and earrings, and pancake make-up an inch thick. She had been praying at a tomb. As Aunt Joom got up from her prostrate position with a chillingly feminine wiggle of the hips, I could see Khun

Chuad Snit's photograph, a frayed blackandwhite thing in a goldbordered frame, in the light of Aunt Joom's votive candles. I was infuriated to learn that Joey had been right about the location of the monument.

"Oh, don't worry, darling," said Aunt Joom, as she applied yet another layer of lipstick, "I'm not here to steal your lottery dream. Your greatgreataunt never much liked me anyway. It's the exorcism, you know … across the way. Khun Phairoj, who's hired the priciest Brahmin to help rid his sister-in-law of the curse of—"

"We met him," Joey interjected.

"Well, he made a pledge to the FourFacedBrahma shrine next to the Erawan hotel that, if the exorcism worked, he'd have a troupe of dancers immediately perform 'The Dance of the Celestial Chickens" … well, a group of us girls is standing by in case everything works out as planned."

"I see." I wasn't surprised; transvestites are always in demand as dancers, as they can switch roles with ease.

"Just don't sleep next to me," Joey jested.

Aunt Joom laughed. "We *katoeys* always make white people queasy, I don't know why. But while I'm here … why don't I buy you some meatballs? You look like you're starving."

"I've got a Big Mac," I said.

"Bah! That stuff'll give you Reagan's Revenge every time."

"I'd love some meatballs," said Joey, and the two of them went off, hand in hand, cracking obscene jokes about meatballs, leaving me alone with my Big Mac, my Snickers bar, and the spirits of my ancestors.

* * *

First I took out the *saisin* the exorcist had given me—better safe than sorry. I looped it around some bushes so that the cord made a sacred circle around my greatgreataunt's memorial. The carnival atmosphere had subsided. It was time for serious business; communion with the supernatural. The moon had disappeared behind a highrise that towered over the temple wall. In the distance, the exorcism was going on; most of the crowd, including my aunt, had gone to watch, leaving only the dedicated lottery-dreamers. Joey, stuffed with *luk chin* in chili sauce, had gone to sleep with his Walkman, and there was a buzz of Metallica coming from around his head.

Carefully I lit seven josssticks and seven candles. I arranged the candles beneath my greatgreataunt's photograph. I lifted my folded palms to my lips and murmured a prayer to the Lord Buddha, then hung a *puangmalai* wreath of jasmine petals across the tombstone. Soft sounds in the night: the stridulant crickets and the snoring dreamers, the faroff music of the exorcism and the fartheroff traffic along the overpass. As far as I could see, I was the only one awake. I was alone, the still center of the crowded city.

What was I to say to my great-great-aunt?

I gazed at the photograph in its brass frame. I had seen the picture before—we had one like it in a family album at home—but it was nothing like the withered betelnutchewing crone of my childhood memories. This was a young woman. Her hair was like a woman on a videotape box I'd once seen at Joey's house— Claudette Colbert in *Cleopatra*. She wore Western-style clothes—the hcight of twenties fashion—and I remembered that she had once been the third minor wife of a provincial functionary of the government of His Divine Majesty the Sixth Rama. We'd been somebody back in those days! Our karma had certainly taken a sad turn for the worse, with my father forced to eke out a living collecting bribes from traffic violators, unable to afford the down payment even on a oneroom condominium.

I put my hands together in the *phnom mue* gesture and addressed the photograph in tones of deepest humility: "Great-Great-Aunt," I said, "things really aren't going too well for your descendants at the moment."

Light flickered. Had the photograph been smiling a moment before? Somehow the monument seemed taller, the fragrance of incense more pungent. I felt a chill. There were spirits present. Somewhere. The cold tickled the base of my spine. Even though it was a hot tropical night and the dark air pregnant with impending rain. The cold moved up the small of my back.

"Great-Great-Aunt!" I said. "You're frightening me! Don't you remember me, the one you used to give the little bags of money to twice a year?" The photograph wavered … or was it the candlelight, the wisps of incense? "Listen, we really have to win that lottery," I said urgently. "We're getting farther and farther behind on the rent. My father drinks too much and he spends the rest of his money gambling on boxers. I know you don't like my grandmother because she accused you of being a whore for agreeing to be the mistress of a government official, but it was just your ticket out of the village and into the provincial capital—and it wasn't her fault your husband died of syphilis! I know you always thought my father was a layabout, and I know how disappointed you were that my mother married him ... but it's all karma anyway. So show compassion to me, honored Great-Great-Aunt, and even if you don't tell me the number for the jackpot, at least give us one of the lesser prizes, enough to scrape by for a month or two while my father gets his life back together again."

A peal of thunder made me jump. I looked around, panicking. Joey was still asleep. A slithering sound in the grass nearby. A snake? I listened. Only the crickets. I made sure that the protective *saisin* was securely fastened. No evil spirit would dare profane such a barrier. I listened carefully again. No snakes ... only the moist wind rifling the leaves of the mango trees next to the cemetery wall.

"Khun Chuad?" I said. "Are you listening to me?"

There was thunder, more distant. My heart was thumping. The grass was whispering. I unrolled the sleeping bag and lay on it with my head propped up against the stone. My stomach growled. I was getting nervous. I wolfed down the candy bar and the cold Big Mac. I could hear the chanting of the exorcist, somewhere far away. I burped. "Excuse me," I whispered, hoping that my venerable ancestor would not take offense. "I shouldn't have eaten my food so fast. Grandmother is always telling me to chew slowly—"

I stopped.

There was someone standing just beyond the *saisin* ... a woman. She was young. A strange perfume emanated from her. She wore a traditional *phasin* of black silk. Her lips were red and glossy, her hair done in that 1920's flapper style ... she was a living, breathing incarnation of the photograph of my Great-Great-Aunt Snit. And yet …

"My favorite grandnephew," she said. Very softly. Shook her head. The moonlight danced in her soft dark hair. "Come to me … I always loved you best."

There was something not quite right about her…

My heartbeat quickened. I felt hot and cold all over and suddenly I realized I was beginning to get an erection. I breathed in perfume mingled with incense and it intoxicated me. How could this be? I got up … took a tentative step towards her ……

Something grabbed my foot.

"Joey! Let go!"

"Stay inside the sacred circle, you idiot!"

"But it's my great-great—"

He leaped off his sleeping bag, tried to restrain me. I freed myself. The vision of my ancestor shimmered in the humid air. He lurched after me but his limp made him trip over a stone. Just as I reached the *saisin*, he managed to get hold of my ankles. I stretched out my arms toward the woman as she floated toward me in a cloud of mist. Her eyes glittered. She grasped my hands … she was cold … colder than ice … I screamed.

At that moment, with my friend trying to pull me back into the circle and the spirit trying to pull me out, I felt the first pangs of Reagan's Revenge. A moist, noisy fart tore through my sphincter. I could have died of embarrassment. I looked up into eyes that were glowing like charcoal embers. The hands gripped tighter, burning my wrists. Joey tugged with all his might, his back against the tomb.

"Let go, one of you," I gasped. "Or I'll crap in my pants!"

"Don't do that!" Joey shouted. "Can't you see, that's exactly what it wants you to do!"

I didn't think I could hold it for another second. I was going to defile my great-great-aunt's tomb and I was never going to receive her blessing now. I had to get away ... find a good spot, maybe among the mango trees ...

I wriggled free of Joey and was pulled across the sacred cord. No sooner was I clear of its protection than I saw that the hands that gripped me were no hands ... they were the slimy, prehensile tongue of a *phii krasue*! "The Lord Buddha protect me!" I said. The tongue tightened its hold, squeezing my arms like a hungry python. I could see the face. Bits of skull showed through the torn flesh. Yellow goo spewed from pustulant_sores. The *phii krasue's* esophagus and intestines flailed about on the grass like a mass of serpents.

"Get back inside the circle!" Joey screamed. I turned around. Rising from the tomb in a miasma of candlelit incense fumes was the skeletal form of GreatGreatAunt Snit! The ghost looked at me, its finger pointing straight at me, and I felt all the terror I'd felt when I was three years old and being ushered into her presence, and I knew I was going to shit myself but I didn't dare do so because I knew that the *phii krasue* wanted to feast upon my excrement ...

Where was Joey? He was nowhere to be seen. His voice had been coming from the place where my great-great-aunt's ghost now stood, her shroud flapping in the wind. The *phii krasue's* intestines were inching up my leg. I couldn't move my hands. I struggled. Sweat was pouring down my neck and mingling with the creature's slime. My wrists were getting so slick that the demon's tongue was losing its purchase. I managed to ease my hand toward my chest, reached into my shirt, pulled out one of my grandmother's amulets.

The *phii krasue* screamed! The tongue slithered away and on the creature's forehead was a fuming burn mark in the shape of the Lord Buddha! I got up as the evil spirit tumbled onto the grass. The scream was waking up all the lottery-dreamers. Flashlights were coming on all around me. The pain was pounding at my abdomen. I was flushed with embarrassment. The *phii krasue* circled me warily, now and then trying to lasso my ankles with its tongue.

"The Lord Buddha preserve us! It's a *phii krasue*!" someone shouted. My writhing assailant and I stood in a pool of flashlight beams.

"How dare you wake me up?" came another voice from behind another tombstone. "I've two more digits to go!"

"Joey!" I screamed. But Joey was not there. In his place loomed the specter of my greatgreataunt, impassively watching me in my shame.

I had to find a bush, a tree, some secluded spot—

I started to run.

"It's after the boy!" someone shouted.

"It must be that spirit they've been exorcizing down at the other end of the cemetery."

"After it!"

I ran. Tripping over gravestones, stopping now and then to brandish an amulet behind me. Others were right behind me ... some waving their own amulets, some there just to enjoy the spectacle ... the meatball vendor was back too, cheerfully hawking as we ran. I sprinted, clutching my stomach.

Dragon's Fin Soup

Voices in the distance ... there was the exorcism in full swing, by the side of the canal! There was Shri Narayan Dass on a dais above the throng, sitting in the lotus position in his white exorcizing robes, chanting up a storm, with clouds of incense whirling about his face. Statues of Hindu gods glared down from a plinth behind him. Sacred exorcizing music, tinkling xylophones, and wailing oboes, poured out of a portable CD player. I saw Aunt Joom, in her dancing costume, ready to go on; Khun Phairoj, the sponsor of the exorcism, sat in a big rattan chair, a fat man looking even fatter in his white Yves St. Laurent suit. A length of *saisin* cord wound round and round the nearby trees and through the folded palms of all the celebrants in the ritual. The exorcist was in the throes of a *khao song*, foaming at the mouth and spewing forth sublimely incomprehensible utterances as the spirits of celestial beings held his *vinyaan* in thrall.

In the throes of a somewhat more earthly need, I hardly had time to take in the splendor of the situation ... although I did notice Mrs. Friedberg in the audience, holding the *saisin* in one hand while feverishly taking notes with the other.

It was Aunt Joom who saw me first. "It's Samraan! And the *phii krasue* is after him!" she shrieked.

The screaming became contagious. Panicking, people were crawling over each other in their haste to reach the gate. Aunt Joom, wringing her hands, stood looking this way and that. "Aunt Joom ... I've got Reagan's Revenge!" I screamed. "That's why it's after me!"

Suddenly there came an eerie voice from high above, from the platform on which the spirit doctor had been meditating. "Don't hold it in anymore, boy! We can assuage the creature's hideous hunger and trap it at the same time!"

"Yes, sir," I shouted. "I'll try." There was no need to try. I had begun to *khii laad* the moment I heard the voice of Shri Narayan Dass.

"You must now be running toward me!" came the spirit doctor's voice, high-pitched, ethereal, plaintive. "Come to me ... try to let it out just a bit at a time ..." I stumbled forward with the *phii krasue* hobbling my left leg. The creature's clammy tongue slid up and down my calf. It fed frenziedly, propelled by the filthy obsession that was the sole purpose of its existence. The exorcist came stomping down the steps, holding aloft an image of a many-headed Hindu deity. With his other hand he twirled a length of *saisin*, like a bullroper in a western. An acolyte struggled to keep up, carrying a huge silver bowl of lustral water. Behind him came the crowd. The creature fed. I could hardly breathe as the wet guts twined around my stomach, pumping me for more.

They were all around me now ... how could Joey be sleeping through all this? ... cheering on the exorcist as he bore down on the monster and me. Dipping a sheaf of twigs into the lustral water, intoning a sacred prayer to Yama, the god of the underworld, Shri Narayan Dass began asperging us both. The chanting crescendoed.

"Be at peace now, evil spirit! Go and be reborn in a decent human shape!"

With each shower, I felt the creature shudder, its grip tightening. I tried to scream but only a squawk came out. Finally the exorcist, standing over us as we thrashed, began flagellating us with the sacred twigs,

Dragon's Fin Soup

chanting wildly, foaming at the mouth, his eyes completely white.

The crowd gasped. The *phii krasue* began to scream ... a heartrending cry, the cry of a woman in pain ... I felt the intestines relax their hold on me. I turned. Smoke billowed upward toward the moon. The sacred waters struck me; I felt all my uncleanness melt from me ... I slid onto the grass ... I saw the monster slowly begin to transform into the corpse of a beautiful woman ... Khun Mayurii, the unfortunate woman whose karma had caused her to walk the earth as the lowliest of demons ...

I heard Aunt Joom's voice from somewhere in the throng. "For the sake of mercy, give the boy something to eat!" That was the last thing I wanted. I lay on my back, against the soft earth, watching the clouds stream across the face of the moon. A few more drops fell on my face ... surely not the lustral waters. No. The monsoon was about to break. We were all going to be drenched. A few more drops. People were murmuring, looking hastily around for shelter, and I could see Khun Phairoj, kneeling, weeping beside the body of his late sister-in-law.

It was at that moment that I saw Joey Friedberg. He was walking slowly toward me out of the darkness. He walked strangely, with the grace of a woman. Actually he wasn't walking at all. He was gliding. Floating toward me on a carpet of mist.

"Joey," I said softly, "how could you have slept through all that? The exorcism—the *phii krasue*—"

"*Samraan*," Joey said. It was a haunting voice, a voice out of some past life ... the voice of a beautiful woman, rich against the patter of impending rain.

"Joey—you didn't turn into a *katoey*, did you?" It had never occurred to me that the Americans had any people like my Aunt Joom.

"*No, my child—*"

"You're possessed!"

"*You're dreaming*," Joey said, and enveloped me in incense fumes. The corpse of Khun Mayurii was melting and the people around about us were draining into the dark sky. He took me by the hand—his hand was soft and caked with perfume-powder—and led me out of my body. We climbed up the tombstones and climbed to the clouds on a staircase of heavenly rain. The gates of the sky swung open and I saw winged *apsaras* on lotus pads, singing in endless praise of Phra Indra, King of Heaven, each one with breasts glistening like ripe mangoes after rainfall. Music of celestial xylophones mingled with Metallica, from Joey's Walkman.

"*I am not what I seem to be*," Joey said, looking into my eyes.

Suddenly I realized that he had become imbued with the *vinyaan* of my great-great-aunt. Appalled at my previous rudeness, I fell down prostrate at the nearest cloudbank and placed my palms between his feet. "*Sadhu, sadhu*, honored ancestor" I, said piteously, "don't be mad at me because I didn't recognize you straight away. Please look with favor upon our family's distress …"

Joey Friedberg looked off into the distance. Far away, silhouetted against the moon, was a pavilion. I could see gods and angels moving against the moonlight as in a shadow play. I could see the cemetery below us. Dozens of people had sought shelter under the mango trees. The exorcist stood, waving his arms,

Dragon's Fin Soup

intoning over the place where the *phii krasue* had fallen. Khun Phairoj was summoning the dancers; he had pledged a dance of thanksgiving, and rain or no rain the dance would now have to occur. Aunt Joom and the other transvestites, in their soggy finery, were coming out into the rain. There was some kind of altercation; but presently the music started up, and the *katoeys* danced—though the grace of their movements was somewhat hampered by their umbrellas. In heaven, too, there was dancing; *apsaras* flitted by, strewing us with jasmine petals, and we were bathed in sourceless light.

"*I could give you the winning lottery number if I really wanted to,*" said Khun Chuad Snit, "*but the wheel of karma moves in mysterious ways, and even if I told it you, it wouldn't make any difference.*"

The ways of dead people are not our ways. They have a very oblique way of expressing themselves, and often they'll tell you something that can be interpreted many ways; it gives them a way out while preserving their reputation for infallibility. Nevertheless, I asked her what she meant.

"*Joey Friedman will take care of you,*" she said. My American friend twitched, as though he were trying to dislodge my great-great-aunt's *vinyaan*.

"Why Joey?" I said. I didn't want him taking care of me. It was an annoying habit of his that I'd been trying to wean him off since knowing him.

"*Well you may ask*," she said. "*But you see, I am Joey Friedberg.*"

"You are—"

"*He is my reincarnation.*"

"Oh, come on! That's the dumbest thing I ever heard. They don't even have reincarnation in America!"

"*Now, now,*" she said, and smiled through Joey's lips, the smile of an indulgent old woman. "*All living things are part of the eternal cycle of karma … I must admit that I was a little nonplussed to find myself being reborn in the body of a* farang, *but then I'm afraid I did a terrible thing in my last life …*"

I listened in horrified fascination, eager to learn what monstrous crime she had committed to be reincarnated so far from the City of Angels the Divine Metropolis Etc. Etc. "*I killed a cockroach,*" she said ruefully.

"But everyone kills cockroaches!"

"*Ah, but this particular cockroach happened to be a reincarnation of my grandfather, you see. One must always be very careful about the wanton destruction of life; one never knows who it might be. Think about it next time you step on an ant.*"

"But … Great-Great-Aunt Snit … Joey's older than me! How could he possibly be you? You died after he was born …" I had her there, I thought. She'd never talk her way out of that one.

"*The fact of the matter is, I spent quite a while in the underworld, going through the usual tortures, being punished for the usual minor offenses like adultery and so on. There is in the underworld an enormous chamber, something like a border immigration center, where the new souls come in. I happened to be in charge of the—as it were—immigrant register one day, when they brought in the soul of a young American boy who was in a car accident. He had been in a coma for a year, and his soul had been flitting back and forth at the border of the kingdom of death. He was crying and carrying on so, but I couldn't send him back; the dictates of Yama, the Death Lord, are irreversible. I prostrated myself before His Dread Majesty and said, 'But my Lord, there is a loophole. The boy's brain is dead, and the* farang, *in their mechanistic way, consider him gone for good; but we Thais know that it is the heart that is the seat of life, and the boy's heart is still beating.'* Which was almost true—there was a machine that was beating in place of his heart. *The Death Lord, who has a macabre sense of humor, began laughing uproariously; then he said to me, 'Your compassion for this child is commendable, and goes a long way toward mitigating the evil for which you were cast into the underworld. I can't send him back, but maybe I could commute your sentence. If as you say, the* farang *soul is dead but the Thai is not, I suppose I could simply send a Thai* vinyaan *to occupy the child's body, and no one will be the wiser. For I am a servant of the teaching of the Lord Buddha, and it is my duty to reward compassion by hastening your soul in its trillion-year journey towards enlightenment.' Then Lord Yama waved his hands,—poof!—I was reborn."*

"That is the weirdest thing I have ever heard," I said.

"*It is all part of the great chain of being,*" my great-great-aunt said, shrugging. "*Take it or leave it.*"

"But the lottery tickets—"

"*It's out of my hands.*"

"But you know the winning number! You as much as said so! Wait ... does that mean Joey knows?"

"*Hard to say. The conscious mind has little knowledge of past lives.*"

Her voice was getting fainter. To my dismay, we were plummeting back to the earth. I could see the whole of the city whirling beneath me ... the great palace of the Chakri Kings, the glittering shopping malls and freeways, the great river choked with houseboats in the shadow of the Temple of Dawn ...

"Joey …" Desperation flooded me. I had failed! How could I face my parents, knowing they would have to give up their apartment? "Joey!" I was shaking him now, gripping his shoulders as he convulsed under the spell of possession …

I was still shaking him as the dream faded away.

The canal was still swollen from the torrent, but the rain had ended as abruptly as it had started; that is how the monsoon rains are. I came to, still shaking Joey, who was rubbing his eyes. "Did I miss something?" he said. It was still dark … not even midnight.

"We can go home now," I said. "It's useless. You're my great-great-aunt, and we're not going to win the lottery anyway."

"Why not?" Joey said. "HK 2516635—that's the winning serial number, isn't it? I assume you got it too."

I gaped at him.

"It's early yet," he said. "Maybe we can catch the midnight showing of *Alien* before we go home." He looked at me. "How'd you manage to stay so dry, little brother?"

* * *

HK 2516635. By an amazing stroke of karma, we found that lottery ticket the next morning at the stationery store at the head of the *soi*. Joey and I bought the whole ticket and split it in half.

A day later, a group of us gathered to watch the drawing on television. We were at the Friedbergs' house: my grandmother, my parents, my little sister, and some raucous friends of the Friedbergs from the American embassy. We sat around the television set

Dragon's Fin Soup

while Aunt Joom served us elegant *hors d'oeuvres* and Coke. A revolution was going on that day; the embassy people were sitting around pontificating about it, quite oblivious to the antics of the announcer. They were playing a music video in between each drawing, and the suspense was mounting ... mounting ... mounting ...

The Friedbergs' friends droned on: "Who's going to get into power this time?"... I got interviewed by CNN this afternoon."... "That new field marshal, what's his name, really seems to have the support of the CIA ..."

"Shut up, you guys!" Joey said. "Anyone who's lived here can tell you that this revolution's gonna fizzle out before dawn."

"Yeah, revolutions only work in October," I said. After all, I distinctly remembered the last five. "Coups in other months are always abortive."

"Army's got to have something to do," my father said, guzzling a Singha beer.

"How anyone can be interested in such things is beyond me," my mother said, as she vigorously pounded shrimp paste in a mortar and pestle, stinking up the entire living room. "What possible difference can it make when Their Divine Majesties are the true heart of the Siamese people?" Meanwhile, my grandmother, serenely confident of victory, was ignoring the entire thing, merely humming away to herself, one of those peasant melodies.

Everyone started arguing, and it was a moment before Aunt Joom noticed our winning number pop up on the screen. "Merciful Buddha!" she shrieked. "Be quiet everyone! Look! It's come! It's the number!"

"We're rich," my father said softly.

I didn't even mind that it was really Joey who had come up with the winning number. We were going to have our new condominium after all—my father was going to get a new car—everything was going to be all right after all!

At that moment, the army took over the television station and announced that there would be a few changes.

We watched in horror as a general in a shiny uniform came on the air and informed us that, because of tampering by certain high officials, it had become necessary to declare the lottery void. The above mentioned high officials would all be resigning in the morning, and his humble self the general had been asked to form a new government to preside over the aftermath of the scandal. He apologized for the revolution, but things would be back to normal in the morning.

"I know that general!" I said. "That's Khun Phairoj ... the man whose sister-in-law I ..."

My father shook his head. "It's not even October."

"Does that mean we're not going to be rich?" said my little sister Kaew.

"On the contrary," said Mrs. Friedberg. I may as well tell you now. I've obtained a big grant from the Ford Foundation to study your grandmother's peasant songs. It's not much by Ford Foundation standards, but your share of it could come to ... say, a million baht." General excitement all around.

"Besides, honored father," I said, "I rescued the prime minister's sister-in-law from wandering the earth as a *phii krasue*. Surely you can get a promotion out of that."

Dragon's Fin Soup

I heard Joey calling from the balcony. "Awesome, Samraan! There are tanks rolling up the main road."

"Here we go again," my father said.

I went to join my friend. Two tanks were processing up the street on their way to seize the government. It was another humdrum evening in the Divine Metropolis. The street was crowded with food-vendors, shoppers, laughing students; no one but Joey seemed to notice the revolution. The monsoon rain was about to come again. The air was heavy with moisture and gasoline fumes and the fragrance of ripening bananas.

Joey watched the tanks starry-eyed, transfixed. It's a quality I had grudgingly come to admire in the Americans: their ability to feel as though everything around them, no matter how many times the world has seen it, is happening for the first time. They have a spanking-newness about them, a sense of wonder. Perhaps it is simply that in their country they rarely have revolutions, exorcisms, or lotteries. I don't know.

I did know, however, that the spirit of my great-great-aunt had come to rest in the body of my friend. That she had shown that I was still her favorite descendant by arranging for the money we had prayed for to come to us—in spite of the lottery being rigged. The heart of the Lord of Death had been moved, the Ford Foundation mobilized, continents and oceans traversed, all this so that my family's karma could be fulfilled.

So awed was I by the cosmic grandeur of our personal lives, and so overcome with gratitude, that I fell on my knees in front of my great-great-aunt's latest incarnation and placed my folded palms between Joey Friedberg's feet. Thank you for protecting me, honored

Great-Great-Aunt, I thought, thank you in the name of the Lord Buddha.

"Why the fuck are you doing *that*?" Joey said, bemused and confused.

"You really don't know, do you?" I studied his face for any trace of remembrance of that night's vision. There was nothing, as is proper ... the conscious mind cannot suffer the burden of so many past lives, or it would go mad.

"Well, at least my little brother's treating me with proper respect at last."

"He sure is." For once I didn't mind being called the little brother of a *farang*, "He sure is."

The Steel American

The steel American was different from all the others. Not that there was any real doubt that he was an American. He spoke English, after all, not Russian; besides, the Russians had just come through the village the week before with their annual promises of tractors and medicine.

He was different because he came alone. Because he was completely encased in platelets of jointed steel, like a television robot. And because he came to *me*. He was *my* American.

On the crest of the hill, past the old stone temple where the man who used to be my husband had meditated, hardly moving, for the last ten years, there was a waterfall where the women used to bathe, mornings, coyly draped in their sarongs. Behind the waterfall was a cave most people were afraid to enter, for it was inhabited by a malevolent spirit, but I've always been good with spirits. The back of the cave abuts onto a deep, still pool at the bottom of a well of rock. Nobody knew about this pool except me. My mother showed it to me the day after I had my first period, and she told me that its waters contained the secret of our family's youthful appearance. Indeed, until the day she died, my mother had an inexplicably smooth complexion, and it seemed that she aged all at once, within minutes, just before she passed away. It could have been the water, but then again my mother was a shaman; it could have been some other magic.

I too was beautiful. No need for false modesty in a story like this. Yet, in his fortieth year, my husband had turned from me, left me sleeping, crawled out of the mosquito net, climbed the hill, entered the sacred brotherhood of *sangkha*. I was a widow and not a widow.

And every morning at sunrise I bathed in the secret pool, waiting, perhaps, though I did not know for whom I waited. Until I met the steel American.

It was the morning after the last Russian left. I had left my *panung* in the cave. That was one of the reasons I kept the pool so secret; although I was a married woman, I loved to bathe naked, like a child. In this private place, I could let the cool water invade every cranny of my body. As I stood embracing myself, it seemed sometimes that the water itself loved me. It was alive and it made me come alive. It touched places my husband had never learned to touch. It made me forget the shame of having been forsaken.

But not for long. I climbed back up into the cave. Sunrise was pouring down the limestone well. I sat in a shaft of light, drying my hair with my husband's old *Phakomaah*. The void inside me ached. I wanted to pray to the guardian *vinyaan* of the hill, but I did not know what to wish for.

Dragon's Fin Soup

At that moment, I heard a crash—iron on rock—like a kettle clattering on the stove. I turned and saw the steel American. At first I didn't think he was human at all; the metal he wore glowed pink and orange in the circle of morning light. The television in the village had not worked in a long time, but I remembered the movie with the robot. No doubt robots were commonplace in America. At first I assumed he was no longer working; perhaps, like transistor radios, he ran on batteries. I did not cover myself, since he did not seem to me to be sentient, but merely a simulacrum of a man.

At that moment the visor slipped and I found myself staring into his eyes. It was too late for modesty, so I just stood there and gaped. The eyes were the color of the secret pool itself: sometimes brown, sometimes blue, depending on the light; a wisp of golden hair straggled from the helmet. His cheeks were lined and hollow; he seemed to have endured many lifetimes' suffering; but his eyes were the eyes of a boy. I thought he was beautiful, and I was ashamed that I thought him beautiful, and it brought back the memory of my husband, sitting in the lotus position in a pavilion at the monastery and gazing for hours at some inner beauty I could never impersonate. And I began to weep.

"Demons," said the steel American, "when you are tired of cajoling, you try tears. But I won't be moved."

I could understand him after a fashion because I had been learning to read the Bible with Father O'Malley.

"What are you doing here?" I said. "You're exhausted … wounded too. You're not a deserter, are you?"

"Of course not," he said. "Get thee behind me."

I can't ... you're leaning against the wall."

"Temptress! Whore of Babylon!" he gasped, and then he slumped back again. Father O'Malley used those words sometimes; it was hard to tell whether they were meant for insult or for lovemaking. Why would a wounded American call me names? I recovered enough of my sense of proprieties to slip my *panung* back on and tuck the fabric around my silver belt, and to throw on my blouse; then I took my plastic *khan* and filled it from the secret pool; then I knelt over him—he was stretched on the cavern floor, his hands clasped together like a corpse prepared for cremation—whispered an ancient formula for making lustral water, threw in a few petals from some wildflower that bloomed from a crack in the rock—I sprinkled the magic liquid over him and waited for him to awaken.

This time, he was a lot more civil.

"Are you an angel?" he said.

"Good," I said. "The last time I was a demoness." I went on sprinkling the water and whispering the meaningless syllables that came unbidden to my lips.

"What country is this?"

"That's a good question," I said. "The Russians have told us we're in a liberated zone; you people have told us we're part of a great free nation; all I know is that this mountain is called Doi Xang, that we're a village of Thai speakers, that below us there's a village where they speak Hmong. We're not actually *in* a country, though everyone around us thinks we're in *his*. We grow opium and raise pigs and ducks. I know that there's a war going on a few kilometers down the mountain, to the northeast of us. Sometimes, at night, we can look down on the flaming jungle and smell the smoke; it's a choking chemical smell mixed with the odor of burning flesh. When the television worked, we sometimes used to see news about the war. But we could never figure out what it was about, so we would switch over to "Lost in Space" or "Leave it to Beaver." But then, you see, the war doesn't touch us. Nothing does, not even the monsoon. It's because our temple is built over one of the sources of the river."

The steel American looked at me, wide-eyed and only half-comprehending. I eased his helmet off and his hair, matted and unkempt, fell on to his shoulders. A rancid odor came from inside his iron casing. I wondered how long it had been since he'd removed his armor. I tried to tug off one of his gauntlets. He pushed me away. "No!" he said. "I've sworn to live inside this metal shell until the day my quest is fulfilled."

"I see. It's a bargain you've made with your god." That was easy to understand; I had tried to deal with the Four-Faced Brahma for winning lottery numbers, but I never seemed to come up with the right offering. Or perhaps it was his way of telling me that my special powers were not meant to benefit myself, but the whole village.

"But it's not good for you," I said … "what you're wearing wasn't designed for the tropics. Your god would surely understand."

"I'm afraid not," said the steel American. "He's a hard god. Harder than the steel I gird myself with."

"I know," I said, thinking of Father O'Malley, tormenting himself whenever a woman crossed his mind.

"They said I would travel far and wide. And it's true. I've traversed the burning desert of time itself, and

I'm still no closer to my goal. They said there'd be a castle of temptation atop a mountain, and a sorceress."

"Well, this is a castle of sorts, and I did tempt you. Though I didn't mean to. And I *am* a sorceress. I know how to curse, and how to heal. Though for healing I usually prefer penicillin."

"Your words are dark," he said. "Tell me your name, mysterious lady."

"My name is Mali," I said. "*Jasmine*." He looked at me with the kind of longing a pubescent boy has; he did not even know the nature of his longing.

"I am Sir Perceval."

"Should I call you Sir, or Mr. Perceval?"

"Tempt me no more," he said. I clutched his metal hands in mine. "I hurt so much I think I'm dying."

"We can heal you," I said. "It's the least we can do."

"But I have to find the Grail!"

"*You* want the Grail?" I said. Foreboding gnawed at me. Of all the things demanded of us through the years, by the CIA and the Russians and the Vietnamese and the missionaries and the land-stealers, this was the first time someone had asked for something we actually possessed. And it was the one thing we could not give, because it would mean the death of our way of life.

"There's nothing for you here," I said. "When your wounds have healed, you can go on your way. Though you've wandered so far astray in space and time that I don't see how you can find your way back."

"You're lying," said the steel American. His jointed fingers dug into my hands and stained them with blood and rust. "You're the sorceress they told me of. This is the castle atop the hill, and this is the stream that heals all wounds."

I gazed into his eyes and knew that in his purity he saw past my dissembling. What could I tell him? "Yes," I said, staring past him at the sweating limestone, "yes, I was lying. I am that sorceress."

I had to move him out of the cave myself; I didn't want anyone to find out about the secret pool. He was delirious by then; our conversation had taken place in a moment of relative lucidity. After I had dragged him out to the other side of the waterfall, I saw my daughter Pailin pounding the washing by the side of the stream while her half-brother, Smaan, sat watching from the back of a water buffalo. I called out to them.

"We've got a new visitor," I said.

My daughter gathered her washing; Smaan went running back to get help; they managed to heft him onto the village chief's Land Rover, and we drove him down to the temple hospice.

I left him lying on a straw mat, in between a pregnant woman and a man with a gangrenous leg, who had crawled all the way to our village from a prison camp in the hope of being healed.

I didn't want him up and about and frightening the villagers, so I placed a sleeping spell over his eyes, and I told Smaan and his friends that if they said anything to anyone I would make sure they were reincarnated as cockroaches; they nodded and ran off to play among the ruined pagodas that jutted from the wild grass like the mountain's teeth. He would sleep at least until evening; by then, perhaps I would have a plan.

My daughter sat cross-legged, mixing a love potion on the veranda of our house, her baby slung across her back. Smaan was still trying to fix the television—had been trying since he was 12 years old and he was 17 now.

The baby squalled. "Oh, mother, hold her for me," Pailin said.

I took the child in my arms. "You're using my mortar and pestle," I said. I wish you'd use your own things when you do experiments,"

She was pounding furiously: locusts, hemp, toadstools, a little horse fat. "Your things have more magic than mine do," she said, "and I need the strongest I can get."

She seemed barely older than my grandchild. I wondered whether she, too, would age all at once, in the minutes before her death. Although the baby was half-Russian—we hadn't been able to save the father—no one dared ridicule my daughter, because they were afraid I would send a spirit in the night.

"You don't need to attract a husband yet; you're only 13."

She smiled and looked away. There was no need to remind me that she had been offered 5,000 baht for a two-year contract at a brothel in Chiang Rai.

"The new American," she said, "is the most beautiful man I have ever seen." Suddenly I noticed a strand of blond hair in the mixture and I realized that my daughter was in love. With a man who was forbidden to make love! I knew what it was like to love such a man, and my heart ached for her.

"Don't think about him. He's made a bargain with Phra Yesu, the Christian god; he is not allowed to remove his iron skin."

"That's ridiculous, Younger Mother," said Smaan. "How can he shit?"

Dragon's Fin Soup 97

"Who knows?" I said. "A sliding panel, perhaps."

"Well," said my daughter, "if he can have a sliding panel for that, he might just as easily have a sliding panel for the other."

"That's absurd," I said, but then I thought, why not? The Americans are not entirely human. The Vietnamese, the Montagnards, even the Russians are easier to fathom.

* * *

I went to see Father O'Malley first, because of all our visitors he was the craziest. Madmen are best at penetrating to the core of things.

The father's church, like all the other buildings in the village, was on stilts, and thatched. It was the time of the year that we hang phallic fetishes from the eaves of our houses to make sure that the earth renews itself. The sandalwood phallus brushed my face as I walked onto the veranda. I knew Father O'Malley would remove it as soon as he found it, but someone would soon sneak another one back up; there are some things that you just don't trifle with.

I washed my feet from the rainwater jar and left my sandals in front of the threshold; then I took some holy water, crossed myself, and genuflected as I went inside. O'Malley sat on the altar, scratching his head: a fat, balding, sweaty man. An electric fan, powered by the battery of a van that idled outside, blew right in his face; the rest of the church was stifling hot. The air was thick with opium smoke.

"Oh, Mali," he said. "Come for your reading lessons? Or perhaps You're in need of religious succor? It's Sunday, isn't it? So hard to keep track."

"You haven't kept track for five years, Father." It had been that long since O'Malley staggered into our village, gibbering about women being raped to death and babies sliced in two. There were no wounds in his flesh, but his soul seemed ravaged beyond repair; even now he had barely begun to heal. We couldn't in all compassion send him back out, so he was allowed to build his church, though of course no one worshipped there.

"We were studying "The Apocalypse," weren't we?" he said, reaching behind the altar for a weather-beaten Bible.

"Yes. But I don't want to read about religion today. Can we go back to what we were looking at last week ... the Arthurian romances?"

He laughed. There was a whole pile of books— mostly reclaimed from corpses found rotting in the jungle—and among them was *A Child's Treasury of Arthurian Tales*. That was where I'd first read about the Grail, and that was how I had been certain that it was in our village.

He opened that book and I got into position, that is to say I lay, face up, on the altar and unclasped my silver belt, and undid the buttons on my blouse. Father O'Malley discreetly turned his back and faced the bamboo crucifix. One hand held the book open; the other reached behind, grasped at the air for a few moments before landing, by accident it seemed, on my exposed breast. Lightly the fingers drummed as Father O'Malley read to me and I listened, filling in the words I couldn't understand with my own vision of how things must have been in the olden times ...

> *Phra Yesu, the Christian god, who was an incarnation of the god Vishnu, made his disciples drink his blood from a silver cup called the Holy Grail. It was a magic blood which could heal the universe. But Phra Yesu was attached to material things and could not free himself from the sexual desire for Mary Magdalene, who was an incarnation of Maya, the deceiving one, who tempted Buddha under the Bo tree. So Phra Yesu was made to suffer crucifixion instead of being granted enlightenment. And the silver cup was lost.*

This was the gist of what I gleaned from the priest's discourse. I could not make out all the words, but oh, the severe beauty of their sounds! I loved the clash and grinding of those English consonants, the elusive imprecision of those vowels. Father O'Malley's left hand had worked its way to my pubes now, and his index finger was warily circling my clitoris. I tried to concentrate on puzzling out the story, but his touch had already begun to tease the waters within me.

> *The Fisher King lay wounded in his castle …*

"Yes, Yes," I said, "but who is Sir Perceval?"
"Let me find where it talks about him."

Softly his left hand skimmed the hair of my pubis. I trembled. I was thinking of the first time my husband touched me. He'd started to waken my body and then without warning he shuddered and fell still … the mosquito netting hung heavy, drenched with the moisture of night. Lizards barked as they darted from cupboard to cupboard. I lay awake while my new husband slept; sometimes, through the wire-mesh window, the sky lit up with the soundless fire of the distant war; I was 16; my husband was 35; I cried as I fingered the amulet I wore to ward off the spirits that cluster around at night, when we are most vulnerable. In those days, the war was still far away. These days we could hear it as well as see the flashes in the jungle.

> *The pure fool came to Klingsor's stronghold ... the maidens danced around him, displaying their wanton charms and daring him to fall into temptation ...*

Father O'Malley dropped his book. He sighed. Perhaps he had ejaculated beneath that sweat-soaked cassock of his. Abruptly he knelt at the altar, retrieved a bundle of *mayom* branches that he kept tied up next to his bag of frankincense; he unbuttoned his cassock, stripped down to his waist, and, gazing intently at the face of Phra Yesu on the cross, began whipping himself furiously. He showed more passion than when he had furtively caressed me. I lay on the altar, unfulfilled, just as I had with my husband. This was how our reading lessons generally ended up.

When Father O'Malley finished flagellating himself, he eased his cassock back over his bruised flesh, went to the back, and got a bottle of Coke and two glasses. I buttoned myself up quickly and joined him in one of the pews, sipping my soda and watching him try to ignore his pain.

"I don't know why you beat yourself afterwards," I said. "Surely you know that the sex drive can't simply be flogged away."

"Then how does your husband manage?"

"He's a holy man," I said, and looked at the floor.

"So am I," said Father O'Malley. He too looked at the floor. A gecko ran past with a struggling dragonfly in its mouth.

"Perhaps you were a holy man once," I said, "but you have fallen from grace. Or so you claim."

"We are all fallen," he said.

"Don't you want to make love to me just once? Don't you feel hypocritical, clutching the book of learning with your right hand and groping me with your left, and feeling so filthy afterwards that you have to flagellate yourself?"

"Of course I want to make love to you," he said, his voice trembling, "but that is between you and your husband. It's what God has ordained."

"I'm afraid my husband is journeying toward the extinguishment of desire. And I'm left out."

To distract him, and to prevent him from falling prey to his temptation and having to hurt himself again; I told him about the steel American and his quest for the Grail. I told him that the man lay up at the hospice, lost in an enchanted sleep.

"He was wearing armor?" Father O'Malley paged through the King Arthur book until he found what purported to be a picture of Sir Perceval.

"That's him!" I said. "But more emaciated. And then the artist doesn't do justice to his eyes. His eyes stare right past things as though they're not there. I wasn't even sure he felt anything when he saw me naked." A thought occurred to me. "He hasn't come to take you back, has he? I mean, you are a deserter after all. Or a spy,"

"It's nothing like that. It's just that … well, he's not real anyway. He's like everything else in this damned village … an illusion. You know as well as I do that I can't go back ... that you're all part of some Twilight Zone-like hallucination that I'm having ... that I'm really out in that jungle with my left arm shattered, drowning in a swamp of leeches ... my death is still going on, a split second stretched out to forever."

"There, there," I said, stroking his hand. "Of course we're an illusion. Life itself is an illusion, according to the Lord Buddha. My husband could tell you more." A feature of Father O'Malley's madness was that he believed he was dead, and that this place was some kind of psychedelic purgatory. "But you'll want to be on hand when he wakes up. He might need another American to talk to."

"He'd be English, not American."

"Makes no difference ... American, Russian, Martian, suit yourself." "Maybe he'll need spiritual counseling," Father O'Malley said.

"You really miss being a priest, don't you? I mean, you haven't made any converts here ... except for Nit, the village idiot, and she thinks that drinking the sacramental wine is just another word for giving you a blowjob."

"I've failed her. But I can't go back. I don't have the guts to face ... what's out there. Beyond the—"

A sacred *saisin* ran the perimeter of the village. Every evening I would walk all the way around, making sure the cord was taut, looping it through banana trees and bamboo thickets, whispering the words that keep away evil. O'Malley was convinced that beyond the *saisin* was another universe, a world more real than ours.

Leaving the church, I saw that Smaan and his friends were kicking something around. It was a human

Dragon's Fin Soup

head. Russian from the headgear. I yelled at them to stop.

"The head is the seat of the soul," I said. "Show some respect. The pigs will eat it if you don't give it a decent cremation."

"But we found it outside the *saisin*," said Smaan. "And it's only a *farang's* head anyways."

I glared at him, and at length he lifted the head up high, like a flag, and the boys, marched off toward the jungle, whistling "She's Got a Ticket To Ride."

I had an exorcism and a childbirth that afternoon, so it was almost evening by the time I went in to look at the Holy Grail.

* * *

I don't know how long the Holy Grail had been in our village. Before the Grail, there had been other relics. There used to be a herb called moly that could cure even death; a bearded adventurer named Gilgamesh had come for it. That was in my mother's time. Or maybe my grandmother's. We had a golden fleece once, but all that remained of it was a shiny hank of wool.

The Holy Grail took many forms. It was never that shimmering golden chalice hovering in the air, haloed with rainbow light, like in

Father O'Malley's book. There were times when its power had resided in a broken Coke bottle. But for a few years now it had been that lowliest of household objects, the *khan* we use for drawing from the stoneware jars, tall as a ten-year-old boy, that we set out for catching the waters of the monsoon. Sir Perceval had already seen the Grail; he had come within a finger's breadth of touching it.

There was a locked room in the temple that held these treasures. The women of my family had held the key to the room since the beginning, before there was even a temple, before the Indians came to our country and converted the people to the teachings of Buddha: in the days when everyone listened to the spirits of tree and rock. In those days they didn't need people like me to interpret the language of spirits. Then we learned from the Buddhist missionaries that the spirits were illusions; that we ourselves are but shadows.

Nothing exists.

In the main hall of the temple I knelt with three joss sticks before the ten-meter-long reclining image of Lord Buddha. I said my *namo dasa* three times, stuck the joss sticks in the burner, drank in the sweet smell of incense. Then, making sure no one could see me, I crawled on my hands and knees under the tiers of altars stacked high with fruit and flowers and fresh eggs, and I crept underneath the statue, past the stucco hem of Lord Buddha's robe, until I faced the wall with the faded fresco of a gateway guarded by angels.

The key was a mantra that I repeated three times; then I was inside the room.

The room that was also the well of rock above the pool of still cool water.

The plastic *khan* I had bought at the Sunday market in the next village for 25 satang … which I'd filled with healing water and sprinkled over the steel American … it lay on a slab of rock beside the pool, where I'd last left it. I felt an overwhelming relief. The relic had a mind of its own; there were times when it refused to be found.

Dragon's Fin Soup

I held the *khan* in my cupped hands. The room spun around me. I muttered the mantra three times in reverse and presently I found myself outside, treading across the stepping stones to the pavilion beside the stream.

My husband sat there in his saffron robes, in the lotus position, on a reed mat; my stepson, his *phakomaah* hitched up, stood thigh-deep in the water casting a fishing-net.

I prostrated myself before him, keeping my distance so that he would not be polluted by the touch of a woman.

"Holiness," I said, "there's a new American. He's asking for the Grail."

"Then you must give it to him," he said.

There were those in the village who believed that my husband neither ate nor slept, and that he had sustained the lotus position for over ten years. I knew better, but you can't argue with superstition.

"How can I?" I said. "We gave away the golden fleece. We gave away the golden apples of the sun. The magical herb. The mistletoe. The urn of the demon's heart,"

"We are a very giving people."

My stepson held a wriggling fish in both hands. He held it up, laughing. "Breakfast, honored father!" he said.

"Don't wave it at me now," said my husband. "Temptation, you know." For monks may not eat after midday.

"But," I said, "everyone for miles around knows that this is the village that heals. The war rages around us and we're untouched. Wounded men come crawling past the *saisin* and we cure them. Without the Grail—"

"Oh, nonsense. It's just an old plastic bowl that you bought for 25 satang."

My husband placed his prayer fan in front of his face and chanted for about half an hour. The words of the mantra, spoke of transience and the insubstantiality of fleshly desires. Smaan gutted fish and tossed them into a bucket. The pavilion smelled of sandalwood and night-blooming jasmine; moisture was condensing out of the evening air.

At length my husband stopped his chanting. He continued the conversation as though no time had elapsed at all. "You see," he said, "we are in the business of fulfilling secret desires ... that's why the travelers come here ... and that's why they often find it so hard to leave. That is how the ones who come here are healed. That is why some cannot be healed ... they just don't have the yearning to be healed."

"I can't believe that Father O'Malley's secret desire is to fumble around inside a woman's *panung* ... and to whip himself afterwards."

"Yet he won't get up and walk away."

"If that is what he really wants, though, doesn't it mean his mind is sick and that we haven't succeeding in healing him at all?"

"It's not our place to say who is sick and who is whole."

As always, my husband spoke in riddles; as always, I knew that the answer to my dilemma lay somewhere in his words. He launched into another bout of chanting. I wanted to fling myself at him and shout, "What about *my* secret desire, what about my need for you to come back down from the mountain and put your arms around me and make me fully a woman?" But I knew he would only answer with an enigmatic smile.

"I'm taking the fish home for Pailin to cook," Smaan said, and he started to lope downhill, swinging the bucket and whistling.

"The boys were kicking around a human head this afternoon," I said. "Any moment, the barrier's going to break and the horrors beyond the *saisin* are going to leak into our world … don't you care about that?"

A bomber passed overhead. Behind the next ridge of mountains, the evening sky was bright with the aurora of warfare.

My husband said, "Remember the story of King Vessandar, who gave away his very children—those most precious to him—to a beggar, because he had managed to free himself even from love itself, that most persistent of desires. It was only when he had relinquished even love that he was free to be reborn as the Lord Buddha."

* * *

I went down to the hospice. I cured a lame child, and I let a man die in peace who had been consumed by tuberculosis, whose every breath was agony. Then I went to the room where Sir Perceval lay. Father O'Malley was already there; he sat beside the knight with open Bible, peering at the words in the light of a kerosene lamp.

On the walls, the frescoes of heaven and hell seemed to dance.

"Back off," I said. "I'm going to wake him now."

I waved my hands over the steel American's eyes.

"Don't listen to the woman," Father O'Malley said to him as he stirred. "She is a seductress; she'll lead you away from your quest." Always woman the evil one, woman the temptress, sex as the ultimate darkness; I marveled at the alienness of Christian thinking.

The eyes opened. They fixed on me. I knew that I was beautiful, like my mother, and that no man save my husband could resist me. I wondered whether he could still be moved by carnal passion or whether, inside that cage of steel, he had succumbed to atrophy. I had to know, because it was the only way to keep my village safe from him.

"You're the angel who tempted me by the pool," he said.

"Is the Grail the thing that you truly desire?"

"Yes." But the eyes told me a different story, and I dared hope that I could win my people a reprieve from the entropy that afflicts all transient things.

"Then I'll have to give it to you," I said. "This village is the place that rewards all seekers with the object of their quest. If the Grail is what you truly desire, meet me at midnight at the secret pool, the one only you and I know about."

I left so Father O'Malley could hear the knight's confession.

* * *

I found my daughter still concocting her potion, and I told her I was going to have to borrow it.

"Oh, mother," she said. "At your age." I was 29 years old. "You know it will only work if there's something there to work with,"

"I believe there is."

"Oh, mother! *I* wanted that man to make love to me! All day I've been dreaming about the milk-white skin beneath the steel, unburned by the sun and moon. It's cruel of you to take him from me."

"Trust me, Pailin." I embraced her. I was glad now that she had used my implements to make the potion. "There will be others. Your time will come."

I sat in meditation until I felt the spirit of my mother, and her mother before her, and so on, back to the beginning of time, take possession of me, one at a time. At midnight I walked back uphill to the temple, crawled behind the giant statue of Lord Buddha, and murmured the mantra that opened the wall to the secret pool beyond the cave.

The steel American was already there, kneeling by the side of the water, his hands clasping his sword. He had doffed his helmet as was proper in the presence of the divine. When I appeared, on the rock in the center of the pool, with my *panung* bound tightly about my breasts, he looked up.

"I have brought you your heart's desire," I said. The same words that my ancestresses spoke to the world's great wanderers. I held out to him the plastic *khan* filled with my daughter's potion.

"I knew you were an angel," said Sir Perceval. "I've kept myself pure. I've done everything I knew how to try to be worthy of this moment. *Deo gracias.*" Humbly he stretched his hands out to receive the relic.

I held the plastic bowl in my hand and I knew what he saw: a jeweled chalice, cunningly wrought, floating on a cloud of light. I stood above him as he knelt.

"Look into my eyes," I said, and as he gazed up at me and the moon behind me I poured the sacred water and the love potion over him so that the liquid grazed his lips and scalded the scales of reality from his eyes ... and I said, "Perceval, Perceval, I am here to give you the thing you most desire. You have fulfilled your vow and you no longer need that armor. Free yourself, Sir Perceval." I did not add, *Free me*, but I felt myself strain against the cage of my ensorcellment, the cage I had crafted around myself, the cage of my self-inflicted shame ... and the pure fool, whose eyes betrayed his true desires because he did not have the art of dissembling, he cried out, "Yes, I have fulfilled my vow!" and all at once the armor seemed to melt from him and scatter across the cool still water like a million beads of quicksilver.

Oh, he was beautiful. His skin was so pale it seemed to be wrought from the very moonlight. His penis was like a fetish carved from teakwood. His hair streamed up toward the stars as though drawing upon their brilliance. And his eyes—in the moments before they lost their innocence—were the eyes of a child. I knew then that I loved him, had always loved him even before I knew he existed for me to love.

I unloosed the knot that held my *panung* over my breasts and it too swirled away; and he seized the bowl and drained the potion and then he kissed me; and I was awakened; and we made love, in the circle of moonlight, in the water that churned and lashed and trickled in time to our passion as though it were one with the waters inside us, our blood, our sweat, our sexual fluids. I was beautiful and I knew that he found me beautiful; I knew that my breasts were ripe and fragrant as young mangoes, and my breath as

Dragon's Fin Soup

intoxicating as the jasmine of the evening. I gave him all I had withheld from other men. The void that no one had filled, I let him fill; took him into myself, like a mother receiving her child back into the womb and saying to it, *Do not be born, for the world is full of suffering*. It was my last and finest magicking.

And afterwards, when I held him in my arms, feeling the water's turbulence die down, I watched the steel American grow old and withered and disintegrate into the pool ... his eyes last of all, still fixed on mine even as his flesh lost all its substance ... I watched him fade into the past whence he had come ... and I still held the plastic *khan* in my hand, and knew that the village would endure.

* * *

Our television sputtered to life soon after that. But my eyes became too dim to watch it, and now I sit on the steps where visitors leave their shoes, chewing betel nut and letting my grandchildren describe the images they see. On this television, they tell me, brutal images of war alternate with reruns of "I Love Lucy."

Today Father O'Malley came to visit me. He walks with a cane now. We read together from the book of the apocalypse, and for old times' sake he touched me; we made love as old people do, getting more comfort from our closeness than excitement.

"Will the steel American ever be back?" I mused, as we lay together beneath the mosquito netting.

"How should I know? I'm only a deserting army chaplain, not a shamaness,"

The *saisin* had been brought in closer to the village, and now, when we walked over to the stream, it was rare to find that it was not red with human blood, or there were no bloated corpses floating slowly toward the main river. "Do you still believe that our village isn't real?"

"Yes," he said. "If I leave, I will find that a thousand years have passed, or that I am dead and buried."

Afterwards, he did not whip himself. He is coming to terms with his secret nature.

Tomorrow is my husband's funeral. Everybody is happy, as he led an exemplary life and we are glad to hasten him toward nirvana.

I no longer bathe in the sacred pool. For me there is no cave behind the waterfall. The mantra in the temple no longer works; it ceased to work shortly after I told my daughter the secret.

But I still try to go back. For, though I loved him and killed him, though I fulfilled his desire by relinquishing my own, though I lied to him by telling him the truth, and betrayed all that he believed in ... I cannot exorcise him from my mind. All my life I waited for the void to be filled, only to find that no void can be filled, no hunger satiated, until the day the soul steps away from the ceaseless cycle of *sansara* and dissolves in the cool still pool at the heart of the world.

Sometimes I toy with the idea of leaving the village. Beyond the *saisin* there are many roads. Perhaps, circling back on myself, I will find the steel American again, and my own young self, unchanged, still charged with magic.

Chui Chai

The living dead are not as you imagine them. There are no dangling innards, no dripping slime. They carry their guts and gore inside them, as do you and I. In the right light they can be beautiful, as when they stand in a doorway caught between cross-shafts of contrasting neon. Fueled by the right fantasy, they become indistinguishable from us. Listen. I know. I've touched them.

In the eighties I used to go to Bangkok a lot. The brokerage I worked for had a lot of business there, some of it shady, some not. The flight of money from Hong Kong had begun and our company, vulture that it was, was staking out its share of the loot. Bangkok was booming like there was no tomorrow. It made Los Angeles seem like Peoria. It was wild and fast and frantic and frustrating. It had temples and buildings shaped like giant robots. Its skyline was a cross between Shangri-La and Manhattan. For a dapper yuppie executive like me there were always meetings to be taken, faxes to fax, traffic to be sat in, credit cards to burn. There was also sex.

There was Patpong.

I was addicted. Days, after hours of high-level talks and poring over papers and banquets that lasted from the close of business until midnight, I stalked the crammed alleys of Patpong. The night smelled of sewage and jasmine. The heat seeped into everything. Each step I took was colored by a different neon sign. From half-open nightclub doorways buttocks bounced to jaunty soulless synthrock. Everything was for sale; the women, the boys, the pirated software, the fake Rolexes. Everything sweated. I stalked the streets and sometimes at random took an entrance, took in a live show, women propelling ping-pong balls from their pussies, boys butt-fucking on motorbikes. I was addicted. There were other entrances where I sat in waiting rooms, watched women with numbers around their necks through the one-way glass, soft, slender brown women. Picked a number. Fingered the American-made condoms in my pocket. Never buy the local ones, brother, they leak like a sieve.

I was addicted. I didn't know what I was looking for. But I knew it wasn't something you could find in Encino. I was a knight on a quest, but I didn't know that to find the Holy Grail is the worst thing that can possibly happen.

I first got a glimpse of the Grail at Club Pagoda, which was near my hotel and which is where we often liked to take our clients. The club was on the very edge of Patpong, but it was respectable—the kind of place that serves up a plastic imitation of *The King and I*, which is, of course, a plastic imitation of life in ancient Siam ... artifice imitating artifice, you see. Waiters

Dragon's Fin Soup

crawled around in mediaeval uniforms, the guests sat on the floor, except there was a well under the table to accommodate the dangling legs of lumbering white people. The floor show was eminently sober … it was all classical Thai dances, women wearing those pagoda-shaped hats moving with painstaking grace and slowness to a tinkling, alien music. A good place to interview prospective grant recipients, because it tended to make them very nervous.

Dr. Frances Stone wasn't at all nervous though. She was already there when I arrived. She was preoccupied with picking the peanuts out of her *gaeng massaman* and arranging them over her rice plate in such a way that they looked like little eyes, a nose, and a mouth.

"You like to play with your food?" I said, taking my shoes off at the edge of our private booth and sliding my legs under the table across from her.

"No," she said, I just prefer them crushed rather than whole. The peanuts I mean. You must be Mr. Leibowitz."

"Russell."

"The man I'm supposed to charm out of a few million dollars." She was doing a sort of coquettish pout, not really the sort of thing I expected from someone in medical research. Her face was ravaged, but the way she smiled kindled the memory of youthful beauty. I wondered what had happened to change her so much; according to her dossier, she was only in her mid-forties.

"Mostly we're in town to take," I said, "not to give. R&D is not one of our strengths. You might want to go to Hoechst or Berli Jucker, Frances."

"But Russell …" She had not touched her curry, but the peanuts on the rice were now formed into a perfect human face, with a few strands of sauce for hair. "This is not exactly R&D. This is a discovery that's been around for almost a century-and-a-half. My great-grand-father's paper—"

"For which he was booted out of the Austrian Academy? Yes, my dossier is pretty thorough, Dr. Stone; I know all about how he fled to America and changed his name."

She smiled. "And my dossier on you, Mr. Leibowitz, is pretty thorough too," she said, as she began removing a number of compromising photographs from her purse.

A gong sounded to announce the next dance. It was a solo. Fog roiled across the stage, and from it a woman emerged. Her clothes glittered with crystal beadwork, but her eyes outshone the yards of cubic zirconia. She looked at me and I felt the pangs of the addiction. She smiled and her lips seemed to glisten with lubricious moisture.

"You like what you see," Frances said softly.

"I—"

"The dance is called *Chui Chai*, the dance of transformation. In every Thai classical drama, there are transformations—a woman transforming herself into a rose, a spirit transforming itself into a human. After the character's metamorphosis, he performs a *chui chai* dance, exulting in the completeness and beauty of his transformed self."

I wasn't interested, but for some reason she insisted on giving me the entire story behind the dance. "This particular *chui chai* is called *Chui Chai Benjakai* … the demoness Benjakai has been despatched by the

Dragon's Fin Soup

demon king, Thotsakanth, to seduce the hero Rama ... disguised as the beautiful Sita, she will float down the river toward Rama's camp, trying to convince him that his beloved has died ... only when she is placed on a funeral pyre, woken from her death-trance by the flames, will she take on her demonic shape once more and fly away toward the dark kingdom of Lanka. But you're not listening."

How could I listen? She was the kind of woman that existed only in dreams, in poems. Slowly she moved against the tawdry backdrop, a faded painting of a palace with pointed eaves. Her feet barely touched the floor. Her arms undulated. And always her eyes held me. As though she were looking at me alone. Thai women can do things with their eyes that no other women can do. Their eyes have a secret language.

"Why are you looking at her so much?" said Frances. "She's just a Patpong bar girl ... she moonlights here ... classics in the evening, pussy after midnight."

"You know her?" I said.

"I have had some ... dealings with her."

"Just what is it that you're doing research into, Dr. Stone?"

"The boundary between life and death," she said. She pointed to the photographs. Next to them was a contract, an R&D grant agreement of some kind. The print was blurry. "Oh, don't worry, it's only a couple of million dollars ... your company won't even miss it ... and you'll own the greatest secret of all ... the tree of life and death ... the apples of Eve. Besides, I know your price and I can meet it." And she looked at the dancing girl. "Her name is Keo. I don't mind procuring if it's in the name of science."

Suddenly I realized that Dr. Stone and I were the only customers in the Club Pagoda. Somehow I had been set up.

The woman continued to dance, faster now, her hands sweeping through the air in mysterious gestures. She never stopped looking at me. She *was* the character she was playing, seductive and diabolical. There was darkness in every look, every hand-movement. I downed the rest of my Kloster lager and beckoned for another. An erection strained against my pants.

The dance ended and she prostrated herself before the audience of two, pressing her palms together in a graceful *wai*. Her eyes downcast, she left the stage. I had signed the grant papers without even knowing it.

Dr. Stone said, "On your way to the upstairs toilet ... take the second door on the left. She'll be waiting for you."

I drank another beer, and when I looked up she was gone. She hadn't eaten one bite. But the food on her plate had been sculpted into the face of a beautiful woman. It was so lifelike that ... but no. It wasn't alive. It wasn't breathing.

* * *

She was still in her dancing clothes when I went in. A little girl was carefully taking out the stitches with a seam-ripper. There was a pile of garments on the floor. In the glare of a naked bulb, the vestments of the goddess had little glamor. "They no have buttons on classical dance clothes," she said. "They just sew us into them. Cannot go pee-pee!" She giggled.

The little girl scooped up the pile and slipped away.

Dragon's Fin Soup

"You're...very beautiful," I said. I don't understand why ... I mean, why you *need* to ..."

"I have problem," she said. "Expensive problem. Dr. Stone no tell you?"

"No." Her hands were coyly clasped across her bosom. Gently I pried them away.

"You want I dance for you?"

"Dance," I said. She was naked. The way she smelled was different from other women. It was like crushed flowers. Maybe a hint of decay in them. She shook her hair and it coiled across her breasts like a nest of black serpents. When I'd seen her on stage I'd been entertaining some kind of rape fantasy about her, but now I wanted to string it out for as long as I could. God, she was driving me mad.

"I see big emptiness inside you. Come to me. I fill you. We both empty people. Need filling up."

I started to protest. But I knew she had seen me for what I was. I had money coming out my ass, but I was one fucked up yuppie. That was the root of my addiction.

Again she danced the dance of transforming, this time for me alone. Really for me alone. I mean, all the girls in Patpong have this way of making you think they love you. It's what gets you addicted. It's the only street in the world where you *can* buy love. But that's not how she was. When she touched me it was as though she reached out to me across an invisible barrier, an unbreachable gulf. Even when I entered her she was untouchable. We were from different worlds and neither of us ever left our private hells.

Not that there wasn't passion. She knew every position in the book. She knew them backwards and forwards. She kept me there all night and each act seemed as though it had been freshly invented for the two of us. It was the last time I came that I felt I had glimpsed the Grail. Her eyes, staring up into the naked bulb, brimmed with some remembered sadness. I loved her with all my might. Then I was seized with terror. She was a demon. Yellow-eyed, dragon-clawed. She was me, she was my insatiable hunger. I was fucking my own addiction. I think I sobbed. I accused her of lacing my drink with hallucinogens. I cried myself to sleep and then she left me.

I didn't notice the lumpy mattress or the peeling walls or the way the light bulb jiggled to the music from downstairs. I didn't notice the cockroaches.

I didn't notice until morning that I had forgotten to use my condoms.

* * *

It was a productive trip but I didn't go back to Thailand for another two years. I was promoted off the traveling circuit, moved from Encino to Beverly Hills, got myself a newer, late-model wife, packed my kids off to a Swiss boarding school. I also found a new therapist and a new support group. I smothered the addiction in new addictions. My old therapist had been a strict Freudian. He'd tried to root out the cause from some childhood trauma—molestation, potty training, Oedipal games—he'd never been able to find anything. I'm good at blocking out memories. To the best of my knowledge, I popped into being around age eight or nine. My parents were dead but I had a trust fund.

My best friends in the support group were Janine, who'd had eight husbands, and Mike, a transvestite with a spectacular 'fro. The clinic was in

Dragon's Fin Soup

Malibu so we could do the beach in between bouts of tearing ourselves apart. One day Thailand came up.

Mike said, "I knew this woman in Thailand. I had fun in Thailand, you know? R&R. Lot of transvestites there, hon. I'm not a fag, I just like lingerie. I met this girl." He rarely stuck to the point because he was always stoned. Our therapist, Glenda, had passed out in the redwood tub. The beach was deserted. "I knew this girl in Thailand, a dancer. She would change when she danced. I mean *change*. You shoulda seen her skin. Translucent. And she smelled different. Smelled of strange drugs."

You know I started shaking when he said that because I'd tried not to think of her all this time even though she came to me in dreams. Even before I'd start to dream, when I'd just closed my eyes, I'd hear the hollow tinkle of marimbas and see her eyes floating in the darkness.

"Sounds familiar," I said.

"Nah. There was nobody like this girl, hon, nobody. She danced in a classical dance show and she worked the whorehouses … had a day job too, working for a nutty professor woman … honky woman, withered face, glasses. Some kind of doctor, I think. Sleazy office in Patpong, gave the girls free VD drugs."

"Dr. Frances Stone." Was the company paying for a free VD clinic? What about the research into the secrets of the universe?

"Hey, how'd you know her name?"

"Did you have sex with her?" Suddenly I was trembling with rage. I don't know why. I mean, I knew what she did for a living.

"Did you?" Mike said. He was all nervous. He inched away from me, rolling a joint with one hand and scootching along the redwood deck with the other.

"I asked first," I shouted, thinking, Jesus, I sound like a ten-year-old kid.

"Of *course* not! She had problems, all right? Expensive problems. But she was beautiful, *mm-mm*, good enough to eat."

I looked wildly around. Mr. Therapist was still dozing—fabulous way to earn a thousand bucks an hour—and the others had broken up into little groups. Janine was sort of listening, but she was more interested in getting her suntan lotion on evenly.

"I want to go back," I said. "I want to see Keo again."

"Totally, like, bullshit," she said, sidling up to me. "You're just, like, externalizing the interior hurt onto a fantasy-object. Like, you need to be in touch with your child, know what I mean?"

"You're getting your support groups muddled up, hon," Mike said edgily.

"Hey, Russ, instead of, like, projecting on some past-forgettable female two years back and 10,000 miles away, why don't you, like, fixate on someone a little closer to home? I mean, I've been looking at you. I only joined this support group cause like, support groups are the only place you can find like *sensitive* guys."

"Janine, I'm married."

"So let's have an affair."

I liked the idea. My marriage to Trisha had mostly been a joke; I'd needed a fresh ornament for cocktail parties and openings; she needed security. We hadn't had much sex; how could we? I was hooked on memory. Perhaps this woman would cure me. And I wanted to be cured so badly because Mike's story had jolted me out of the fantasy that Keo had existed only for me.

By now it was the nineties so Janine insisted on a blood test before we did anything. I tested positive. I was scared shitless. Because the only time I'd ever been so careless as to forget to use a condom was ... that night. And we'd done everything. Plumbed every orifice. Shared every fluid.

It had been a dance of transformation all right.

* * *

I had nothing to lose. I divorced my wife and sent my kids to an even more expensive school in Connecticut. I was feeling fine. Maybe I'd never come down with anything. I read all the books and articles about it. I didn't tell anyone. I packed a couple of suits and some casual clothes and a supply of bootleg AZT. I was feeling fine. Fine, I told myself. Fine.

I took the next flight to Bangkok.

The company was surprised to see me, but I was such a big executive by now they assumed I was doing some kind of internal troubleshooting. They put me up at the Oriental. They gave me a 10,000 baht per diem. In Bangkok you can buy a lot for 400 bucks. I told them to leave me alone. The investigation didn't concern them. They didn't know what I was investigating, so they feared the worst.

I went to Silom, Road, where Club Pagoda had stood. It was gone. In its stead stood a brand new McDonalds and an airline ticket office. Perhaps Keo was already dead. Wasn't that what I had smelled on her? The odor of crushed flowers, wilting ... the smell of coming death? And the passion with which she had made love. I understood it now. It was the passion of the damned. She had reached out to me from a place between life and death. She had sucked the life from me and given me the virus as a gift of love.

I strolled through Patpong. Hustlers tugged at my elbows. Fake Rolexes were flashed in my face. It was useless to ask for Keo. There are a million women named Keo. *Keo* means jewel. It also means glass. In Thai there are many words that are used indiscriminately for reality and artifice. I didn't have a photograph and Keo's beauty was hard to describe. And every girl in Patpong is beautiful. Every night, parading before me in the neon labyrinth, a thousand pairs of lips and eyes, sensuous and infinitely giving. The wrong lips, the wrong eyes.

There are only a few city blocks in Patpong, but to trudge up and down them in the searing heat, questioning, observing every face for a trace of the remembered Grail … it can age you. I stopped shaving and took recreational drugs. What did it matter anyway?

But I was still fine, I wasn't coming down with anything.

I was fine. Fine!

And then, one day, while paying for a Big Mac, I saw her hands. I was looking down at the counter counting out the money. I heard the computer beep of the cash register and then I saw them: proffering the hamburger in both hands, palms up, like an offering to the gods. The fingers arched upwards, just so, with delicacy and hidden strength. God, I knew those hands. Their delicacy as they skimmed my shoulder blades, as they glided across my testicles just a hair's breadth away from touching. Their strength when she balled up her fist and shoved it into my rectum. Jesus, we'd done everything that night. I dropped my wallet on the counter, I seized those hands and gripped them, burger and all, and I felt the familiar response. Oh, God, I ached.

"Mister, you want a blowjob?"

It wasn't her voice. I looked up. It wasn't even a woman.

I looked back down at the hands. I looked up at the face. They didn't even belong together. It was a pockmarked boy and when he talked to me he stared off into space. There was no relation between the vacuity of his expression and the passion with which those hands caressed my hands.

"I don't like to do such thing," he said, "but I'm a poor college student and I needing money. So you can come back after 5 p.m. You not be disappointed."

The fingers kneaded my wrists with the familiarity of one who has touched every part of your body, who has memorized the varicose veins in your left leg and the mole on your right testicle.

It was obscene. I wrenched my own hands free. I barely remembered to retrieve my wallet before I ran out into the street.

* * *

I had been trying to find Dr. Frances Stone since I arrived, looking through the files at the corporate headquarters, screaming at secretaries. Although the corporation had funded Dr. Stone's project the records seemed to have been spirited away.

At last I realized that that was the wrong way to go about it. I remembered what Mike had told me, so the day after the encounter with Keo's hands, I was back in Patpong, asking around for a good VD clinic. The most highly regarded one of all turned out to be at the corner of Patpong and Soi Cowboy, above a store that sold pirated software and videotapes.

I walked up a steep staircase into a tiny room without windows, with a ceiling fan moving the same sweaty air around and around. A receptionist smiled at me. Her eyes had the same vacuity that the boy at McDonalds had possessed. I sat in an unraveling rattan chair and waited, and Dr. Stone summoned me into her office.

"You've done something with her," I said.

"Yes." She was shuffling a stack of papers. She had a window; she had an air-conditioner blasting away in the direction of all the computers. I was still drenched with sweat.

The phone rang and she had a brief conversation in Thai that I couldn't catch. "You're angry, of course," she said, putting down the phone. "But it was better than nothing. Better than the cold emptiness of the earth. And she had nothing to lose."

"She was dying of AIDS! And now *I* have it!" It was the first time I'd allowed the word to cross my lips. "You *killed* me!"

Frances laughed. "My," she said, "aren't we being a little melodramatic? You have the virus, but you haven't actually come down with anything."

"I'm fine. Fine."

"Well, why don't you sit down. I'll order up some food. We'll talk."

Dragon's Fin Soup

She had really gone native. In Thailand it's rude to talk business without ordering up food. Sullenly I sat down while she opened a window and yelled out an order to one of the street vendors.

"To be honest, Mr. Leibowitz," she said, "we really could use another grant. We had to spend so much of the last one on cloak-and-dagger nonsense, security, bribes, and so on; so little could be spared for research itself ... I mean, look around you ... I'm not exactly wasting money on luxurious office space, am I?"

"I saw her hands."

"Very effective, wasn't it?" The food arrived. It was some kind of noodle thing wrapped in banana leaves and groaning from the weight of chili peppers. She did not eat; instead, she amused herself by rearranging the peppers in the shape of ... "The hands, I mean. Beautiful as ever. Vibrant. Sensual. My first breakthrough."

I started shaking again. I'd read about Dr. Stone's great-grandfather and his grave robbing experiments. Jigsaw corpse's brought to life with bolts of lightning. Not life. A simulacrum of life. Could this have happened to Keo? But she was dying. Perhaps it was better than nothing. Perhaps...

"Anyhow. I was hoping you'd arrive soon, Mr. Leibowitz. Because we've made up another grant proposal. I have the papers here. I know that you've become so important now that your signature alone will suffice to bring us ten times the amount you authorized two years ago.

"I want to see her."

"Would you like to dance with her? Would you like to see her in the *chui chai* one more time?"

* * *

She led me down a different stairwell. Many flights. I was sure we were below ground level. I knew we were getting nearer to Keo because there was a hint of that rotting flower fragrance in the air. We descended. There was an unnatural chill.

And then, at last, we reached the laboratory. No shambling Igors or bubbling retorts. Just a clean, well-lit basement room. Cold, like the vault of a morgue. Walls of white tile; ceiling of stucco; fluorescent lamps; the pervasive smell of the not-quite-dead.

Perspex tanks lined the walls. They were full of fluid and body parts. Arms and legs floating past me. Torsos twirled. A woman's breast peered from between a child's thighs. In another tank, human hearts swirled, each neatly severed at the aorta. There was a tank of eyes. Another of genitalia. A necklace of tongues hung suspended in a third. A mass of intestines writhed in a fourth. Computers drew intricate charts on a bank of monitors. Oscilloscopes beeped. A pet gibbon was chained to a post topped by a human skull. There was something so outlandishly antiseptic about this spectacle that I couldn't feel the horror.

"I'm sorry about the decor, Russell, but you see, we've had to forgo the usual decoration allowance." The one attempt at dressing up the place was a frayed poster of *Young Frankenstein* tacked to the far wall. "Please don't be upset at all the body parts," she added. "It's all very macabre, but one gets inured to it in med school; if you feel like losing your lunch, there's a small restroom on your left … yes, between the eyes and the

Dragon's Fin Soup

tongues." I did not feel sick. I was feeling ... excited. It was the odor. I knew I was getting closer to Keo.

She unlocked another door. We stepped into an inner room.

Keo was there. A cloth was draped over her, but seeing her face after all these years made my heart almost stop beating. The eyes. The parted lips. The hair, streaming upward toward a source of blue light ... although I felt no wind in the room. "It is an electron wind," said Dr. Stone. "No more waiting for the monsoon lightning. We can get more power from a wall socket than Great-Grandfather Victor could ever dream of stealing from the sky."

And she laughed the laughter of mad scientists.

I saw the boy from McDonalds sitting in a chair. The hands reached out toward me. There were electrodes fastened to his temples. He was naked now, and I saw the scars where the hands had been joined at the wrists to someone else's arms. I saw a woman with Keo's breasts, wired to a pillar of glass, straining, heaving while jags of blue lightning danced about her bonds. I saw her vagina stitched onto the pubis of a dwarf, who lay twitching at the foot of the pillar. Her feet were fastened to the body of a five-year-old boy, transforming their grace to ungainliness as he stomped in circles around the pillar.

"Jigsaw people!" I said.

"Of course!" said Dr. Stone. "Do you think I would be so foolish as to bring back people whole? Do you not realize what the consequences would be? The legal redefinition of life and death ... wills declared void, humans made subservient to walking corpses ... I'm a scientist, not a philosopher."

"But who are they now?"

"They were nobody before. Street kids. Prostitutes. They were dying, Mr. Leibowitz, dying! They were glad to will their bodies to me. And now they're more than human. They're many persons in many bodies. A gestalt. I can shuffle them and put them back together, oh, so many different ways ... and the beautiful Keo. Oh, she wept when she came to me. When she found out she had given you the virus. She loved you. You were the last person she ever loved. I saved her for you. She's been sleeping here, waiting to dance for you, since the day she died. Oh, let us not say *died*. The day she ... she ... I am no poet, Mr. Leibowitz. Just a scientist."

I didn't want to listen to her. All I could see was Keo's face. It all came back to me. Everything we had done. I wanted to relive it. I didn't care if she was dead or undead. I wanted to seize the Grail and clutch it in my hands and own it.

Frances threw a switch. The music started. The shrilling of the *pinai*, the pounding of the *taphon*, the tinkling of marimbas and xylophones rang in the *chui chai* music. Then she slipped away unobtrusively. I heard a key turn in a lock. She had left the grant contract lying on the floor. I was alone with all the parts of the woman I'd loved. Slowly I walked toward the draped head. The electron wind surged; the cold blue light intensified. Her eyes opened. Her lips moved as though discovering speech for the first time ...

"*Rus ... sell.*"

On the pizza-faced boy, the hands stirred of their own accord. He turned his head from side to side and the hands groped the air, straining to touch my face. Keo's lips were dry. I put my arms around the drape-shrouded body and kissed the dead mouth. I could feel my hair stand on end.

"*I see big emptiness inside you. Come to me. I fill you. We both empty people. Need filling up.*"

"Yes. Jesus, Yes."

I hugged her to me. What I embraced was cold and prickly. I whisked away the drape. There was no body. Only a framework of wires and transistors and circuit boards and tubes that fed flasks of flaming reagents.

"*I dance for you now.*"

I turned. The hands of the McDonalds boy twisted into graceful patterns. The feet of the child moved in syncopation to the music, dragging the rest of the body with them. The breasts of the chained woman stood firm, waiting for my touch. The music welled up. A contralto voice spun plaintive *melismas* over the interlocking rhythms of wood and metal. I kissed her. I kissed that severed head and lent my warmth to the cold tongue, awakened passion in her. I kissed her. I could hear chains breaking and wires slithering along the floor tiles.

There were hands pressed into my spine, rubbing my neck, unfastening my belt. A breast touched my left buttock and a foot trod lightly on my right. I didn't care that these parts were attached to other bodies. They were hers. She was loving me all over. The dwarf that wore her pudenda was climbing up my leg. Every part of her was in love with me. Oh, she danced. We danced together. I was the epicenter of their passion. We were empty people but now we drank our fill. Oh, God, we danced. Oh, it was a grave music, but it contented us.

And I signed everything, even the codicil.

* * *

Today I am in the AIDS ward of a Beverly Hills hospital. I don't have long to wait. Soon the codicil will come into effect, and my body will be preserved in liquid nitrogen and shipped to Patpong.

The nurses hate to look at me. They come at me with rubber gloves on so I won't contaminate them, even though they should know better. My insurance policy has disowned me. My children no longer write me letters, though I've paid for them to go to Ivy League colleges. Trisha comes by sometimes. She is happy that we rarely made love.

One day I will close my eyes and wake up in a dozen other bodies. I will be closer to her than I could ever be in life. In life we are all islands. Only in Dr. Stone's laboratory can we know true intimacy, the mind of one commanding the muscles of another and causing the nerves of a third to tingle with unnameable desires. I hope I shall die soon.

The living dead are not as you imagine them. There are no dangling innards, no dripping slime. They carry their guts and gore inside them, as do you and I. In the right light they can be beautiful, as when they stand in the cold luminescence of a basement laboratory, waiting for an electron stream to lend them the illusion of life. Fueled by the right fantasy, they become indistinguishable from us.

Listen. I know. I've loved them.

The Bird Catcher

There was this other boy in the internment camp. His name was Jim. After the war, he made something of a name for himself. He wrote books, even a memoir of the camp that got turned into a Spielberg movie. It didn't turn out that gloriously for me.

My grandson will never know what it's like to be consumed with hunger; hunger that is heartache. Hunger that can propel you past insanity. But I know. I've been there. So has that boy Jim; that's why I really don't envy him his Spielberg movie.

After the war, my mother and I were stranded in China for a few more years. She was penniless, a lady journalist in a time when lady journalists only covered church bazaars; a single mother at a time when "bastard" was more than a bad word.

You might think that at least we had each other, but my mother and I never intersected. Not as mother and son, not even as Americans awash in great events and oceans of Asian faces. We were both loners. We were both vulnerable.

That's how I became the boogieman's friend.

He's long dead now, but they keep him, you know, in the Museum of Horrors. Once in a generation, I visit him. Yesterday, I took my grandson Corey. Just as I took his father before him.

The destination stays the same, but the road changes every generation. The first time I had gone by boat, along the quiet back canals of the old city. Now there was an expressway. The toll was forty baht—a dollar—a month's salary that would have been, back in the fifties, in old Siam.

My son's in love with Bangkok—the insane skyline, the high-tech blending with the low-tech, the skyscraper shaped like a giant robot, the palatial shopping malls, the kinky sex bars, the bootleg software arcades, the whole tossed salad. And he doesn't mind the heat. He's a big-time entrepreneur here, owns a taco chain.

I live in Manhattan. It's quieter.

I can be anonymous. I can be alone. I can nurse my hunger in secret.

Christmases, though, I go to Bangkok. This Christmas, my grandson's eleventh birthday, I told my son it was time. He nodded and told me to take the chauffeur for the day.

So, to get to the place, you zigzag through the world's raunchiest traffic, then you fly along this madcap figure-eight expressway, cross the river where stone demons stand guard on the parapets of the Temple of Dawn, and then you're suddenly in this sleazy alley. Vendors hawk bowls of soup and pickled guavas. The directions are on a handwritten placard attached to a street sign with duct tape.

Dragon's Fin Soup

It's the Police Museum, upstairs from the local morgue. One wall is covered with photographs of corpses. That's not part of the museum, it's a public service display for people with missing family members to check if any of them have turned up dead. Corey didn't pay attention to the photographs; he was busy with Pokémon.

Upstairs, the feeling changed. The stairs creaked. The upstairs room was garishly lit. Glass cases along the walls were filled with medical oddities, two-headed babies and the like, each one in a jar of formaldehyde, each one meticulously labeled in Thai and English. The labels weren't printed, mind you. Handwritten. There was definitely a middle-school show-and-tell feel about the exhibits. No air-conditioning. And no more breeze from the river like in the old days; skyscrapers had stifled the city's breath.

There was a uniform, sick-yellow tinge to all the displays … the neutral cream paint was edged with yellow … the deformed livers, misshapen brains, tumorous embryos all floating in a dull yellow fluid … the heaps of dry bones an orange-yellow, the rows of skulls yellowing in the cracks … and then there were the young novices, shaven-headed little boys in yellow robes, staring in a heat-induced stupor as their mentor droned on about the transience of all existence, the quintessence of Buddhist philosophy.

And then there was Si Ui.

He had his own glass cabinet, like a phone booth, in the middle of the room. Naked. Desiccated. A mummy. Skinny. Mud-colored, from the embalming process, I think.

A sign—handwritten, of course—explained who he was: *See Ui. Devourer of Children's Livers in the 1950s.*

My grandson reads Thai more fluently than I do. He sounded out the name right away.

Si Sui Sae Ung.

"It's the boogieman, isn't it?" Corey said. But he showed little more than a passing interest. It was the year Pokémon Gold and Silver came out. So many new monsters to catch, so many names to learn.

"He hated cages," I said.

"Got him!" Corey squealed. Then, not looking up at the dead man, "I know who he was. They did a documentary on him. Can we go now?"

"Didn't your maid tell you stories at night? To frighten you? 'Be a good boy, or Si Ui will eat your liver'?"

"Gimme a break, Grandpa. I'm too old for that shit." He paused. Still wouldn't look up at him. There were other glass booths in the room, other mummified criminals: a serial rapist down the way. But Si Ui was the star of the show.

"Okay," Corey said, "she did try to scare me once. Well, I was like five, okay? Si Ui. You watch out, he'll eat your liver, be a good boy now. Sure, I heard that before. Well, he's not gonna eat my liver now, is he? I mean, that's probably not even him; it's probably like wax or something."

He smiled at me. The dead man did not.

"I knew him," I said. "He was my friend."

"I get it!" Corey said, back to his Gameboy. "You're like me in this Pokémon game. You caught a monster once. And tamed him. You caught the most famous monster in Thailand."

"And tamed him?" I shook my head. "No, not tamed."

"Can we go to McDonald's now?"

Dragon's Fin Soup

"You're hungry."

"I could eat the world!"

"After I tell you the whole story."

"You're gonna talk about the Chinese camp again, Grandpa? And that kid Jim, and the Spielberg movie?"

"No, Corey, this is something I've never told you about before. But I'm telling you so when I'm gone, you'll know to tell your son. And your grandson."

"Okay, Grandpa."

And finally, tearing himself away from the video game, he willed himself to look.

The dead man had no eyes; he could not stare back.

* * *

He hated cages. But his whole life was a long imprisonment. Without a cage, he did not even exist.

Listen, Corey. I'll tell you how I met the boogieman.

Imagine I'm 11 years old, same as you are now, running wild on a leaky ship crammed with coolies. They're packed into the lower deck. We can't afford the upper deck, but when they saw we were white, they waved us on up without checking our tickets. It looks more interesting down there. And the food's got to be better. I can smell a Chinese breakfast. That oily fried bread, so crunchy on the outside, dripping with pig fat … yeah.

It's hot. It's boring. Mom's on the prowl. A job or a husband, whichever comes first. Everyone's fleeing the communists. We're some of the last white people to get out of China.

Someone's got a portable charcoal stove on the lower deck, and there's a toothless old woman cooking congee, fanning the stove. A whiff of opium in the air blends with the rich gingery broth. Everyone down there's clustered around the food. Except this one man. Harmless-looking. Before the Japs came, we had a gardener who looked like that. Shirtless, thin, by the railing. Stiller than a statue. And a bird on the railing. Also unmoving. The other coolies are ridiculing him, making fun of his Hakka accent, calling him simpleton.

I watch him.

"Look at the idiot," the toothless woman says. "Hasn't said a word since we left Swatow."

The man has his arms stretched out, his hands cupped. Frozen. Concentrated. I suddenly realize I've snuck down the steps myself, pushed my through all the Chinese around the cooking pot, and I'm halfway there. Mesmerized. The man is stalking the bird, the boy stalking the man. I try not to breathe as I creep up.

He pounces. Wrings the bird's neck in one swift liquid movement, a twist of the wrist, and he's already plucking the feathers with the other hand, ignoring the death-spasms. And I'm real close now. I can smell him. Mud and sweat. Behind him, the open sea. On the deck, the feathers, a bloody snowfall.

He bites off the head and I hear the skull crunch.

I scream. He whirls. I try to cover it up with a childish giggle.

He speaks in a monotone. Slowly. Sounding out each syllable, but he seems to have picked up a little pidgin. "Little white boy. You go upstairs. No belong here."

"I go where I want. They don't care."

He offers me a raw wing.

Dragon's Fin Soup

"Boy hungry?"

"Man hungry?"

I fish in my pocket, find half a liverwurst sandwich. I hold it out to him. He shakes his head. We both laugh a little. We've both known this hunger that consumes you; the agony of China is in our bones.

I say, "Me and Mom are going to Siam. On account of my dad getting killed by the Japs and we can't live in Shanghai anymore. We were in a camp and everything." He stares blankly and so I bark in Japanese, like the guards used to. And he goes crazy.

He mutters to himself in Hakka which I don't understand that well, but it's something like, "Don't look 'em in the eye. They chop off your head. You stare at the ground, they leave you alone." He is chewing away at raw bird flesh the whole time. He adds in English, "Si Ui no like Japan man."

"Makes two of us," I say.

I've seen too much. Before the internment camp, there was Nanking. Mom was gonna do an article about the atrocities. I saw them. You think a two-year-old doesn't see anything? She carried me on her back the whole time, papoose-style.

When you've seen a river clogged with corpses, when you've looked at piles of human heads, and human livers roasting on spits, and women raped and set on fire, well, Santa and the Tooth Fairy just don't cut it. I pretended about the Tooth Fairy, though, for a long time. Because, in the camp, the ladies would pool their resources to bribe Mr. Tooth Fairy Sakamoto for a little piece of fish.

"I'm Nicholas," I say.

"Si Ui." I don't know if it's his name or something in Hakka.

I hear my mother calling from the upper deck. I turn from the strange man, the raw bird's blood trailing from his lips. "Gotta go." I turn to him, pointing at my chest, and I say, "Nicholas."

Even the upper deck is cramped. It's hotter than Shanghai, hotter even than the internment camp. We share a cabin with two Catholic priests who let us hide out there after suspecting we didn't have tickets.

Night doesn't get any cooler, and the priests snore. I'm down to a pair of shorts and I still can't sleep. So I slip away. It's easy. Nobody cares. Millions of people have been dying and I'm just some skinny kid on the wrong side of the ocean. Me and my mom have been adrift for as long as I can remember.

The ship groans and clanks. I take the steep metal stairwell down to the coolies' level. I'm wondering about the birdcatcher. Down below, the smells are a lot more comforting. The smell of sweat and soy-stained clothing masks the odor of the sea. The charcoal stove is still burning. The old woman is simmering some stew. Maybe something magical ... a bit of snake's blood to revive someone's limp dick, crushed tiger bones, powdered rhinoceros horn ... to heal pretty much anything. People are starving, but you can still get those kind of ingredients. I'm 11, and I already know too much.

They are sleeping every which way, but it's easy for me to step over them even in the dark. The camp was even more crowded than this, and a misstep could get you hurt. There's a little bit of light from the little clay stove.

I don't know what I'm looking for. Just to be alone, I guess. I can be more alone in a crowd of

Dragon's Fin Soup 141

Chinese than up there. Mom says things will be better in Siam. I don't know.

I've threaded my way past all of them. And I'm leaning against the railing. There isn't much moonlight. It's probably past midnight but the metal is still hot. There's a warm wind, though, and it dries away my sweat. China's too far away to see, and I can't even imagine Boston anymore.

He pounces.

Leather hands rasp my shoulders. Strong hands. Not big, but I can't squirm out of their grip. The hands twirl me around and I'm looking into Si Ui's eyes. The moonlight is in them. I'm scared. I don't know why, really, all I'd have to do is scream and they'll pull him off me. But I can't get the scream out.

I look into his eyes and I see fire. A burning village. Maybe it's just the opium haze that clings to this deck, making me feel all weird inside, seeing things. And the sounds. I think it must be the whispering of the sea, but it's not, it's voices. Hungry, you little Chink? And those leering, bucktoothed faces. Like comic book Japs. Barking. The fire blazes. And then, abruptly, it dissolves. And there's a kid standing in the smoky ruins. Me. And I'm holding out a liverwurst sandwich. Am I really than skinny, that pathetic? But the vision fades. And Si Ui's eyes become empty. Soulless.

"Si Ui catch anything," he says. "See, catch bird, catch boy. All same." And smiles, a curiously captivating smile.

"As long as you don't eat me," I say.

"Si Ui never eat Nicholas," he says. "Nicholas friend."

Friend? In the burning wasteland of China, an angel holding out a liverwurst sandwich? It makes me smile. And suddenly angry. The anger hits me so suddenly I don't even have time to figure out what it is. It's the war, the maggots in the millet, the commandant kicking me across the yard, but more than that it's my mom, clinging to her journalist fantasies while I dug for earthworms, letting my dad walk out to his death. I'm crying and the birdcatcher is stroking my cheek, saying, "You no cry now. Soon go back America. No one cry there." And it's the first time someone has touched me with some kind of tenderness in … in … in … I dunno, since before the invasion. Because Mom doesn't hug, she kind of encircles, and her arms are like the bars of a cage.

* * *

So, I'm thinking this will be my last glimpse of Si Ui. It's in the harbor at Klong Toey. You know, where Anna landed in *The King and I*. And where Joseph Conrad landed in *Youth*.

So all these coolies, and all these trapped Americans and Europeans, they're all stampeding down the gangplank, with cargo being hoisted; workmen trundling; fleets of those bicycle pedicabs called *samlors*; itinerant merchants with bales of silk and fruits that seem to have hair or claws; and then there's the smell that socks you in the face—gasoline and jasmine and decay and incense. Pungent salt squid drying on racks. The ever-present fish sauce, blending with the odor of fresh papaya and pineapple and coconut and human sweat.

And my mother's off and running—with me barely keeping up—chasing after some waxed-mustache

Dragon's Fin Soup

British doctor guy with one of those accents you think's a joke until you realize that's really how they talk.

So I'm just carried along by the mob.

"You buy bird, little boy?" I look up. It's a wall of sparrows, each one in a cramped wooden cage. Rows and rows of cages, stacked up from the concrete high as a man, more cages hanging from wires, stuffed into the branch-crooks of a mango tree. I see others buying the birds for a few coins, releasing them into the air.

"Why are they doing that?"

"Good for your karma. Buy bird, set bird free, shorten your suffering in your next life."

"Swell," I say.

Further off, the vendor's boy is catching them, coaxing them back into cages. That's got to be wrong, I'm thinking as the boy comes back with ten little cages hanging on each arm. The birds haven't gotten far. They can barely fly. Answering my unspoken thought, the bird seller says, "Oh, we clip wings. Must make living too, you know."

That's when I hear a sound like the thunder of a thousand wings. I think I must be dreaming. I look up. The crowd has parted. And there's a skinny little shirtless man standing in the clearing—his arms spread wide like a Jesus statue—only you can barely see a square inch of him because he's all covered in sparrows. They're perched all over his arms like they're telegraph wires or something, and squatting on his head, and clinging to his baggy homespun shorts with their claws. And the birds are all chattering at once, drowning out the cacophony of the mob.

Si Ui looks at me. And in his eyes I see ... bars. Bars of light, maybe. Prison bars. The man's trying to tell me something. I'm trapped.

The crowd that parted all of sudden comes together and he's gone. I wonder if I'm the only one who saw. I wonder if it's just another aftereffect of the opium that clogged the walkways on the ship.

But it's too late to wonder; my mom has found me, she's got me by the arm and she's yanking me back into the stream of people. And in the next few weeks I don't think about Si Ui at all. Until he shows up—just like that—in a village called Thapsakae.

* * *

After the museum, I took Corey to Baskin-Robbins and popped into Starbucks next door for a frappuccino. Visiting the boogieman is a draining thing. I wanted to let him down easy. But Corey didn't want to let go right away.

"Can we take a boat ride or something?" he said. "You know I never get to come to this part of town." It's true. The traffic in Bangkok is so bad that they sell little car toilets so you can go while you're stuck at a red light for an hour. This side of town—Thonburi, the old capital—is a lot more like the past. But no one bothers to come. The traffic, they say, always the traffic.

We left the car by a local pier, hailed a river taxi, just told him to go, anywhere, told him we wanted to ride around. Overpaid him. It served me right for being me, an old white guy in baggy slacks, with a facing-backwards-Yankees-hat-toting blond kid in tow.

When you leave the river behind, there's a network of canals, called *klongs*, that used to be the arteries and capillaries of the old city. In Bangkok proper, they've all [mostly] been filled in. But not here. The further from the main waterway we floated, the further back in time. Now the *klongs* were fragrant with jasmine, with stilted houses rearing up behind thickets of banana and bamboo. And I was remembering more.

Rain jars by the landing docks … lizards basking in the sun … young boys leaping into the water.

"The water was a lot clearer," I told my grandson. "And the swimmers weren't wearing those little trunks … they were naked."

Recently—fearing to offend the sensibilities of tourists—the Thai government made a fuss about little boys skinny dipping along the tourist riverboat routes. But the river is so polluted now, one wonders what difference it makes.

They were bobbing up and down around the boat. Shouting in fractured English. Wanting a lick of Corey's Baskin-Robbins. When Corey spoke to them in Thai, they swam away. Tourists who speak the language aren't tourists anymore.

"You used to do that, huh, Grandpa?"

"Yes," I said.

"I like the Sports Club better. The water's clean. And they make a mean chicken sandwich at the poolside bar."

I only went to the sports club once in my life. A week after we landed in Bangkok, a week of sleeping on a pew at a missionary church, a week wringing out the same clothes and ironing them over and over.

"I never thought much of the Sports Club," I said.

"Oh, Grandpa, you're such a prole." One of his father's words, I thought, smiling.

"Well, I did grow up in Red China," I said.

"Yeah," he said. "So what was it like, the Sports Club?"

* * *

A little piece of England in the midst of all this tropical stuff. The horse races. Cricket. My mother has a rendezvous with the doctor, the one she's been flirting with on the ship. They have tea and crumpets. They talk about the Bangkok Chinatown riots, and about money. I am reading a battered EC comic that I found in the reading room.

"Well, if you don't mind going native," the doctor says, "there's a clinic, down south a bit; pay wouldn't be much, and you'll have to live with the benighted buggers, but I daresay you'll cope."

"Oh, I'll go native," Mom says, "as long as I can keep writing. I'll do anything for that. I'd give you a blowjob if that's what it takes."

"Heavens," says the doctor. "More tea?"

* * *

And so, a month later, we come to a fishing village nestled in the western crook of the Gulf of Siam, and I swear it's paradise. There's a village school taught by monks, and a little clinic where Mom works, dressing wounds, jabbing penicillin into people's buttocks; I think she's working on a novel. That doctor she was flirting with got her this job because she speaks Chinese, and the village is full of Chinese immigrants—smuggled across the sea—looking for some measure of freedom.

Thapsakae … it rhymes with Tupperware … it's always warm, but never stifling like in Bangkok … always a breeze from the unseen sea, shaking the ripe coconuts from the trees … a town of stilted dwellings, a

Dragon's Fin Soup

tiny main street with storefront rowhouses, fields of neon green rice as far as the eye can see, lazy water buffalo wallowing, and always the canals running alongside the half-paved road, women beating their wet laundry with rocks in the dawn, boys diving in the noonday heat ... the second day I'm there, I meet these kids, Lek and Sombun. They're my age. I can't understand a word they're saying at first. I'm watching them, leaning against a dragon-glazed rain jar, as they shuck their school uniforms and leap in. They're laughing a lot, splashing, one time they're throwing a catfish back and forth like it's some kind of volleyball, but they're like fishes themselves, silvery brown sleek things chattering in a singsong language. And I'm alone, like I was at the camp, flinging stones into the water. Except I'm not scared like I was there. There's no time I have to be home. I can reach into just about any thicket and pluck out something good to eat: bananas, mangoes, little pink sour-apples. My shorts are all torn (I still only have one pair) and my shirt is stained with the juices of exotic fruits, and I let my hair grow as long as I want.

Today I'm thinking of the birds.

You buy a bird to free yourself from the cage of karma. You free the bird, but its wings are clipped and he's inside another cage, a cage circumscribed by the fact that he can't fly far. And the boy that catches him is in another cage, apprenticed to that vendor, unable to fly free. Cages within cages within cages. I've been in a cage before; one time in the camp they hung me up in one in the commandant's office and told me to sing.

Here, I don't feel caged at all.

The Thai kids have noticed me and they pop up from the depths right next to me, staring curiously.

They're not hostile. I don't know what they're saying, but I know I'm soon going to absorb this musical language. Meanwhile, they're splashing me, daring me to dive in, and in the end I throw off these filthy clothes and I'm in the water and it's clear and warm and full of fish. And we're laughing and chasing each other. And they do know a few words of English; they've picked it up in that village school, where the monks have been ramming a weird antiquated English phrasebook down their throats.

But later, after we dry off in the sun and they try to show me how to ride a water buffalo, we sneak across the *gailan* field and I see him again. The Birdcatcher, I mean. *Gailan* is a Chinese vegetable like broccoli, only without the bushy part. The Chinese immigrants grow it here. They all work for this one rich Chinese man named Tae Pak, the one who had the refugees shipped to this town as cheap labor.

"You want to watch TV?" Sombun asks me.

I haven't had much of a chance to see TV. He takes me by the lead and pulls me along, with Lek behind him, giggling. Night has fallen. It happens really suddenly in the tropics, boom and it's dark. In the distance, past a wall of bamboo trees, we see glimmering lights. Tae Pak has electricity. Not that many private homes have. Mom and I use kerosene lamps at night. I've never been to his house, but I know we're going there. Villagers are zeroing in on the house now, walking sure-footedly in the moonlight. The stench of night-blooming jasmine is almost choking in the compound. A little shrine to the Mother of Mercy stands by the entrance, and ahead we see what passes for a mansion here; the wooden stilts and the thatched roof with the pointed eaves, like everyone else's house,

Dragon's Fin Soup

but spread out over three sides of a quadrangle, and in the center a ruined pagoda, whose origin no one remembers.

The usual pigs and chickens are running around in the space under the house, but the stairway up to the veranda is packed with people, kids mostly, and they're all gazing upward. The object of their devotion is a television set, the images on it ghostly, the sound staticky and in Thai in any case … but I recognize the show … it's "I Love Lucy." And I'm just staring and staring. Sombun pushes me up the steps. I barely remember to remove my sandals and step in the trough at the bottom of the steps to wash the river-mud off my feet. It's really true. I can't understand a word of it but it's still funny. The kids are laughing along with the laughtrack.

Well, that's when I see Si Ui. I point at him. I try to attract his attention, but he too, sitting cross-legged on the veranda, is riveted to the screen. And when I try to whisper to Sombun that hey, I know this guy, what a weird coincidence, Sombun just whispers back, "*Jek, Jek*," which I know is a putdown word for a Chinaman.

"I know him," I whisper. "He catches birds. And eats them. Alive." I try to attract Si Ui's attention. But he won't look at me. He's too busy staring at Lucille Ball. I'm a little bit afraid to look at him directly, scared of what his eyes might disclose, our shared and brutal past.

Lek, whose nickname just means "tiny", shudders.

"*Jek, Jek*," Sombun says. The laughtrack kicks in.

* * *

Everything has changed now that I know he's here. On my reed mat, under the mosquito nets every night, I toss and turn, and I see things. I don't think they're dreams. I think it's like the time I looked into Si Ui's eyes and saw the fire. I see a Chinese boy running through a field of dead people. It's sort of all in black and white and he's screaming and behind him a village is burning.

At first it's the Chinese boy but somehow it's me too, and I'm running, with my bare feet squishing into dead men's bowels, running over a sea of blood and shit. And I run right into someone's arms. Hard. The comic-book Japanese villain face. A human heart, still beating, in his hand.

"Hungry, you little Chink?" he says.

"Little Chink. Little *Jek*."

Intestines are writhing up out of disemboweled bodies like snakes. I saw a lot of disemboweled Japs. Their officers did it in groups, quietly, stony-faced. The honorable thing to do.

I'm screaming myself awake. And then, from the veranda, maybe, I hear the tap of my mom's battered typewriter, an old Hermes she bought in the Sunday market in Bangkok for a hundred baht.

I crawl out of bed. It's already dawn.

"Hi, Mom," I say, as I breeze past her, an old *phakomaah* wrapped around my loins.

"Wow! It talks."

"Mom, I'm going over to Sombun's house to play."

"You're getting the hang of the place, I take it."

"Yeah."

"Pick up some food, Nicholas."

Dragon's Fin Soup

"Okay." Around here, a dollar will feed me and her three square meals. But it won't take away the other hunger.

Another lazy day of running myself ragged, gorging on papaya and coconut milk, another day in paradise.

It's time to meet the serpent, I decide.

* * *

Sombun tells me someone's been killed, and we sneak over to the police station. Si Ui is there, sitting at a desk, staring at a wall. I think he's just doing some kind of alien registration thing. He has a Thai interpreter, the same toothless woman I saw on the boat. And a policeman is writing stuff down in a ledger.

There's a woman sitting on a bench, rocking back and forth. She's talking to everyone in sight. Even me and Sombun.

Sombun whispers, "That woman Daeng. Daughter die."

Daeng mumbles, "My daughter. By the railway tracks. All she was doing was running down the street for an ice coffee. Oh, my terrible karma." She collars a passing inspector. "Help me. My daughter. Strangled, raped."

"That Inspector Jed," Sombun whispered to me. "Head of the whole place."

Inspector Jed is being polite, compassionate, and efficient at the same time. I like him. My mom should hang out with people like that instead of the losers who are just looking for a quick lay.

The woman continues muttering to herself. "Nit, Nit, Nit, Nit, Nit," she says. That must be the girl's name. They all have nicknames like that. *Nit* means "tiny", too, like *lek*. "Dead, strangled," she says. "And this town is supposed to be heaven on earth. The sea, the palm trees, the sun always bright. This town has a dark heart."

Suddenly, Si Ui looks up. Stares at her. As though remembering something. Daeng is sobbing. And the policeman who's been interviewing him says, "Watch yourself, Chink. Everyone smiles here. Food falls from the trees. If a little girl's murdered, they'll file it away; they won't try to find out who did it. Because this is a perfect place, and no one gets murdered. We all love each other here … you little *Jek*."

Si Ui has this weird look in his eye. Mesmerized. My mother looks that way sometimes … when a man catches her eye and she's zeroing in for the kill. The woman's mumbling that she's going to go be a nun now, she has nothing left to live for.

"Watch your back, *Jek*," says the policeman. He's trying, I realize, to help this man, who he probably thinks is some kind of village idiot type. "Someone'll murder you just for being a stupid little Chink. And no one will bother to find out who did it."

"Si Ui hungry," says Si Ui.

I realize that I speak his language, and my friends do not.

"Si Ui!" I call out to him.

He freezes in his tracks, and slowly turns, and I look into his eyes for the second time, and I know that it was no illusion before.

Somehow we've seen through each other's eyes.

I am misfit kid in a picture-perfect town with a dark heart, but I understand what he's saying, because though I look all different I come from where he comes

Dragon's Fin Soup

from. I've experienced what it's like to be Chinese. You can torture them and kill them by millions, like the Japs did, and still they endure. They just shake it off. They've outlasted everyone so far. And will till the end of time. Right now in Siam they're the coolies and the laborers, and soon they're going to end up owning the whole country. They endure. I saw their severed heads piled up like battlements, and the river choked with their corpses, and they outlasted it all.

These Thai kids will never understand.

"See Ui hungry!" the man cries.

That afternoon, I slip away from my friends at the river, and I go to the *gailan* field where I know he works. He never acknowledges my presence, but later, he strides further and further from the house of his rich patron, towards a more densely wooded area past the fields. It's all banana trees, the little bananas that have seeds in them, you chew the whole banana and spit out the seeds, *rat-tat-tat*, like a machine gun. There's bamboo, too, and the jasmine bushes that grow wild, and mango trees. Si Ui doesn't talk to me, doesn't look back, but somehow I know I'm supposed to follow him.

And I do.

Through the thicket, into a private clearing, the ground overgrown with weeds, the whole thing surrounded by vegetation, and in the middle of it a tumbledown house, the thatch unpatched in places, the stilts decaying and carved with old graffiti. The steps are lined with wooden cages. There's birdshit all over the decking, over the wooden railings, even around the foot trough. Birds are chattering from the cages, from the air around us. The sun has been searing and sweat is running down my face, my chest, soaking my *phakomaah*.

We don't go up into the house. Instead, Si Ui leads me past it, toward a clump of rubber trees. He doesn't talk, just keeps beckoning me, the curious way they have of beckoning, palm pointing toward the ground.

I feel dizzy. He's standing there. Swaying a little. Then he makes a little clucking, chattering sound, barely opening his lips. The birds are gathering. He seems to know their language. They're answering him. The chirping around us grows to a screeching cacophony. Above, they're circling. They're blocking out the sun and it's suddenly chilly. I'm scared now. But I don't dare say anything. In the camp, if you said anything, they always hurt you. Si Ui keeps beckoning me: nearer, come nearer. And I creep up. The birds are shrieking. And now they're swooping down, landing, gathering at Si Ui's feet, their heads moving to-and-fro in a regular rhythm, like they're listening to … a heartbeat. Si Ui's heartbeat. My own.

An image flashes into my head. A little Chinese boy hiding in a closet … listening to footsteps … breathing nervously.

He's poised. Like a snake, coiled up, ready to pounce. And then, without warning, he drops to a crouch, pulls a bird out of the sea of birds, puts it to his lips, snaps its neck with his teeth, and the blood just spurts, all over his bare skin, over the homespun wrapped around his loins, an impossible crimson. And he smiles. And throws me the bird.

I recoil. He laughs again when I let the dead bird slip through my fingers. Pounces again and gets me another.

"Birds are easy to trap," he says to me in Chinese, "easy as children, sometimes; you just have to know their language." He rips one open, pulls out a slippery liver. "You don't like them raw, I know," he says, "but come, little brother, we'll make a fire."

He waves his hand, dismisses the birds; all at once they're gone and the air is steaming again. In the heat, we make a bonfire and grill the birds' livers over it. He has become, I guess, my friend. Because he's become all talkative. "I didn't rape her," he says.

Then he talks about fleeing through the rice fields. There's a war going on around him. I guess he's my age in his story, but in Chinese they don't use past or future, everything happens in a kind of abstract now-time. I don't understand his dialect that well, but what he says matches the waking dreams I've had tossing and turning under that mosquito net. There was a Japanese soldier. He seemed kinder than the others. They were roasting something over a fire. He was handing Si Ui a morsel. A piece of liver.

"Hungry, little Chink?"

Hungry. I understand hungry.

Human liver.

In Asia they believe that everything that will ever happen has already happened. Is that what Si Ui is doing with me, forging a karmic chain with his own childhood, the Japanese soldier?

There's so much I want to ask him, but I can't form the thoughts, especially not in Chinese. I'm young, Corey. I'm not thinking karmic cycles. What are you trying to ask me?

* * *

"I thought Si Ui ate children's livers," said Corey. "Not some dumb old birds'."

We were still on the *klong*, turning back now toward civilization; on either side of us were crumbling temples, old houses with pointed eaves, each one with its little totemic spirit house by the front gate, pouring sweet incense into the air, the air itself dripping with humidity. But ahead, just beyond a turn in the *klong*, a series of eighty-story condos reared up over the banana trees.

"Yes, he did," I said, "and we'll get to that part, in time. Don't be impatient."

"Grandpa, Si Ui ate children's livers. Just like Dracula bit women in the neck. Well like, it's the main part of the story. How long are you gonna make me wait?"

"So you know more than you told me before. About the maid trying to scare you one time, when you were five."

"Well, yeah, Grandpa, I saw the miniseries. It never mentioned you."

"I'm part of the secret history, Corey."

"Cool." He contemplated his Pokémon, but decided not to go back to monster trapping. "When we get back to the Bangkok side, can I get another caramel frappuccino at Starbucks?"

"Decaf," I said.

* * *

That evening I go back to the house and find Mom in bed with Jed, the police detective. Suddenly, I don't like Jed anymore.

She barely looks up at me; Jed is pounding away and oblivious to it all; I don't know if Mom really knows I'm there, or just a shadow flitting beyond the

Dragon's Fin Soup

mosquito netting. I know why she's doing it; she'll say that it's all about getting information for this great novel she's planning to write, or research for a major magazine article, but the truth is that it's about survival; it's no different from that concentration camp.

I think she finally does realize I'm there; she mouths the words "I'm sorry" and then turns back to her work. At that moment, I hear someone tapping at the entrance, and I crawl over the squeaky floor-planks, Siamese style (children learn to move around on their knees so that their head isn't accidentally higher than someone of higher rank) to see Sombun on the step.

"Can you come out?" he says. "There's a *ngaan wat*."

I don't know what that is, but I don't want to stay in the house. So I throw on a shirt and go with him. I soon find out that a *Ngaan Wat* is a temple fair, sort of a cross between a carnival and a church bazaar and a theatrical night out.

Even from a mile or two away we hear the music, the tinkling of marimbas and the thud of drums, the wail of the Javanese oboe. By the time we get there, the air is drenched with the fragrance of pickled guava, peanut pork skewers, and green papaya tossed in fish sauce. A makeshift dance floor has been spread over the muddy ground and there are dancers with rhinestone court costumes and pagoda hats, their hands bent back at an impossible angle. There's a Chinese opera troupe like I've seen in Shanghai, glittering costumes, masks painted on the faces in garish colors, boys dressed as monkeys leaping to-and-fro; the Thai and the Chinese striving to outdo each other in noise and brilliance. And on a grill—being tended by a fat woman—pigeons are barbecuing, each one on a mini-spear of steel. And I'm reminded of the open fire and the sizzling of half-plucked feathers.

"You got money?" Sombun says. He thinks that all *farangs* are rich. I fish in my pocket and pull out a few saleungs, and we stuff ourselves with pan-fried *roti* swimming in sweet condensed milk.

The thick juice is dripping from our lips. This really is paradise. The music, the mingled scents, the warm wind. Then I see Si Ui. There aren't any birds nearby, not unless you count the pigeons charring on the grill. Si Ui is muttering to himself, but I understand Chinese, and he's saying, over and over again, "Si Ui hungry, Si Ui hungry." He says it in a little voice and it's almost like baby talk.

We wander over to the Chinese opera troupe. They're doing something about monkeys invading heaven and stealing the apples of the gods. All these kids are somersaulting, tumbling, cartwheeling, and climbing up onto each other's shoulders. There's a little girl, nine or ten maybe, and she's watching the show. And Si Ui is watching her. And I'm watching him.

I've seen her before, know her from that night we squatted on the veranda staring at American TV shows. Was Si Ui watching her even then? I tried to remember. Couldn't be sure. Her name's Juk.

Those Chinese cymbals, with their annoying *boing-boing-boing* sound, are clashing. A man is intoning in a weird singsong. The monkeys are leaping. Suddenly I see, in Si Ui's face, the same expression I saw on the ship. He's utterly still inside, utterly quiet, beyond feeling. The war did that to him. I know. Just like it made my mom into a whore, and me into … I don't know … a bird without a nesting place … a lost boy.

Dragon's Fin Soup 159

And then I get this … irrational feeling. That the little girl is a bird, chirping to herself, hopping along the ground, not noticing the stalker.

So many people here. So much jangling, so much laughter. The town's dilapidated pagodas sparkle with reflected colors, like stone Christmas trees. Chinese opera rings in my ears. I look away, when I look back they are gone. Sombun is preoccupied now, playing with a two-saleung top that he just bought. Somehow I feel impelled to follow. To stalk the stalker.

I duck behind a fruit stand and then I see a golden deer. It's a toy, on four wheels, pulled along on a string. I can't help following it with my eyes as it darts between hampers full of rambutans and pomelos.

The deer darts toward the cupped hands of the little girl. I see her disappear into the crowd, but then I see Si Ui's face too; you can't mistake the cold fire in his eyes.

She follows the toy. Si Ui pulls. I follow, too, not really knowing why it's so fascinating. The toy deer weaves through the ocean of feet. Bare feet of monks and novices, their saffron robes skimming the mud. Feet in rubber flip-flops, in the wooden sandals the *Jek* call *kiah*. I hear a voice: "Juk, Juk!" And I know there's someone else looking for the girl, too. It's a weird quartet, each one in the sequence known only to the next one. I can Si Ui now, his head bobbing up and down in the throng because he's a little taller than the average Thai, even though he's so skinny. He's intent. Concentrated. He seems to be on wheels himself, he glides through the crowd like the toy deer does. The woman's voice, calling for Juk, is faint and distant; she hears it, I'm sure, but she's ignoring her mother or her big sister. I only hear it because my senses are sharp now, it's like the rest of the temple fair's all out of focus now, all blurry, and there's just the four of us. I see the woman now—it must be a mother or aunt, too old for a sister—collaring a roti vendor and asking if he's seen the child. The vendor shakes his head, laughs. And suddenly we're all next to the pigeon barbecue, and if the woman was only looking in the right place she'd see the little girl, giggling as she clambers through the forest of legs, as the toy zigzags over the dirt aisles. And now the deer has been yanked right up to Si Ui's feet. And the girl crawls all the way after it, seizes it, laughs, looks solemnly up at the face of the Chinaman.

"It's him! It's the Chink!" Sombun is pointing, laughing. I'd forgotten he was even with me.

Si Ui is startled. His concentration snaps. He lashes out. There's a blind rage in his eyes. Dead pigeons are flying everywhere.

"Hungry!" he screams in Chinese. "Si Ui hungry!"

He turns. There is a cloth stall nearby. Suddenly he and the girl are gone amid a flurry of billowing sarongs. And I follow.

Incense in the air, stinging my eyes. A shaman gets possessed in a side aisle, his followers hushed. A flash of red. A red sarong, embroidered with gold, a year's wages, twisting through the crowd. I follow. I see the girl's terrified eyes. I see Si Ui with the red cloth wrapped around his arms, around the girl. I see something glistening, a knife maybe. And no one sees. No one but me.

Juk! Juk!

I've lost Sombun somewhere. I don't care. I thread my way through a bevy of *ramwong* dancers, through men dressed as women and women dressed as

Dragon's Fin Soup

men. Fireworks are going off. There's an ancient wall, the temple boundary, crumbling ... and the trail of red funnels into black night ... and I'm standing on the other side of the wall now, watching Si Ui ride away in a pedicab, into the night. There's moonlight on him. He's saying something; even from far off I can read his lips; he's saying it over and over: "Si Ui hungry, Si Ui hungry."

* * *

So they find her by the side of the road with her internal organs missing. And I'm there too, all the boys are at dawn, peering down, daring each other to touch. It's not a rape or anything, they tell us. Nothing like the other girl. Someone has seen a cowherd near the site, and he's the one they arrest. He's an Indian, you see. If there's anyone the locals despise more than the Chinese, it's the Indians. They have a saying: if you see a snake and an Indian, kill the *babu*.

Later, in the market, Detective Jed is escorting the Indian to the police station, and they start pelting him with stones, and they call him a dirty Indian and a cowshit eater. They beat him up pretty badly in the jail. The country's under martial law in those days, you know. They can beat up anyone they want. Or shoot them.

But most people don't really notice, or care. After all, it is paradise. To say that it is not, aloud, risks making it true. That's why my mom will never belong to Thailand; she doesn't understand that everything there resides in what is left unsaid.

* * *

That afternoon I go back to the rubber orchard. He is standing patiently. There's a bird on a branch. Si Ui is poised. Waiting. I think he is about to pounce. But I'm too excited to wait. "The girl," I say. "The girl, she's dead, did you know?"

Si Ui whirls around in a murderous fury, and then, just as suddenly, he's smiling.

"I didn't mean to break your concentration," I say.

"Girl soft," Si Ui says. "Tender." He laughs a little.

I don't see a vicious killer. All I see is loneliness and hunger.

"Did you kill her?" I say.

"Kill?" he says. "I don't know. Si Ui hungry." He beckons me closer. I'm not afraid of him. "Do like me," he says. He crouches. I crouch too. He stares at the bird. And so do I. "Make like a tree now," he says, and I say, "Yes. I'm a tree." He's behind me. He's breathing down my neck. Am I the next bird? But somehow I know he won't hurt me.

"Now!" he shrieks. Blindly, instinctively, I grab the sparrow in both hands. I can feel the quick heart grow cold as the bones crunch. Blood and birdshit squirt into my fists. It feels exciting, you know, down there, inside me. I killed it. The shock of death is amazing, joyous. I wonder if this is what grownups feel when they do things to each other in the night.

He laughs. "You and me," he says, "now we same-same."

He shows me how to lick the warm blood as it spurts. It's hotter than you think. It pulses, it quivers, the whole bird trembles as it yields up its spirit to me.

And then there's the weirdest thing. You know that hunger, the one that's gnawed at me, like a wound that won't close up, since we were dragged to that camp … it's suddenly gone. In it's place there's a kind of nothing.

The Buddhists here say that heaven itself is a kind of nothing. That the goal of all existence is to become as nothing.

And I feel it. For all of a second or two, I feel it. "I know why you do it," I say. "I won't tell anyone, I swear."

"Si Ui knows that already."

Yes, he does. We have stood on common ground. We have shared communion flesh. Once a month, a Chinese priest used to come to the camp and celebrate mass with a hunk of maggoty man to, but he never made me feel one with anyone, let alone God.

The blood bathes my lips. The liver is succulent and bursting with juices.

Perhaps this is the first person I've ever loved.

The feeling lasts a few minutes. But then comes the hunger, swooping down on me, hunger clawed and ravenous. It will never go away, not completely.

* * *

They have called in an exorcist to pray over the railway tracks. The mother of the girl they found there has become a nun, and she stands on the gravel pathway lamenting her karma. The most recent victim has few to grieve for her. I overhear Detective Jed talking to my mother. He tells her there are two killers. The second one had her throat cut and her internal organs removed … the first one, strangulation, all different … he's been studying these cases, these ritual killers, in American psychiatry books. And the cowherd has an alibi for the first victim.

I'm only half-listening to Jed, who drones on and on about famous mad killers in Europe. Like the Butcher of Hanover, Jack the Ripper. How their victims were always chosen in a special way. How they killed over and over, always a certain way, a ritual. How they always got careless after a while, because part of what they were doing came from a hunger, a desperate need to be found out. How after a while they might leave clues … confide in someone … how he thought he had one of these cases on his hands, but the authorities in Bangkok weren't buying the idea. The village of Thapsakae just wasn't grand enough to play host to a reincarnation of Jack the Ripper.

I listen to him, but I've never been to Europe, and it's all just talk to me. I'm much more interested in the exorcist, who's a Brahmin, in white robes, hair down to his feet, all nappy and filthy, a dozen flower garlands around his neck, and amulets tinkling all over him.

"The killer might confide in someone," says Jed, "someone he thinks is in no position to betray him, someone perhaps too simple-minded to understand. Remember, the killer doesn't know he's evil. In a sense, he really can't help himself. He doesn't think the way we think. To himself, he's an innocent."

The exorcist enters his trance and sways and mumbles in unknown tongues. The villagers don't believe the killer's an innocent.

They want to lynch him.

Women washing clothes find a young girl's hand bobbing up and down, and her head a few yards

Dragon's Fin Soup

downstream. Women are panicking in the marketplace. They're lynching Indians, Chinese, anyone alien. But not Si Ui; he's a simpleton, after all. The village idiot is immune from persecution because every village needs an idiot.

The exorcist gets quite a workout, capturing spirits into baskets and jars.

Meanwhile, Si Ui has become the trusted *Jek*, the one who cuts the *gailan* in the fields and never cheats anyone of their two-saleung bundle of Chinese broccoli.

I keep his secret. Evenings, after I'm exhausted from swimming all day with Sombun and Lek, or lazing on the back of a water buffalo, I go to the rubber orchard and catch birds as the sun sets. I'm almost as good as him now. Sometimes he says nothing, though he'll share with me a piece of meat, cooked or uncooked; sometimes he talks up a storm. When he talks pidgin, he sounds like he's a half-wit. When he talks Thai, it's the same way, I think. But when he goes on and on in his Hakka dialect, he's as lucid as they come. I think. Because I'm only getting it in patches.

One day he says to me, "The young ones taste the best because it's the taste of childhood. You and I, we have no childhood. Only the taste."

A bird flies onto his shoulder, head tilted, chirps a friendly song. Perhaps he will soon be dinner.

Another day, Si Ui says, "Children's livers are the sweetest, they're bursting with young life. I weep for them. They're with me always. They're my friends. Like you."

Around us, paradise is crumbling. Everyone suspects someone else. Fights are breaking out in the marketplace. One day it's the Indians, another day the

Chinks, the Burmese. Hatred hangs in the air like the smell of rotten mangoes.

And Si Ui is getting hungrier.

My mother is working on her book now, thinking it'll make her fortune; she waits for the mail, which gets here sometimes by train, sometimes by oxcart. She's waiting for some letter from Simon and Schuster. It never comes, but she's having a ball, in her own way. She stumbles her way through the language, commits appalling solecisms, points her feet, even touches a monk one time, a total sacrilege … but they let her get away with everything. *Farangs*, after all, are touched by a divine madness. You can expect nothing normal from them.

She questions every villager, pores over every clue. It never occurs to her to ask me what I know.

We glut ourselves on papaya and curried catfish.

"Nicholas," my mother tells me one evening, after she's offered me a hit of opium, her latest affectation, "this really is the Garden of Eden."

I don't tell her that I've already met the serpent.

* * *

Here's how the day of reckoning happened, Corey:

It's mid-morning and I'm wandering aimlessly. My mother has taken the train to Bangkok with Detective Jed. He's decided that her untouchable *farang-ness* might get him an audience with some major official in the police department. I don't see my friends at the river or in the marketplace. But it's not planting season, and there's no school. So I'm playing by myself,

Dragon's Fin Soup

but you can only flip so many pebbles into the river, and tease so many water buffaloes.

After a while I decide to go and look for Sombun. We're not close, he and I, but we're thrown together a lot; things don't seem right without him.

I go to Sombun's house; it's a shabby place, but immaculate, a row house in the more "citified" part of the village, if you can call it that. Sombun's mother is making chili paste, pounding the spices in a stone mortar. You can smell the sweet basil and the lemongrass in the air. And the betelnut, too; she's chewing on the intoxicant; her teeth are stained red-black from long use.

"Oh," she says, "the *farang* boy."

"Where's Sombun?"

She doesn't know quite what to make of my Thai, which has been getting better for months. "He's not home, Little Mouse," she says. "He went to the *Jek's* house to buy broccoli. Do you want to eat?"

"I've eaten, thanks, Auntie," I say, but for politeness' sake I'm forced to nibble on bright green *sali* pastry.

"He's been gone a long time," she said, as she pounded. "I wonder if the Chink's going to teach him to catch birds."

"Birds?"

And I start to get this weird feeling. Because I'm the one who catches birds with the Chinaman, I'm the one who's shared his past, who understands his hunger. Not just any kid.

"Sombun told me the Chink was going to show him a special trick for catching them. Something about putting yourself into a deep state of *samadhi*, reaching out with your mind, plucking the life-force with your mind. It sounds very spiritual, doesn't it? I always took the Chink for a moron, but maybe I'm misjudging him; Sombun seems to do a much better job," she said. "I never liked it when they came to our village, but they do work hard."

Well, when I leave Sombun's house, I'm starting to get a little mad. It's jealousy, of course, childish jealousy; I see that now. But I don't want to go there and disrupt their little bird-catching session. I'm not a spoilsport. I'm just going to pace up and down by the side of the *klong*, doing a slow burn.

The serpent came to me! I was the only one who could see through his madness and his pain, the only one who truly knew the hunger that drove him! That's what I'm thinking. And I go back to tossing pebbles, and I tease the gibbon chained by the temple's gate, and I kick a water buffalo around. And, before I knew it, this twinge of jealousy has grown into a kind of rage. It's like I was one of those birds, only in a really big cage, and I'd been flying and flying and thinking I was free, and now I've banged into the prison bars for the first time. I'm so mad I could burst.

I'm playing by myself by the railway tracks when I see my mom and the detective walking out of the station. And that's the last straw. I want to hurt someone. I want to hurt my mom for shutting me out and letting strangers into her mosquito net at night. I want to punish Jed for thinking he knows everything. I want someone to notice me.

So that's when I run up to them and I say, "I'm the one! He confided in me! You said he was going to give himself away to someone and it was me, it was me!"

Dragon's Fin Soup

My mom just stares at me, but Jed becomes very quiet. "The Chinaman?" he asks me.

I say, "He told me children's livers are the sweetest. I think he's after Sombun." I don't tell him that he's only going to teach Sombun to catch birds, that he taught me too, that boys are safe from him because like the detective told us, we're not the special kind of victim he seeks out. "In his house, in the rubber orchard, you'll find everything," I say. "Bones. He makes the feet into a stew," I add, improvising now, because I've never been inside that house. "He cuts off their faces and dries them on a jerky rack. And Sombun's with him."

The truth is, I'm just making trouble. I don't believe there's dried faces in the house or human bones. I know Sombun's going to be safe, that Si Ui's only teaching him how to squeeze the life force from the birds, how to blunt the ancient hunger. Him instead of me. They're not going to find anything but dead birds.

There's a scream. I turn. I see Sombun's mother with a basket of fish, coming from the market. She's overheard me, and she cries, "The Chink is killing my son!" Faster than thought, the street is full of people, screaming their anti-Chink epithets and pulling out butcher knives. Jed's calling for reinforcements. Street vendors are tightening their *phakhomas* around their waists.

"Which way?" Jed asks, and suddenly I'm at the head of an army, racing full tilt toward the rubber orchard, along the neon green of the young rice paddies, beside the canals teeming with catfish, through thickets of banana trees, around the walls of the old temple, through the fields of *gailan* ... and this too feeds my hunger. It's ugly. He's a Chinaman. He's the village idiot. He's different. He's an alien. Anything is possible.

We're converging on the *gailan* field now. They're waving sticks. Harvesting sickles. Fishknives. They're shouting, "Kill the Chink, kill the Chink." Sombun's mother is shrieking and wailing, and Detective Jed has his gun out. Tae Pak, the village rich man, is vainly trying to stop the mob from trampling his broccoli. The army is unstoppable. And I'm their leader, I brought them here with my little lie. Even my mother is finally in awe.

I push through the bamboo thicket and we're standing in the clearing in the rubber orchard now. They're screaming for the *Jek's* blood. And I'm screaming with them.

Si Ui is nowhere to be found. They're beating on the ground now, slicing it with their scythes, smashing their clubs against the trees. Sombun's mother is hysterical. The other women have caught her mood, and they're all screaming now, because someone is holding up a sandal ... Sombun's.

A little Chinese boy hiding in a closet.

The image flashes again. I must go up into the house. I steal away, sneak up the steps, respectfully removing my sandals at the veranda, and I slip into the house.

A kerosene lamp burns. Light and shadows dance. There is a low wooden platform for a bed, a mosquito net, a woven rush mat for sleeping; off in a corner, there is a closet.

Birds everywhere. Dead birds pinned to the walls. Birds' heads piled up on plates. Blood spatters on the floor-planks. Feathers wafting. On a charcoal stove in one corner, there's a wok with some hot oil and garlic,

Dragon's Fin Soup

and sizzling in that oil is a heart, too big to be the heart of a bird.

My eyes get used to the darkness. I see human bones in a pail. I see a young girl's head in a jar, the skull sawn open, half the brain gone. I see a bowl of pickled eyes.

I'm not afraid. These are familiar sights. This horror is a spectral echo of Nanking, nothing more.

"Si Ui," I whisper. "I lied to them. I know you didn't do anything to Sombun. You're one of the killers who does the same thing over and over. You don't eat boys. I know I've always been safe with you. I've always trusted you."

I hear someone crying. The whimper of a child.

"Hungry," says the voice. "Hungry."

A voice from behind the closet door.

The door opens. Si Ui is there, huddled, bone-thin, his *phakomaah* about his loins, weeping, rocking.

Noises now. Angry voices. They're clambering up the steps. They're breaking down the wall planks. Light streams in.

"I'm sorry," I whisper. I see fire flicker in his eyes, then drain away as the mob sweeps into the room.

* * *

My grandson was hungry, too. When he said he could eat the world, he wasn't kidding. After the second decaf frappuccino, there was Italian ice in the Oriental's coffee shop, and then, riding back on the Skytrain to join the chauffeur who had conveniently parked at the Sogo mall, there was a box of Smarties. Corey's mother always told me to watch the sugar, and she had plenty of Ritalin in stock—no prescription needed here—but it was always my pleasure to defy my daughter-in-law and leave her to deal with the consequences.

Corey ran wild in the skytrain station, whooping up the staircases, yelling at old ladies. No one minded. Kids are indulged in Babylon East; little blond boys are too cute to do wrong. For some, this noisy, polluted, chaotic city is still a kind of paradise.

My day of revelations ended at my son's townhouse in Sukhumvit, where maids and nannies fussed over little Corey and undressed him and got him in his Pokémon pajamas as I drained a glass of Beaujolais. My son was rarely home; the taco chain consumed all his time. My daughter-in-law was a social butterfly; she had already gone out for the evening, all pearls and Thai silk. So it fell to me to go into my grandson's room and to kiss him goodnight and goodbye.

Corey's bedroom was little piece of America, with its *Phantom Menace* drapes and its Playstation. But on a high niche, an image of the Buddha looked down; a decaying garland still perfumed the air with a whiff of jasmine. The air conditioning was chilly; the Bangkok of the rich is a cold city; the more conspicuous the consumption, the lower the thermostat setting. I shivered, even as I missed Manhattan in January.

"Tell me a story, Grandpa?" Corey said.

"I told you one already," I said.

"Yeah, you did," he said wistfully. "About you in the Garden of Eden, and the serpent who was really a kid-eating monster."

All true. But as the years passed I had come to see that perhaps I was the serpent. I was the one who mixed lies with the truth, and took away his innocence. He was a child, really, a hungry child. And so was I.

"Tell me what happened to him," Corey said. "Did the people lynch him?"

"No. The court ruled that he was a madman, and sentenced him to a mental home. But the military government of Field Marshal Sarit reversed the decision, and they took him away and shot him. And he didn't even kill half the kids they said he killed."

"Like the first girl, the one who was raped and strangled," Corey said, "but she didn't get eaten. Maybe that other killer's still around." So he had been paying attention after all. I know he loves me, though he rarely says so; he had suffered an old man's ramblings for one long air conditioning-free day, without complaint. I'm proud of him, can barely believe I've held on to life long enough to get to know him.

I leaned down to kiss him. He clung to me; and, as he let go, he asked me sleepily, "Do you ever feel that hungry, Grandpa?"

I didn't want to answer him; so, without another word, I slipped quietly away.

That night, I wandered in my dreams through fields of the dead; the hunger raged; I killed, I swallowed children whole and spat them out; I burned down cities; I stood aflame in my self-made inferno, howling with elemental grief; and in the morning, without leaving a note, I took a taxi to the airport and flew back to New York.

To face the hunger.

Diamonds Aren't Forever

A priceless Ming vase skidded down the marble steps. Fortunately, Rapi, the more swift-footed of the two mezzanine maids, was pushing a mop past the landing at just that moment; she caught it one-handed and, not missing a beat, set it down at the table by the window overlooking the teak pavilion by the canal, where I was just settling down to enjoy a quick breakfast of rice soup, pickled quails' eggs, dried sugar-roasted pork, and ice capuccino.

"I'm sorry, sir," said the maid.

"'What the hell's going on?" I said, turning the vase over and noting that it belonged to the reign of the Emperor Chien Lung. I had only been in Bangkok for a week, and had yet to regain my bearings.

"It's the *khunying*," the maid said. "I think she's lost her earrings again. Oh, dear, here comes another." The vase's identical twin came whizzing through the air, narrowly missing a gorgeous, though armless, Khmer statue of an *apsara* or celestial woman, which stood mounted on a plinth in the center of the landing.

Dragon's Fin Soup

The vase shattered against the far wall. "Oh, dear, oh, dear," said the maid, and scurried after the shards.

As she scooped them into a dustpan, she turned to me and went on, "Don't panic, Mr. Shapiro. All these antiques are fakes. The master has lent all the real ones to the Metropolitan Museum in New York. His nerves, you know."

The master, Dr. Sukhrip, was my host for this trip. I had met him at a curator's luncheon in New York, where he had given a brief speech on the subject of fourteenth-century Siamese lintels. After welcoming me with a lavish dinner, he had promptly disappeared, leaving me to root about his estate—a palatial complex of Somerset Maugham-like splendor—while he flew off to Singapore to tryst with one of his innumerable wives.

I had been going to the Orient since the 1950s, first as an intrepid young archaeologist's apprentice, then as a buyer for the Metropolitan's Southeast Asian collection, and now as a private dealer in rare art. But I had never been a guest in one of these huge aristocratic family compounds, and I was often at a loss.

I had any number of chauffeurs and servants at my disposal, and I can speak the language tolerably well; but even figuring out which of the 17 dining rooms, pavilions, pantries, and lunch nooks breakfast was going to be served in each morning was an ordeal. It had never, so far, been served in the same place.

My hostess the *khunying* (which is a minor title of Thai nobility) was seldom seen except on her way to some society function.

"Does the *khunying* often lose her earrings?" I asked Rapi, who was now kneeling at the low table—I still couldn't quite get used to all this groveling—and refilling my orange juice glass. "What happens next?"

"Oh," she said, "at about ten o'clock she will conclude that one of the servants has stolen them. At 11, there'll be a police investigation where they'll find us all innocent. At 12, she'll insist that the investigation hasn't been thorough enough. At one, we'll all take lie detector tests and pass. At two, the tarot card reader will arrive, if she's in town. By five, she'll be calling the shaman."

"Shaman?" I said, my interest piqued.

"Mae Thiap, the shaman," Rapi said. "She's a peasant from the northeast. She's very good at finding things. She usually gets the earrings on the first try; but if she doesn't, the *khunying* will have nightmares, forget the lie detector test results, and wake up suspecting one of the servants again, and then the whole chain of events recycles, you see."

At that point, a bloodcurdling scream issued forth from behind us. A door slammed.

"Rapi, you impertinent bitch! How often have I told you not to chatter to the honored guests? This isn't the Beaver Bar in Patpong."

Rapi rapidly folded her palms in the universal Thai gesture of respect and said, "Terribly sorry, Khunying."

"My own fault, Midge," I said. I asked her a few questions."

Midge, as her American friends called her, stood about 4'11", had the complexion of a fine Sung dynasty porcelain, delicately pouting lips, slender fingers, and enough jewelry to sink the *Titanic*.

"Asking a few questions!" she began in a fury. Then, morphing instantaneously into the perfect hostess, she said, "Is everything all right, Mervin? What time will you need the car? I'm afraid you'll have to take the Benz; I'll need the Rolls to escort the servants to the police station." Then, with renewed rage: "Perfidious lice! Robbing me blind! Fifty American dollars a week I pay these fools, and I can't buy their bloody loyalty!"

"Earrings, was it?" I said.

She turned to me. "And not some silly bauble either; these were three carat blue-whites, worth around 800,000 baht."

A quick calculation told me that this sum could purchase the services of one of these maids for approximately 12 years and four months. I whistled. "Oh, it's not that they're worth that much," she said, "it's just … oh! the sense of violation! that one of these creatures actually slunk into my bedroom in the middle of the night … it's just too appalling. I'm so sorry about disturbing your breakfast, Moreton—"

"Marvin."

"—perhaps you'd care for some *prosciutto melone*? My cousin just brought back a couple of whole ones from Italy, and I know you can never get decent gourmet food in America—"

"It's all right, thanks. I've got a meeting with a Burmese smuggler at noon, and you know they'll be plying me with—"

"Burmese? Better take some diarrhea pills, just in case. Rapi, go and fetch the big blue bottle from the inner bathroom … not the Valium. And the crocodile stilettos for the police station, I think … fourteenth ones from the left, third shelf, sixth shoe cabinet."

The maid disappeared silently, and after pursing her lips becomingly for a few minutes, so did the *khunying*. It occurred to me that a woman who could pinpoint the exact location of every specimen in her Imeldaesque shoe collection could surely keep track of a pair of earrings.

My rendezvous was a mile away—an hour and a half in Bangkok's stultifying traffic. It was almost evening when I returned, and my chauffeur-driven Mercedes pulled up at the wrought-iron gates at the same time as the shaman came roaring up on the back of a Harley.

The front lawn of the estate was packed. Various staff members were emoting, weeping, gawking, and chattering as police sergeants wandered around interrogating and taking notes.

I left my shoes at the door and was about to go up to my suite when Midge accosted me. "Oh, good, you're here," she said, while simultaneously speaking in Thai into two cellular phones. "You'll probably enjoy the shaman."

I realized we were right on schedule. "Where?" I said.

"Follow the smell of incense," she said. "I'll join you in a moment. Do you want tea sent up?"

She vanished before I could answer her, trailing a cloud of *Samsara*.

Incense wafted down from an upper story. As I hesitated, the shaman came trampling past, surrounded by servants bearing silver platters laden with cloth, fruit, flowers, and hardboiled eggs. Her entourage included a little blind boy wearing a traditional *jongkabaen* costume and a white-robed Brahmin priest bearing aloft a silver bowl, as well as a piper, a drummer, and a boy banging on an upturned brass bath bucket. From a lone woman on the back of a motorcycle, she had somehow metastasized into a garish, noisy carnival.

Midge's *faux* Louis Quinze bedroom suite, which she did not share with my host, her husband, took up most of the third floor of the mansion. I sat down at a divan, and a tray of tea and cucumber sandwiches appeared miraculously in front of me. It was served by Rapi, her eyes downcast, on properly bended knee; but when no one was looking, she boldly gazed into my eyes and, with a twinkle, said, "Right on schedule, Mr. Shapiro, you see."

The entourage was setting up shop in an anteroom. Meanwhile, the shaman joined me on the divan. She was a stately woman wrapped in an embroidered *panung*, held in place by a silver belt, and had a no-nonsense look about her, like a *yenta* on steroids.

"Oh, an American," she muttered to the maid. "I'll have to charge extra."

"I'm afraid I speak Thai," I said.

She giggled at my atrocious accent, then said, "Well in that case, of course, we'll only be charging the down-home rate. Unless you're an anthropologist, of course." She downed an entire cup of tea, and plucked an amulet out of her capacious bosom. "Take this," she said to me, and handed it over. It depicted an intertwined couple—outrageously pornographic, really. "You look as if you might need a little, ah, supernatural assistance in your love life."

"Very kind of you," I said. I peered at it. I couldn't tell if it was old without a magnifying glass. Such fetishes can fetch a fairly decent price in New York, however, so I pocketed it. She waited, presumably for a donation of some kind, but I didn't feel like playing the game.

"You Americans all alike," she cackled in English. "Always show me, show me. All right, tonight you have big, wonderful sex. Then donation. My card." Her business card had a cellular number as well as a fax number, and included the legend "*As seen on Letterman.*"

At that point, the *khunying* showed up. She had changed into a casual silk pants suit and slightly less jewelry.

"Oh, Mae Thiap," she said, "I'm so glad you could come!"

"It's nothing, my dear," said the shaman. "And you last saw your earrings where?"

"I don't know, I don't know." said Midge. "It's those beastly servants, I swear! There's not an honest domestic left in all of Bangkok; the foreigners have hired them all away at grossly inflated wages. I was coming home from the big charity ball, you know, at the Dusit. I'm sure I still had the earrings then. Unless I took them off in the bathroom. But why would I have done that? Or maybe I wasn't even wearing them." Her confusion was genuine, and very discomfiting. "I mean, it's not as if they went *poof!* and just vanished from my ears, is it?"

"Of course not, my dear," she said. "Let's all concentrate our minds." An assistant brought a tray of joss-sticks and garlands. Apparently, I was supposed to join in, so I took seven incense sticks and lit them.

"This part's simply grand," Midge said, clutching my forearm excitedly. "She becomes possessed by the god Phra Isuan—Shiva—who as you know is Lord of the Dance. Then, in the personage of

Dragon's Fin Soup

the god, she dances around wildly until she's able to see the true location of every object in the world."

"What if they're not in this room? What if they're stolen?" I said.

"Phra Isuan will rearrange the fabric of reality," said Midge, "and make whatever has happened un-happen. After all, he is the God of Destruction."

"I see," I said dubiously.

The little blind boy came in and presented us with a bowl of sand in which to plant our incense sticks. The room was getting smoky. I tried to look appropriately meditative for a few minutes before carefully placing the sticks in the bowl.

"All right," said Mae Thiap. "Now, children, you must remember that life is a dream; the world is an illusion; that which we call reality is held in place by the chains of karma; but there's a certain elasticity in those chains, and that's what we must rely on. Now, Khunying, if you would kindly concentrate on the earrings ... try to conjure up a mental picture of them in your mind, a picture so crystal-clear that I won't have any trouble plucking it from the maelstrom of your thoughts."

Midge closed her eyes. She folded her palms, blushed a little; her delicate features made me think of celestial women painted on faded murals in the temples of the North of Thailand, one of which I had managed to get smuggled out of the country to a museum in Berlin last year. Not an easy task; to get a mural out, in pieces, you have to dismantle the temple. Crossed a lot of palms with silver that month.

From the antechamber, the pipe, drums, and gong began a bloodcurdling caterwauling. Attendants began a kind of chanting and clapping. The Brahmin priest intoned in singsongy Sanskrit, now and then pausing to asperge us all with lustral water.

As the music crescendoed, Mae Thiap, underwent a bizarre transformation. She leaped up. Her arms and legs contorted into strange attitudes and impossible angles. Sideways, she skittered across the carpet. She spun. I could have sworn she had at least four arms. She somersaulted. Her hefty bosom seemed to have a life of its own. She stamped her feet, which jingled with brass anklets. The drums were speeding up now, and at the final crash of the upturned bucket, she was suddenly seated in lotus position on the Sealy posturepedic under the silken canopy of the four-poster, her arms folded tight across her chest, her neck bobbing up and down like a jack-in-the-box's.

She spoke in a booming voice, the way flying saucer people speak in fifties science fiction movies. "The earrings," she declared majestically, "all right here."

She pointed to one of the pillows.

Abruptly, the music came to a stop. Slowly, Mae Thiap returned to a semblance of human form, then fainted.

There was a moment's silence. The air-conditioners hummed. The trails of incense began to settle.

Midge scurried over to the pillow. She lifted it up. Then, with a look of triumph on her face, she held aloft the earrings. "Oh, Mae Thiap, you've done it!" she cried. She knelt beside the prostrate shaman and performed a ritual obeisance and, perhaps because in Thailand one's head may never be higher than the head of a social superior, everyone in the room immediately fell on his knees as well. Except, of course, for me, the token Ugly American. I sat there, staring in bewilderment at the sea of backs that encircled the fat supine, heaving woman with a fleck of froth on her lips.

* * *

That night, I awoke from a fitful sleep to find Rapi inexplicably scrubbing the floor.

"What on earth are you doing?"

Startled, she dropped her mop. "Oh, I'm so terribly sorry … I don't know what's come over me. I must have been walking in my sleep again. I'll leave at once."

She did not leave until dawn.

* * *

Obviously, there was something to this Mae Thiap's powers. In New York, one wouldn't think of calling in a shaman to find missing objects, but here in Bangkok, you're always right at the borderland of the mundane and the supernatural. I mean, here's a city with fax machines and smog and expressways and buildings shaped like giant robots and the world's highest concentration of shopping malls and all that, but the twentieth century's just skin deep; scratch it and you're in the primeval past. I love it. Keeps my mind working.

I was musing on all these things as I gazed at the sleek sleeping young body of the mezzanine maid.

The earrings were an impressive enough feat, but to cause this nubile thing to jump into the bed of a shopworn, sagging, middle-aged Semite was more amazing still. It had to be the amulet.

And if this woman could locate missing earrings, what about something bigger? With the 12-hour time difference, it was too late to call New York now. I was going to have to wait until after dinner. I had 12 hours or so to cook up a dastardly plan.

* * *

I met the *khunying* for lunch at the Picasso, a post-modernist cafe on Sathorn Road whose exterior was a large-scale stucco recreation of one of those brown cubist paintings. Inside, there were pillars that were three-dimensional reconstructions of the *Demoiselles D'Avignon*, and the walls were a sort of colorized *Guernica*-in-the-round. It was a monument to the cultural hubris of Bangkok in the nineties.

And the *khunying* was attired to match: she had the earrings, of course, and a drop-dead Chanel suit set off by a Versace purse of Olympian proportions. It needed to be that big to carry both her cellular phones, which rang continuously during the beluga, and only slowed down when we reached the rack of lamb.

"So how exactly *do* you know my husband, Melvin?" she asked me. I had given up correcting her on my name; I realized now that pretending not to know it was just some roundabout way of insulting her absent husband.

"In New York," I said, "he presented a very fine piece of twelfth-century celadon to the museum's Southeast Asian collection; we've corresponded, on and off, ever since."

"Oh, I see," she said. "You launder his money."

I tried to ignore that, and went on, "And I'm sorry I haven't had a chance to thank him for his hospitality …"

"Oh, I'm sure he's already forgotten," she said. "His whole life seems to consist of trysting with that trollop in Singapore."

We consumed the rack of lamb in silence.

"So you're sort of an Indiana Jones, type, then?" she asked me at last.

"Hardly. But I *have* been known to find … objects."

"Lost objects. Like Mae Thiap,"

"Ones that have been lost for centuries. But I don't use magic."

I daresay not; Americans are never any good at magic. No offense, but you're all just too closed-minded."

"I'm not," I said. "Not after what I saw yesterday." And experienced last night, for that matter. But I wasn't sure how Midge would feel about a bed-hopping maid, so I didn't mention it. "That shaman," I went on, "this … Mae Thiap. Where did you find her?"

"Oh, she's from up north somewhere … all my friends use her. She's not bad, and it's a hell of a spectacle for only 500 baht. Where in America can you have such a show for twenty bucks? But why do you ask? Have you lost something recently?"

"Found something, more like," I said, remembering the delicious night I had just enjoyed, though the memory was becoming more and more elusive, like a dream that slips through your fingers when you try to grasp it. "She's a fascinating lady."

"Would you like to see her again? We can fax her if you like; I've got my Newton in my bag."

"Has she ever recovered … *big* objects?" I fingered the obscene fetish in my coat pocket.

I don't know … well, there was my cousin's Maserati, but there was some doubt as to whether it was actually the right car, you see, and anyway it was stolen again a week later."

Very interesting.

"But what I don't quite understand is … didn't you look under that pillow *before* you called her in … even before you called the police? I mean, it was a pretty obvious place to have mislaid your earrings …"

"The gods work in mysterious ways, Mordred; such things are beyond me. Yes, I looked there. They must have been there the whole time. Sometimes, if you look at something all the time, you miss the obvious."

That was true enough. But it seemed to me that this was a little more complicated than just locating where an object had been lost. There was something else … telekinesis, perhaps. Fixing on the object's true essence, somehow, making it pop through the ether and materialize in its designated place. It was pretty exciting, I thought, as I distractedly munched my *crêpes suzette* and Midge chatted away on both cellulars.

* * *

The journey to Mae Thiap's house was by canal. We were on the Thonburi side of the city, far from the places where tourists congregate; we had to park the Mercedes at the Oriental Hotel and catch a water-taxi. My companions were the *khunying* herself, who had managed to get the evening off from her taxing round

Dragon's Fin Soup

of charity balls, and Rapi, the maid, who had been brought along to carry the various garlands, incense-sticks, fruit, and hardboiled eggs that always seemed to accompany these operations.

I asked Midge about the eggs. "Some of the gods don't like them," she said, "because the higher up they are, the more likely they are to be vegetarians; but with the lesser spirits, they're pretty much *de rigeur*. The *jao thii*, for example, who inhabits the spirit house at the end of our front lawn,"

"But Phra Isuan's pretty big, isn't he? You can't get much higher than Shiva."

"Don't take any of it too seriously, Melrose! We are all Buddhists here in Thailand, which means we don't really believe in gods at all. They're just part of the illusion of reality; they're subject to the laws of karma, too."

"You mean it's all a dream."

"Nothing exists," she agreed, as Rapi poured her a glass of Moët Chandon from the magnum in the ice bucket.

Visitors don't see this side of Bangkok much. The boat eased down the narrow *klongs*, bordered by stilted wooden houses; children leaped naked from overhanging branches, laughing at us; a crone in a passing sampan sold me ice-cold coconut juice.

We docked at one of the wooden houses. The air was heavy with the fragrances of incense, jasmine, and mango. After leaving our shoes on the stoop, we went into a small waiting room that was crammed with suppliants.

"Do we have to wait?" Midge said querulously, but soon the little blind boy emerged from the inner chamber to tell us we could skip to the head of the line. Money talks.

Inside, the walls were lined with statues of Hindu gods, and there were shelves of jars full of strange concoctions: love philters and the like, no doubt. The shaman was sleeping on a huge heap of pillows, snoring cacophonously, and the blind boy gently prodded her awake.

"Ah," she said, "the *khunying* has lost her earrings again?"

"Well, actually, no," said Midge, as we crawled into appropriate positions of respect, "it's my friend Marty from America. He's lost something. Well, he hasn't lost it, exactly. It's more that he's never found it, although he knows it has to be around somewhere."

"It's a simple thing, really," I said, pulling out a series of photographs that had just been faxed to me that afternoon. I have a client in Los Angeles who owns a very interesting set of Buddha images. They date from the late Ayuthaya Period, they're about an inch or so tall, and there are 55 in all, each one representing a different *pang* or attitude of the Lord Buddha. It's an absolutely superb collection, possibly the *only* miniature compendium of all the traditional postures of Buddha images done by a single sculptor—"

"But there are 56," said Mae Thiap. "Everyone knows that."

"Yes, indeed," I said. "The one that was never excavated from the site is the *pang peut lok*, the Buddha revealing the three worlds."

"Excavated!" Mae Thiap said. "Stolen, you mean. You're trying to get me to cooperate in the stripping of our national treasures from archaeological sites? You appalling little man."

Dragon's Fin Soup

I gulped. Every now and then one runs across one of those *rah-rah* do-gooders who wants to repatriate all the antiquities, but to be honest they tend to be starry-eyed Caucasians straight out of Smith College, rather than the more pragmatic natives.

"I'm terribly sorry for offending—" I began, rooting around for some shred of political correctness with which to redeem myself.

"It'll cost a little more," said Mae Thiap. "Let's say, a thousand baht."

"Forty bucks!" I exclaimed in astonishment.

"All right, 900."

"You'd strip a national treasure for 900 baht?" I said.

"My child," she said wearily, "life is a dream. Reality is but a figment of the imagination, a baseless fabric, a thing of no substance. And yet, we must keep the wheel of karma turning, must we not? I am merely an instrument of the gods. By the way, I trust that your sex life has improved somewhat?" At which the maid could not help giggling, and the *khunying* shot her a look of disapproval.

Then, all at once, the mountain of flesh was dancing up a storm, and the music started banging and tooting from the next room.

She hurled herself across the room with startling agility, working her hands and feet into attitudes more contorted than the 56 *pangs* of the Buddha. It was hard to believe that so much poundage could possess so much terpsichorean talent. She somersaulted, cartwheeled, and tied herself into knots. She didn't even appear to sweat, and sure enough, I was starting to swear she had four arms, though doubtless it was the after images of her gestures.

The dance went on a lot longer than before, and I was afraid that the god might give her a coronary before departing her body, but just as I thought she would give out, she shuddered to a stop.

The booming voice of the god spoke to me.

"At the antique shop in the arcade of the Hyatt," said the Lord of the Dance, "on the right-hand side, second shelf down, you will find your missing Buddha image. Go straight there in the morning, though; it has been mislabeled, and is being sold as a modern reproduction, so someone may grab it first."

We all prostrated ourselves, made the appropriate offerings, and took the canal taxi back to civilization.

* * *

That night, I woke just before dawn, only to find the lovely Rapi weeping in the moonlight that poured in through the window that overlooked an ancient temple and a large Pizza Hut. She was exquisite in her nakedness; I watched her for a long time before deciding to disturb her melancholy.

"Is everything all right?" I said.

"I suppose so, Master," she said. "I'm just sitting here bewailing my terrible karma, and wondering how many thousands of lives I'm going to have to live through before I can be rich and carefree like the *khunying*."

"There's little I can say," I said. "Except to point out that I don't think the *khunying's* that happy. Money's not everything. I mean, she's got a husband who's a cad, and … a terrible fear of loneliness, too, I suspect."

"Money's not everything! Easy for you to say. You entice me into your bed with a love-spell, and next week you'll be getting on that plane and going back to America, and where does that leave me? It's not like you're going to marry me."

"You're right," I said, feeling like a bit of a user myself. "It isn't as if I'm going to marry you."

"Of course you're not, Mr. Shapiro," she said. "Americans always say they come from a classless society; but we all find out pretty soon that that's bullshit.

She was doing a pretty good guilt job on me, almost as good as my mother. This was beginning to sound like the annual *hannukah* phone call from Miami. "You're right," I said.

"And anyway, since this entire relationship is just based on a magic spell, you probably don't even like me."

"What are you getting at?"

"You beast! You're gray and withered, and your nose is like a parrot's beak. And to top it all, you're a criminal who gets rich by ransacking other people's cultures."

"That's all very true, but—"

"I hate you!" She flung herself at me, and began pummeling me with her fists. "I hate you, I hate you!" Then she wept passionately, until there was nothing for it but to shake out my weary member one more time and make whoopie till dawn.

* * *

To my amazement, the *objet d'art* in question was exactly where Mae Thiap said it would be, and for a mere hundred dollars, I claimed possession of it. What with bribing a few more officials for the papers necessary for exporting antiquities, and a few other miscellaneous expenses, I was pretty certain I could clear $200,000 for this one.

I was ecstatic. I took Midge out to lunch, dropped a couple hundred bucks on giant crabs flown in from Australia, went down to Fed Ex to ship the relic off to my client, and called the bank to tell them to await an enormous wire transfer within 24 hours.

Then I retired to the *khunying's* estate to figure out what I should get Mae Thiap to locate next. So many lost masterworks in the world. Imagine if she could dredge up, say, the complete poems of Sappho—even *one* complete poem of Sappho!—or a lost *Pieta* of Michelangelo. And why stop at art? What about the True Cross ... the Holy Grail the Ark of the Covenant?

My hands were shaking as I gulped down my chrysanthemum tea and watched a Madonna music video in the *khunying's* capacious television room. By now, everyone in the household staff knew that I was having a relationship with Rapi, and schedules had been shuffled so that she could spend more time with me. So she was serving my tea with downcast eyes, every inch the serving wench; after the outburst of the previous night, it was awkward to see her kneeling at my feet, but Thailand is a hierarchical society, and everyone knows his place.

"I wish you wouldn't stare at the floor the whole time," I said.

"I wouldn't presume, Mr. Shapiro," she said.

"What's going on in that complicated brain of yours?"

"Nothing," she said.

I very much doubted that. "Perhaps," I said, "you feel you should give the old classless society a whirl?"

"What do you mean?"

"I'm not saying I'd go so far as to marry you—even at my advanced age, my mother won't let me bring any *schicksehs* home to meet her—but perhaps a live-in position of some kind. You know, in New York, these kinds of things are done all the time."

"You mean, you're offering me a concubine's position?" she said. "That wouldn't be too bad. I'd have to have my own condo though. It wouldn't do to share the house with your major wife; I'm a respectable woman."

"Your own condo, eh? In New York City?"

"Sir, I've heard that the land in New York is almost as expensive as it is in Bangkok, but surely, with the new antiquities you're planning to 'find' it wouldn't be too hard to—"

True enough, I thought. The girl's mind was devious as hell, and she didn't miss a thing. It wouldn't be bad to have her around the place. She'd look pretty glamorous in one of the *khunying's* evening gowns—

"Not to mention the earrings," she said softly.

"You're a mind-reader?"

"Not too hard to read an open book," she said, giggling. "But seriously, it would be wonderful to be your wife, even your minor wife, but there wouldn't be anything I could call my own, would there? The condo, the clothes, the checkbook, it would still be all in your name. I'd only be part of the décor. If only I owned just *one* valuable thing ... a ring ... an amulet ... a pair of three carat earrings ... sometimes I dream about stealing them, you know. I mean, I've been interrogated by the police about them often enough, every time the *khunying* loses them ... once, they even beat me."

"Good heavens," I said, empathizing and simultaneously admiring the artful manner in which I was being manipulated. "How awful! Why didn't you quit?"

"But if I had quit, wouldn't they have assumed that I stole them? No, one accepts a bit of police brutality as part of one's karma. I must have stolen someone's earrings in a past life to have been pistol-whipped for stealing earrings in this one ..."

The woman was brilliant. If she went on in this vein, I'd have my mother swearing she was Jewish. "You're a remarkable woman," I said, trying to sound noncommittal, telling myself that she was right, that this was a sheerly physical thing, a magically induced anyway, and that there wasn't a shred of *reality* to the passion that even now was welling up once more in my brain, my breast, my loins ... oh, she was ravishing ... *and* she had character. She was irresistable. And yet ...

I had to think big. The Ark of the Covenant was all very well, but what about the lost tomb of Alexander the Great? What about the lost treasure of Troy, discovered by Schliemann and spirited behind the Iron Curtain fifty years ago? Could Mae Thiap, perhaps, reassemble lost artifacts as well as find them, so that we could gaze, once more, on the wonders of the ancient world: the Diana of Ephesus, the Hanging Gardens of Babylon? And all for a mere fifty bucks a pop? I imagined she'd need a little more once the scam got going, but who would not mind paying fifty, a hundred even a thousand dollars for the chance to gaze at, say, the Great Pyramid of Khufu with all its limestone facing intact and with the Pharaoh and his treasure still lying around inside?

Dragon's Fin Soup

"You're daydreaming" Rapi said. "Have some more tea, Master."

"Sure," I said, reaching for my cellular phone. "Sure."

* * *

That night, the *khunying's* earrings disappeared again.

That night, the maid disappeared.

I was awakened by a scream. The scream came from some distant part of the mansion. I snapped on the light only to discover that Rapi was gone from my side. Was the magic wearing off? Her scent still clung to the bedsheets. I put on a dressing gown and stepped outside.

The lights were on. The house was in an uproar. Valets, maids, and cooks were scurrying about, rubbing their eyes. A Ming vase almost brained me, but I ducked and it flew into a enormous bronze gong that hung between immense ivories. "What's the matter?" I cried.

But I already knew what it must be.

"Those traitorous, disloyal, scheming, greedy, good-for-nothing servants!" The *khunying*, robed in one of Victoria's sheerest secrets, was stomping about the landing. "Those earrings were only recovered a few days ago, and now they're gone again! Oh, my terrible karma!"

"Midge!" I exclaimed. Sobbing, she flew into my arms.

"You don't know the half of it," she wept. "It's so difficult ... the absentee husband ... trying to manage this beastly estate on a miserable trust fund the size of a rat turd ... and these damned three-carat earrings ... I don't know why I ever bought them."

"Calm down," I said. "You know you always recover them."

"Yes," she said. "But the aggravation! The police! Strip-searching the maids! The lie-detector tests! The shamans!"

"Why not cut to the chase and just fax the shaman now?"

"I can't. You have to do everything by the numbers. If it weren't for due process, the whole structure of reality would collapse."

Well, there was little I could say to that.

"Call a roll call," she commanded one of the valets. "I want to make sure no one's made off with the earrings."

Soon, the entire staff was assembling on the front lawn: sentries, scullery maids, dishwashers, laundry women, gardeners, and so on. I knew there were a lot of people working on the estate, but this seemed endless. It was barely light. The faces were ghostly. They muttered and murmured, but the chirping of crickets and frogs and the buzzing of mosquitoes, not to mention the occasional pile-driver doing overtime at the condos going up on the other side of Sukhumvit, overwhelmed their chatter. One by one they were being made to swear, in front of the *saanphraphum* or spirit house, which held the displaced guardian spirit of the land, that they had not done the dastardly deed, and calling down all sorts of hideous curses unto the seventh generation if they were perjuring themselves. It was an astonishing spectacle. I looked around for Rapi.

I didn't see her I went right into the midst of the throng of servants. There were a dozen of her age and

Dragon's Fin Soup

build, but none was the woman of my wildest sexual fantasies.

I went to the head security guard, who was doing a roll call and marking the names off on a list. "Have you seen Rapi?" I asked him.

"Not yet," he said.

I was beginning to have a sinking feeling. Hadn't Rapi unburdened herself to me only that afternoon? Hadn't she as much as told me that she lusted after the earrings, yearned to possess them, just so she could know what it was like to own something of value? If she had stolen them, had she fled the house? How long would it be until Midge suspected, and how long could a simple country girl elude a police force so adept at obeying the orders of the rich? Somehow I had to help her get away. Somehow I had to deflect suspicion. I had to get the *khunying* to skip the police and go straight to the shaman stage.

At that moment, one of the innumerable Rapi clones—so close, and yet so unlike the real thing—showed up with a cellular phone on a silver platter.

"Hey, Marvin ..." it squawked. "It's Ross. From Los Angeles."

"Great," I said. "I take it the Buddha image arrived?"

"It came this morning! I installed it in its niche. The whole thing has got to be the most gorgeous assemblage of the 56 pangs ever collected ... but ... but ... Marvin ... it's vanished!"

"Vanished?"

"Disappeared out of a locked glass case, in a closed wing of a museum after hours, with 17 security guards, and I began to have a sinking feeling.

How real were the recovered objects? Were they illusions, plucked from the images in our minds? Was it our desperate need to possess these objects that caused Mae Thiap to be able to conjure them out of thin air?

How long did it take for the magic to wear off?

"Midge!" I waved at her as she raged back and forth on the front porch. "Help!" Into the phone I said, "I'll get it back for you. I can't explain how, but I'm absolutely sure that it hasn't gotten far. There's more to this than meets the eye."

"Telling me," said Ross, and hung up with a grunt as the *khunying* approached me, tearful with fury.

"Look, Midge," I said. "Please. This time you're going to have to skip the police investigation." I wondered if Rapi had managed to make it out of Bangkok yet. "My client in LA just called. His Buddha image is missing, too. Let's just fax the shaman and get her over here pronto."

"It's five in the morning," she said. I wonder if we can get her a police escort."

* * *

Breakfast that morning was grim, though served with an even greater sumptuousness that usual, in a teak pavilion, overhung with orchids, that overlooked a pond. At least, one assumed there was a pond beneath the wall-to-wall lotus pads and blossoms. The *khunying* and I were served a rice porridge festooned with giant shrimp and chilies, along with the usual cinnamon-vanilla capuccino.

We didn't speak. We each awaited the arrival of the shamaness. I felt dread and hope in equal measure. Midge maintained a stolid, aristocratic composure,

Dragon's Fin Soup

having far exceeded her quota of *faux* Ming vases. Here, as elsewhere in this household, even a tantrum had to follow set guidelines, or the fabric of the universe would inexorably unravel.

The *khunying* had by now learned that my paramour had absconded. Doubtless she was itching to send the police off after Rapi, but now that those stages had been skipped, there was no turning back. Every effort had to be made to restore a semblance of karmic balance.

"Eight hundred thousand baht," the *khunying* murmured into her capuccino.

I was thinking of the 200,000 dollars. And the Ark of the Covenant. And my lost love. Not necessarily in that order.

At last, the steward could be seen walking across the back lawn. He took off his sandals, entered the pavilion, prostrated himself, and informed the *khunying* that Mae Thiap had been summoned.

* * *

In Midge's bedroom suite, I felt a strange sort of desolation. This was the first time I'd ever been in this room when it only contained three people, and its vastness was a little daunting.

Settling into lotus position on the divan, Mae Thiap said, "I'm afraid there's no entourage today, but this is a little sudden … not to mention irregular. You didn't call the police inspectors first?"

"Other circumstances …" I began.

"I don't know what you're talking about," said the shaman, "but once I am possessed by the god, I'm sure he'll understand everything."

Midge said, "About this unprecedented morning house call there"ll be a little extra in the offering, of course."

Mae Thiap waved it all aside. "You're lucky that this is the twenty-fifth century," she said—it took me a second to remember that the Buddhist Era starts 500 years before our own—"and that I don't actually need a live band." She plucked a CD out of her bosom. "This comes from India," she said, "and there's four tracks: one for summoning Brahma, one for Vishnu, one for Shiva, and one that's sort of a free-for-all. If you wouldn't mind playing track three, there's a dear," she said, handing the CD to Midge, who got up to fiddle with the stereo in the console next to the 55" television. Then she put her hand on my sleeve. "My poor *farang* friend," she said. "The lady is missing her earrings, and your friend in Los Angeles is missing his Buddha image; isn't there something you're missing too? Oh, don't even bother to tell me. The god will see all. What your heart asks, the god will provide. As long as you don't skimp on the offerings." I was about to reply, but she put a finger to her lips. I almost forgot to tell you. You know, once the god is present, you may ask him a question or two. He might answer you, you know. After all, you're a foreigner. How else will you learn anything?"

* * *

The dance was even wilder than before. She spun, she stood on her hands, she jiggled her head back and forth, she defied gravity and seemed to hang in the air as she whirled. Arms snaked hither and thither. Now and then, as her robes flapped, her navel glistened

Dragon's Fin Soup

like a thousand-faceted jewel. She moved so fast there seemed to be two of her ... no, more. She boomeranged across the walls. She swung from the drapes of the four-poster bed. There was nothing I could do but stare.

At length, she assumed the lotus position on the bed ... or was it a couple of inches above the bedspread? ... I couldn't be quite sure. My vision was blurry. Perhaps it was from all the stress. Or maybe it was because one cannot look directly at the gods.

But this time I wanted answers. True answers. Answers about the very nature of reality. "O Shiva," I said, kneeling with folded palms in front of the possessed woman, "you said I could ask a few questions."

"Yes, my child," she said in the resonant, deep tones of god-hood. "I'll answer the questions even before you ask them. The world is an illusion. You want to know whether the earrings I find today are the same earrings that the *khunying* lost? The answer to that is simple: if they are perceived to be the same earrings, why would they not be the same earrings? Do you know, my child, what reality is? It is the confluence of all your private illusions. In a world that is already illusion, does the creation of an illusion within that illusion make that illusion less real than the matrix of illusion that surrounds it?"

It sounded a lot like cheating to me. "But—" I began.

"Rest assured," said the god. "The earrings are under the bed."

"Oh, thank you!" said Midge, awed and relieved, and she immediately got down on her hands and knees and started fishing around beneath the posturepedic.

"Rest assured, also, my pale son," the god continued, "that the missing Buddha image is not far from your friend's hands. He will find it on the next shelf, to the left, above where the cabinet with the rest of his collection is. The mahogany shelf now, not the teak. And this time it will last a while. You see, your friend couldn't quite believe his luck when he opened the package. Illusions, as you know, are fed by the power of our own beliefs. As you Americans say, dreams can come true if you want them badly enough …"

"But this is cheating!" I blurted out. "What you're really doing is creating the objects anew, but they're illusions so they're unstable or something, and after a while they pop out of existence, and then the owner thinks they've been mislaid and they end up calling you in to create the object all over again, and so Mae Thiap ends up with another forty bucks … it's a great big cosmic scam!"

"Oh, you Westerners are so Western sometimes. Of course it's a scam. The universe is a scam. You think it's all really there because you think you're really there. But you're not, and it's not. A universe lasts a trillion years, and a pair of my earrings lasts a trillion nanoseconds. Both are the stuff of dreams, or dreams within dreams. You should not be too attached to material things, my child. Let them go."

"And—"

"But now I have a question for you, my child. You too are missing something, are you not? Something very important … I would go so far as to call it a piece of your heart. Do you want me to conjure it back up for you? Your faith in her is strong. You can probably keep the illusion going for a lot longer than a few days."

Dragon's Fin Soup

I thought about Rapi: her impertinence, her laughing eyes, the delicate odor of the bedsheets. Could I really get her back just by bribing the gods with a few cheap offerings? But if Phra Isuan made her reappear in my arms, exactly the way she was before she left me, would she just be a simulacrum of Rapi, ready to melt into thin air at any moment? Would I be spending the rest of my life paying protection money to a witch doctor in Bangkok in order to keep my woman?

"No," I said. The god was right. If I caused her to reappear, I would only be clinging to the illusion of her that I'd created for myself. "Let her go," I said softly.

"Very karmically correct," the god said. Then, after writhing a little, and foaming at the mouth, Mae Thiap fell into a dead faint, and the audience with Phra Isuan was over.

* * *

A week went by. I dreamed about Rapi every night. It wasn't going to be that easy to forget, and the love fetish didn't bring me any more women; it had to be one of those magic spells that only works once.

I never quite had the *chutzpah* to arrange for the discovery of the Ark of the Covenant, but I did recover a few major antiquities, thanks to Mae Thiap. I was careful to pick clients who were absolutely fervent in the desire to possess those *objets d'art*, so there was no recurrence of the vanishing Buddha incident—at least not in the first week. I cleared a cool million, and put a down payment on a penthouse in the upper East Eighties, a building that was being converted to condominiums. So you see, I still hoped.

Midge saw me off at Don Muang Airport. She got one of the VIP rooms opened, so we were able to sit around sipping capuccino for a while.

"I'm sorry about that maid," she said to me—my first indication that she had any idea I had been hiding the salami in her house. "You know, sometimes a perfectly good maid will up and run like that. I don't understand it. They have much more fulfilling lives with me than back on the farm. Last year it was one of the janitors."

"It's okay," I said, sipping and looking at my watch.

"What can you do?" she said. "After all, slavery's been abolished." She sounded vaguely regretful about that, even though she couldn't possibly have been around back then.

"Here," I said, and I gave her the love fetish I had received from the shaman. "With your husband *still* away, you could probably use this."

"Wow," she said, "thanks." She made sure I still had Mae Thiap's business card and fax number. I made sure that she was still wearing her earrings. Then she gave me a quick peck on the cheek and abandoned me to my karma.

The plane was stalled on the runway for about half an hour. First class was empty, and I downed a double scotch on the rocks, trying to get numb.

Suddenly the curtain was drawn aside and I saw her. I blinked a few times. I wasn't quite sure at first because she was wearing one of those Chanel suits—just like Midge had in her closet—and a two-hundred-dollar hairdo. I'd never seen her with make-up before, either. But that giggle was unforgettable, and the impertinent stare clinched it.

"How—what the—" I said.

"I sold the earrings," she said.

"But—the *khunying*—she had them on—Mae Thiap—"

I stole the earrings at midnight, while the *khunying* was taking a soak in the jacuzzi. By the time she missed them, I'd already had the meeting with the jeweler. He ripped me off—I only got 500,000 baht for them—but I had to act fast. Once Mae Thiap showed up at the mansion—"

"You sold a jeweler the earrings, knowing that Mae Thiap would cause them to rematerialize in the *khunying's* bedroom and the jeweler would get screwed?"

"Dealing hot property is a risky business," she said, and sat down beside me. "You shouldn't drink so much."

"I almost blew it for you," I said. I got the *khunying* to send for Mae Thiap a good eight hours ahead of schedule."

"Thank god I had already disposed of them."

"I'm really going to marry you," I said in wonderment.

"I know, Mr. Shapiro."

"You know!" I wished she would stop calling me Mr. Shapiro.

She smiled. She was beautiful when she smiled. She had the aristocratic bearing of the *khunying* down pat—after all, she had spent years observing the members of high society from a kneeling position—but when she smiled, she couldn't quite suppress the farm girl in her. She was full of mischief. She had strength. I really did love her, I thought. I didn't want to say it out loud for fear of looking like an idiot.

The airplane started to move. Goodbye, city of high-rises and stagnant canals, city of shopping malls that look like temples and temples that look like shopping malls, city of beautiful and dangerous women, city of cacophony and tranquillity, city of neon night. I had a piece of that city with me always now. I could hardly grasp it.

"Don't you want to know why I'm here?" she said.

"Because I've put a down payment on the condo in Manhattan?"

She laughed again. "No, silly," she said. "It's because you didn't summon me.

"What do you mean?"

"You had the power. You had Mae Thiap. You lost something, and Mae Thiap can restore any missing object. But you didn't ask her to bring me back to you. And you know, she would have, if you had asked. Mae Thiap does not have scruples. She does not have a conscience. At least, not when she is the god. Gods do not have the same morals that mortals do. For the right offering, Shiva would have plucked me from wherever I was, and popped me right back into your arms. You would have had me. Or a reasonable imitation of me. But I would have become a dream within a dream, wouldn't I? I waited for a few days, holed up in a shack in the slums of Klong Toey, with all that cash in a paper bag, thinking, he's going to send for me any minute. But you didn't. And because you didn't, the woman who comes to you now is the same woman you loved before, and the love that I bring to you is not coerced by a magic spell or by your own capacity to weave an illusion of true love. This me is the real me."

Was this Rapi speaking, or was it the voice of the god? I didn't have time to reflect, because she kissed me then, and as I kissed her back we reached cruising altitude, and I started unbuckling her seat belt …

She was real enough for me.

Fiddling for Water Buffaloes

When my brother Lek and I were children we were only allowed to go to Prasongburi once a week. That was the day our mothers went to the marketplace and to make merit at the temple. Our grandmother, our mothers' mother, spent the days chewing betelnut and fashioning intricate mobiles out of dried palm leaves; not just the usual fish shapes, dozens of tiny baby fish swinging from a big mother fish lacquered in bright red or orange, but also more elaborate shapes: spaceships and tigers and mythical beasts, *nagas* that swallowed their own tails. It was our job to sell them to the *thaokae* who owned the only souvenir shop in the town ... the only store with one of those aluminum gratings that you pull shut to lock up at night, just like the ones in Bangkok.

It was always difficult to get him to take the ones that weren't fish. Once we took in a mobile made entirely of spaceships, which our grandmother had copied from one of the American TV shows. (In view of our later experiences, this proved particularly

Dragon's Fin Soup

prophetic.) "Everyone knows," the *thaokae* said (that was the time he admitted us to his inner sanctum, where he would smoke opium from an impressive bong and puff it in our faces) "that a *plataphien* mobile has fish in it. Everyone wants sweet little fishies to hang over their baby's cradle. I mean, those spaceships are a tribute to your grandmother's skill at weaving dried palm leaves, but as far as the tourists are concerned, it's just fiddling for water buffaloes." He meant there was no point in doing such fine work because it would be wasted on his customers.

We ended up with maybe ten baht apiece for my grandmother's labors, and we'd carefully tuck away two of the little blue banknotes (this was in the year 2504 BE, long before they debased the baht into a mere coin) so that we could go to the movies. The American ones were funniest—especially the James Bond ones—because the dubbers had the most outrageous ad libs. I remember that in *Goldfinger* the dubbers kept putting in jokes about the fairy tale of Jao Ngo, which is about a hideous monster who falls into a tank of gold paint and becomes very handsome. The audience became so wild with laughter that they actually stormed the dubbers' booth and started improvising their own puns. I particularly remember that day because we were waiting for the monsoon to burst, and the heat had been making everyone crazy.

Seconds after we left the theater it came all at once, and the way home was so impassable we had to stay at the village before our village, and then we had to go home by boat, rowing frantically by the side of the drowned road. The fish were so thick you could pull them from the water in handfulls.

That was when my brother Lek said to me, "You know, Noi, I think it would be grand to be a movie dubber."

"That's silly, Phii Lek," I said. "Someone has to herd the water buffaloes and sell the mobiles and—"

"That's what we both should do. So we don't have to work on the farm anymore." Our mothers, who were rowing the boat, pricked up their ears at that. Something to report back to our father, perhaps. "We could live in the town. I love that town."

"It's not so great," my mother said.

My senior mother (Phii Lek's mother) agreed. "We went to Chiang Mai once, for the beauty contest. Now there was a town. Streets that wind on and on ... and air conditioning in almost every public building!"

"We didn't win the beauty contest, though," my mother said sadly. She didn't say it, but she implied that that was how they'd both ended up marrying my father. "Our stars were bad. Maybe in my next life—"

"I'm not waiting till my next life," my brother said. "When I'm grown up they'll have air-conditioning in Prasongburi, and I'll be dubbing movies every night."

The sun was beating down, blinding, sizzling. We threw off our clothes and dived from the boat. The water was cool, mud-flecked; we pushed our way through the reeds.

The storm had blown the village's TV antenna out into the paddy field. We watched "Star Trek" at the headsman's house, our arms clutching the railings on his porch, our feet dangling, slipping against the stilts that were still soaked with rain. It was fuzzy and the sound was off, so Phii Lek put on a magnificent performance, putting discreet obscenities into the mouths of Kirk and Spock while the old men laughed and the coils of mosquito incense smoked through the humid evening. At night, when we were both tucked in under our mosquito netting, I dreamed about going into space and finding my grandmother's palm-leaf mobiles hanging from the points of the stars.

* * *

Ten years later they built a highway from Bangkok to Chiang Mai, and there were no more casual tourists in Prasongburi. Some American archaeologists started digging at the site of an old Khmer city nearby. The movie theater never did get air-conditioning, but my grandmother did get into faking antiques; it turned out to be infinitely more lucrative than fish mobiles, and when the *thaokae* died, she and my two mothers were actually able to buy the place from his intransigent nephew. The three of them turned it into an "antique" place (fakes in the front, the few genuine pieces carefully hoarded in the air-conditioned back room) and our father set about looking for a third wife as befit his improved station in life.

My family were also able to buy a half-interest in the movie theater, and that was how my brother and I ended up in the dubbing booth after all. Now, the fact of the matter was, sound projection systems in theaters had become prevalent all over the country by then, and Lek and I both knew that live movie dubbing was a dying art. Only the fact that the highway didn't come anywhere near Prasongburi prevented its citizens from positively demanding talkies. But we were young and, relatively speaking, wealthy; we wanted to have a bit of fun before having the drudgery of marriage and earning a real living thrust upon us. Lek did most of the dubbing—he was astonishingly convincing at female voices as well as male—while I contributed the sound effects and played background music from the library of scratched records we'd inherited from the previous régime.

Since we two were the only purveyors of, well, foreign culture in the town, you'd think we would be the ones best equipped to deal with an alien invasion.

Apparently the aliens thought so too.

Aliens were farthest from my mind the day it happened, though. I was putting in some time at the shop and trying to pacify my three honored parents, who were going at it like cats and dogs in the back.

"If you dare bring that bitch into our house," Elder Mother was saying, fanning herself feverishly with a plastic fan—for our air-conditioning had broken down, as usual—"I'll leave."

"Well," Younger Mother (my own) said, "I don't mind as long as you make sure she's a servant. But if you marry her—"

"Well, *I* mind, I'm telling you!" my other mother shouted. "If the two of us aren't enough for you, I've three more cousins up north, decent, hardworking girls who'll bring in money, not use it up."

"Anyway, if you simply have to spend money," Younger Mother said, "what's wrong with a new pick-up truck?"

"I'm not dealing with that usurious *thaokae* in Ban Kraduk," my father said, taking another swig of his Mekong whiskey, and "and there's no other way of coming up with a down payment … and besides, I happen to be a very horny man."

Dragon's Fin Soup

"All of you shut up," my grandmother said from somewhere out back, where she had been meticulously aging some pots into a semblance of twelfth-century Sawankhalok ware. "All this chatter disturbs my work."

"Yes, Khun Mae," the three of them chorused back respectfully.

My Elder Mother hissed, "But watch out, my dear husband. I read a story in *Siam Rath* about a woman who castrated her unfaithful husband and fed his eggs to the ducks!"

My father sucked in his breath and took a comforting gulp of whiskey as I went to the front to answer a customer.

She was one of those archaeologists or anthropologists or something. She was tall and smelly, as all *farangs* are (they have very active sweat glands); she wore a sort of safari outfit, and she had long hair, stringy from her digging and the humidity. She was scrutinizing the spaceship mobile my grandmother had made ten years ago—it still had not sold, and we had kept it as a memento of hard times—and muttering to herself words that sounded like, "Warp factor five!"

My brother and I know some English, and I was preparing to embarrass myself by exercising that ungrateful, toneless tongue, when she addressed me in Thai.

"Greetings to you, honored sir," she said, and brought her palms together in a clumsy but heartfelt *wai*. I couldn't suppress a laugh.

"Why, didn't I do that right?" she demanded.

"You did it remarkably well," I said. "But you shouldn't go to such lengths. I'm only a shopkeeper, and you're not supposed to *wai* first. But I suppose I should give you 'E for effort,'" (I said this phrase in her language, having learned it from another archaeologist the previous year) "since few would even try as hard as you."

"Oh, but I'm doing my Ph.D. in Southeast Asian aesthetics at UCLA," she said. "By all means, correct me." She started to pull out a notebook.

I had never, as we say, "arrived" in America, though my sexual adventures had recently included an aging, overwhelmingly odoriferous Frenchwoman and the daughter of the Indian *babu* who sold cloth in the next town, and the prospect suddenly seemed rather inviting. Emboldened, I said, "But to really study our culture, you might consider—" and eyed her with undisguised interest.

She laughed. *Farang* women are exceptional, in that one need not make overtures to them subtly, but may approach the matter in a no-nonsense fashion, as a plumber might regard a sewage pipe. "Jesus," she said in English, "I think he's asking me for a date!"

"I understood that," I said.

"Where will we go?" she said in Thai, giggling. "I've got the day off. And the night, I might add. Oh, that's not correct, is it? You should send a go-between to my father, or something."

"Only if the liaison is intended to be permanent," I said quickly, lest anthropology get the better of lust. "Well, we could go to a movie."

"What's showing?" she said. "Why, this is just like back home, and me a teenager again." She bent down, anxious to please, and started to deliver a sloppy kiss to my forehead. I recoiled. "Oh, I forgot," she said. "You people frown on public displays."

"*Star Wars*," I said.

"Oh, but I've seen that twenty times."

Dragon's Fin Soup

"Ah, but have you seen it—dubbed live, in a provincial Thai theater without air-conditioning? Think of the glorious field notes you could write."

"You Thai men are all alike," she said, intimating that she had had a vast experience of them. "Very well. What time? By the way, my name is Mary, Mary Mason."

* * *

We were an hour late getting the show started, which was pretty normal, and the audience was getting so restless that some of them had started an impromptu bawdy-rhyming contest in the front rows. My brother and I had manned the booth and were studying the script. He would do all the main characters, and I would do such meaty roles as the Second Stormtrooper.

"Let's begin," Phii Lek said. "She won't come anyway."

Mary turned up just as we were lowering the house lights. She had bathed (my brother sniffed appreciatively as she entered the dubbing booth) and wore a clean sarong, which did not look too bad on her.

"Can I do Princess Leia?" she said, *wai-ing* to Phii Lek as though she were already his younger sibling by virtue of her as-yet-unconsummated association with me.

"You can *read* Thai?" Phii Lek said in astonishment.

"I have my Masters' in Siamese from Michigan U," she said huffily, and studied under Bill Gedney." We shrugged.

"Yes, but you can't improvise," my brother said.

She agreed, pulled out her notebook, and sat down in a corner. My brother started to put on a wild performance, while I ran hither and thither putting on records and creating sound effects out of my box of props. We began the opening chase scene with Tchaikovsky's *Piano Concerto*, which kept skipping; at last the needle got stuck and I turned the volume down hastily just as my brother (in the tones of the heroic Princess Leia) was supposed to murmur, "Help me, Obi-Wan Kenobi. You're my only hope." Instead, he began to moan like a harlot in heat, screeching out, "Oh, I need a man, I do, I do! These robots are no good in bed!"

At that point Mary became hysterical with laughter. She fell out of her chair and collided with the shoe rack. I hastened to rescue her from the indignity of having her face next to a stack of filthy flip flops, and could not prevent myself from grabbing her. She put her arms around my waist and indecorously refused to let go, while my brother, warming to the audience reaction, began to ad lib ever more outrageously.

It was only after the movie, when I had put on the 45 of the Royal Anthem and everyone had stood up to pay homage to the Sacred Majesty of the King, that I noticed something wrong with my brother. For one thing, he did not rise in respect, even though he was ordinarily the most devout of people. He sat bunched up in a corner of the dubbing booth, with, his eyes darting from side to side like, window wiper.

I watched him anxiously but dared not move until the Royal Anthem had finished playing.

Then, tentatively, I tapped him on the shoulder. "Phii Lek," I said, "it's time we went home."

Dragon's Fin Soup

He turned on me and snarled ... then he fell on the floor and began dragging himself forward in a very strange manner, propelling himself with his chin and elbows along the woven-rush matting at our feet.

Mary said, "Is that something worth reporting on?" and began scribbling wildly in her notebook.

"Phii Lek," I said to my brother in terms of utmost respect, for I thought he might be punishing me for some imagined grievance, "are you ill?" Suddenly I thought I had it figured out. "If you're playing 'putting on the anthropologists,' Elder Sibling, I don't think this one's going to be taken in."

"*You are part of a rebel alliance, and a traitor!*" my brother intoned—in English—in a harsh, unearthly voice. "*Take her away!*"

"That's ... my God, that's James Earl Jones' voice," Mary said, forgetting in her confusion to speak Thai. "That's from the movie we just saw."

"What are we going to do?" I said, panicking. My older brother was crawling, around at my feet, making me feel distinctly uncomfortable because of the elevation of my head over the head of a person of higher status, so I dropped down on my hands and knees so as to maintain my head at the properly respectful level. Meanwhile, he was wriggling around on his belly.

Amid all this, Mary's notebook and pens clattered to the floor and she began to scream.

At that moment, my grandmother entered the booth and stared about wildly. I attempted, from my prone position, to perform the appropriate *wai*, but Phii Lek was rolling around and making peculiar hissing noises. Mary started to stutter, "Khun Yaa, I don't know what happened, they just suddenly started acting this way—"

"Don't you *khun yaa* me," grandmother snapped. "I'm no kin to any foreigners, thank you!" She surveyed the spectacle before her with mounting horror. "Oh, my terrible karma!" she cried. "Demons have transformed my grandsons into dogs!"

* * *

On the street, there were crowds everywhere. I could hear people babbling about mysterious lights in the sky ... portents and celestial signs. Someone said something about the spectacle outside being more impressive than the *Star Wars* effects inside the theater. Apparently the main pagoda of the temple had seemed on fire for a few minutes and they'd called in a fire-fighting squad from the next town. "Who'd have thought of it?" my grandmother was complaining. "A demon visits Prasongburi—and makes straight for my own grandson!"

When we got to the shop—Mary still tagging behind and furiously taking notes on our social customs—the situation was even worse. The skirmish between my father and mothers had crescendoed to an all-out war.

"That's why I came to fetch you, children," my grandmother said. "Maybe you can referee this boxing match." A hefty celadon pot came whistling through the air and shattered on the overhead electric fan. We scurried for cover ... all except my brother, who obliviously crawled about on his hands and knees, occasionally spouting lines from *Star Wars.*

Dragon's Fin Soup

Shrieking, Mary ran after the potshards. "My god, that's thing's 800 years old—"

"Bah! I faked it last week," my grandmother said, forcing the *farang* woman to gape in mingled horror and admiration.

"All right, all right," my father said, fleeing from the back room with my mothers in hot pursuit. I won't marry her ... but I want a little more kindness out of the two of you ... oh, my terrible karma."

He tripped over my brother and went sprawling to the floor. "What's wrong with him?"

"You fool!" my grandmother said. "Your own son has become possessed by demons ... and it's all because of your sexual excesses."

My father stopped and stared at my brother. Then, murmuring a brief prayer to the Lord Buddha, he retired cowering behind the shop counter. "What must I do?"

His wives came marching out behind him. Elder Mother hastened to succor Phii Lek. Younger Mother took in the situation and said, "I haven't seen anyone this possessed since my cousin Phii Daeng spent the night in a graveyard trying to get a vision of a winning lottery ticket number."

"It's all your fault," Phii Lek's mother said, turning wrathfully on my father. "You're all too eager to douse your staff of passion, and now my son has been turned into a monster!" The logic of this accusation escaped me, but my father seemed convinced.

"I'll go and *buat phra* for three months," he said, affecting a tone of deep piety. "I'll cut my hair off tomorrow and enter the nearest monastery. That ought to do the trick. Oh, my son, my son, what have I done?"

"Well," my grandmother said, "a little abstinence should do you good. I always thought you were unwise not to enter the monkhood at twenty like an obedient son should ... cursing me to be reborn on earth instead of spending my next life in heaven as I ought, considering how I've worked my fingers to the bone for you! It's about time, that's what I say. A twenty-year-old belongs in a temple, not in the village scouts killing communists. Time for that when you've done your filial duty ... well, 25 years late is better than nothing."

Seeing himself trapped between several painful alternatives, my father bowed his head, raised his palms in a gesture of respect, and said, "All right, *khun mae yaai*, if that's what you want."

* * *

When my father and the elder females of the family had left to pack his things, I was left with my older brother and with the bizarre American woman, in the antique shop in the middle of the night. They had taken the truck back to the village (which now boasted a good half-dozen motor vehicles, one of them ours) and we were stranded. In the heat of their argument and my father's repentance, they seemed to have forgotten all about us.

It was at that moment that my brother chose to snap out of whatever it was that possessed him.

Calmly he rose from the floor, wiped a few foam-flecks from his mouth with his sleeve, and sat down on the stool behind the counter. It took him a minute or two to recognize us, and then he said, "Well, well, Ai Noi! I gave the family quite a scare, didn't I?"

I was even more frightened now than I had been before. I knew very well that night is the time of spirits, and I was completely convinced that some spirit or another had taken hold of Phii Lek, though I was unsure about the part about my father being punished for his roving eyes and hands. I said, "Yes, Khun Phii, it was the most astonishing performance I've ever seen. Indeed, a bit too astonishing, if you don't mind your Humble Younger Sibling saying so. I mean, do you think they really appreciated it? If you ask me, you were just fiddling for water buffaloes."

"The most amazing thing is this … they weren't even after me!" He pointed at Mary. "They're in the wrong brain! It was her they wanted.

But we all look alike to them. And I was imitating a woman's voice when they were trying to get a fix on the psychic transference. So they made an error of a few decimal places, and—*poof!*—here I am!"

"*Pen baa pai laew*!" I whispered to Mary Mason.

"I heard that!" my brother riposted. "But I am not mad. I am quite, quite sane, and I have been taken over by a *manus tang dao*."

"What's that?" Mary asked me.

"A being from another star."

"Far frigging out! An extraterrestrial!" she said in English. I didn't understand a word of it; I thought it must be some kind of anthropology jargon.

"Look, I can't talk long, but … you see, they're after Mary. One of them is trying to send a message to America … something to do with the Khmer ruins … some kind of artifact … to another of these creatures who is walking around in the body of a professor at

UCLA. This *farang* woman seemed ideal; she could journey back without causing any suspicion. But, you see, we all look alike to them, and—"

"Well, can't you tell whatever it is to stop inhabiting your body and transfer itself to—?"

"Hell, no!" Mary said, and started to back away. "Native customs are all very well, but this is a bit more than I bargained for."

"Psychic transference too difficult … additional expenditure of energy impractical at present stage … but message must get through …". Suddenly he clawed at his throat for a few moments, and then fell writhing to the floor in another fit. "Can't get used to this gravity," he moaned. "Legs instead of pseudopods—and the contents of the stomach make me sick—there's at least fifty whole undigested chilies down here—oh, I'm going to puke—"

"By Buddha, Dharma and Sangkha!" I cried. "Quick, Mary, help me. Give me something to catch his vomit."

"Will this do?" she said, pulling down something from the shelf. Distractedly I motioned her to put it up to his mouth.

Only when he had begun regurgitating into the bowl did I realize what she's done. "You imbecile!" I said. "That's a genuine Ming spittoon!"

"I thought they were all fakes," she said, holding up my brother as he slowly turned green.

"We do have some *genuine* items here," I said disdainfully, "for those who can tell the difference."

"You mean, for *Thai* collectors," she said, hurt.

"Well, what can you expect?" I said, becoming furious. "You come here, you dig up all our ancient treasures, violate the chastity of our women—"

Dragon's Fin Soup

"Look who's talking!" Mary said gently. "Male chauvinist pig" she added in English.

"Let's not fight," I said. "He seems better now … what are we going to do with him?"

"Here. Help me drag him to the back room."

We lifted him up and laid him down on the couch.

We looked at each other in the close, humid, mosquito-infested room. Suddenly, providentially almost, the air-conditioning kicked on. "I've been trying to get it to work all day," I whispered.

"Does this mean—"

"Yes! Soon it will cool enough to—"

She kissed me on the lips. By morning I had "arrived" in America several delicious times, and Mary was telephoning the hotel in Ban Kraduk so she could get her things moved into my father's house.

* * *

The next morning, over breakfast, I tried to explain it all to my elders. On the one hand there was this *farang* woman sitting on the floor, clumsily rolling rice balls with one hand and attempting to address my mothers as *khun mae*, much to their discomfiture; on the other there was the mystery of my brother, who was now confined to his room and refused to eat anything with any chilies in it.

"It's your weird western ways," my grandmother said, eyeing my latest conquest critically. "No chilies indeed! He'll be demanding hamburgers next."

"It's nothing to do with western ways," I said.

"It's a *manus tang dao*," Mary said, proudly displaying her latest lexical gem, "and it's trying to get a message to America, and there's some kind of artifact in the ruins that they need, and they travel by some kind of psychic transference—"

"You Americans are crazy!" my grandmother said, spitting out her betelnut so she could take a few mouthfuls of curried fish. "Any fool can see the boys possessed. I remember my great-uncle had fits like this when he promised a donation of 500 baht to the Sacred Pillar of the City and then reneged on his offer. My parents had to pay off the Brahmins—with interest!—before the curse was lifted. Oh, my karma, my karma!"

"Shouldn't we call in some scientists, or something? A psychiatrist?" Mary said.

"Nothing of the sort!" said my grandmother. "If we can't take care of this in the home, we'll not take care of it at all. No one's going to say my grandson is crazy. Possessed, maybe ... everyone can sympathize with that ... but crazy, never! The family honor is at stake."

"Well, what should we do?" I said helplessly. As the junior member of the family, I had no say in the matter at all. I was annoyed at Mary for mentioning psychiatrists, but I reminded myself that she was, after all, a barbarian, even though she could speak a human tongue after a fashion.

"We'll wait," grandmother said, "and see whether your father's penance will do the trick. If not ... well, our stars are bad, that's all."

* * *

During the weeks to come, my brother became increasingly odd. He would enter the house without even removing his sandals, let alone washing his feet.

Dragon's Fin Soup

When my Uncle Eed came to dinner one night, my brother actually pointed his left foot at our honored uncle's head. I would be most surprised if Uncle Eed ever came to dinner again after such unforgivable rudeness. I was forced to go into town every evening to dub the movies, which I did in so lackluster a manner that our usual audience began walking the two hours to Ban Kraduk for their entertainment. My heart sank when a passing visitor to the shop told me that the Ban Kraduk cinema had actually installed a projection sound system and could show talkies … not only the foreign films, with sound and subtitles, but the new domestic talkies … so you could actually find out what great actors like Mitr and Petchara sounded like! I knew we'd never compete with that. I knew the days of live movie dubbing were numbered. Maybe I could go to Bangkok and get a job with Channel Seven, dubbing "Leave it to Beaver" and "Charlie's Angels." But Bangkok was just about as distant as another galaxy, and I could imagine the fun those city people would have with my hick northern accent.

One night about two weeks later, Mary and I were awakened by my brother, moaning from the mosquito net next to ours. I went across.

"Oh, there you are," Phii Lek said. "I've been trying to attract your attention for hours."

"I was busy," I said, and my brother leered knowingly. "Are you all right? Are you recovered?"

"Not exactly," he said. "But I'm, well, off-duty. The alien'll come back any minute, though, so I can't talk long." He paused. "Maybe that girlfriend of yours should hear this" he said. At that moment Mary crept in beside us, and we crouched together under the netting. The electric fan made the nets billow like ghosts.

"You have to take me to that archaeological dig of yours," he said. "There's an artifact … it's got some kind of encoded information … you have to take it back to Professor Übermuth at UCLA—"

"I've heard of him!" Mary whispered. "He's in a loony bin. Apparently he became convinced he was an extraterre—oh, Jesus!" she said in English.

"He is one," Phii Lek said. "So am I. There are hundreds us on this planet. But my controlling alien's resting right now. Look, Ai Noi, I want you to go down to the kitchen and get me as many chili peppers as you can find. On the *manus tang dao's* home planet the food is about as bland as rice soup."

I hurried to obey. When I got back, he wolfed down the peppers until he started weeping from the influx of spiciness. Suspiciously I said, "If you're really an alien, what about spaceships?"

"Spaceships … we do have them, but they are drones, taking millennia to reach the center of the galaxy. We ourselves travel by tachyon psychic transference. But the device is being sent by drone."

"Device?"

"From the excavation! Haven't you been listening? It's got to be dug up and secretly taken to America and … I'm not sure what or why, but I get the feeling there's danger if we don't make our rendezvous. Something to do with upsetting the tachyon fields."

"I see," I said, humoring him.

"You know what I look like on the home planet, up there? I look like a giant *mangdaa*."

"What's that?" said Mary.

"It's sort of a giant cockroach," I said. "We use its wings to flavor some kinds of curry."

"Yeuch!" she squealed. "Eating insects. Gross!"

"What do you mean? You've been enjoying it all week, and you've never complained about eating insects," I said. She started to turn slightly bluish. A *farang's* complexion, when he or she is about to be sick, is one of the few truly indescribable hues on the face of this earth.

"Help me …" Phii Lek said. "The sooner this artifact is unearthed and loaded onto the drone, the sooner I'll be released from this—oh, no, it's coming back!" Frantically he gobbled down several more chilies. But it was too late. They came right back up again, and he was scampering around the room on all fours and emitting pigeon-like cooing noises.

"Come to think of it," I said, "he is acting rather like a cockroach, isn't he?"

* * *

A week later our home was invaded by nine monks. My mothers had been cooking all the previous day, and when I came into the main living room they had already been chanting for about an hour, their bass voices droning from behind huge prayer fans. The house was fragrant with jasmine and incense.

I prostrated myself along with the other members of the family.

My brother was there too, wriggling around on his belly; his hands were tied up with a sacred rope which ran all the way around the house and through the folded palms of each of the monks. Among them was my father, who looked rather self-conscious and didn't seem to know all the words of the chants yet ... now and then he seemed to be opening his mouth at random, like a goldfish.

"This isn't going to work," I whispered to my grandmother, who was kneeling in the *phabphieb* position with her palms folded, her face frozen in an expression of beatific piety. "Mary and I have found out what the problem is, and it's not possession."

"*Buddhang sarnang gacchami,*" the monks intoned in unison.

"What are they talking about?" Mary said. She was properly prostrate, but seemed distracted. She was probably uncomfortable without her trusty notebook.

"I haven't the faintest, idea. It's all in Pali or Sanskrit or something," I said.

"*Namodasa phrakhavato arahato—*" the monks continued inexorably.

At length they laid their prayer fans down and the chief *luangphoh* doused a spray of twigs in a silver dipper of lustral water and began to sprinkle Phii Lek liberally.

"It's got to be over soon," I said to Mary. "It's getting toward noon, and you know monks are not allowed to eat after 12 o'clock."

As the odor of incense wafted over me and the chanting continued, I fell into a sort of trance. These were familiar feelings, sacred feelings. Maybe my brother was in the grip of some supernatural force that could be driven out by the proper application of Buddha, Dharma, and Sangkha. However, as the *luangphoh* became ever more frantic, waving the twigs energetically over my writhing brother to no avail, I began to lose hope.

Dragon's Fin Soup

Presently the monks took a break for their one meal of the day, and we took turns presenting them with trays of delicacies. After securing my brother carefully to the wall with the sacred twine, I went to the kitchen, where my grandmother was grinding fresh betelnut with a mortar and pestle. To my surprise, my father was there too. It was rather a shock to see him wearing a saffron robe and bald, when I was so used to seeing him barechested with a *phakomaah* loosely wrapped about his loins, and with a whiskey bottle rather than a begging bowl in his arms. I did not know whether to treat him as father or monk. To be on the safe side, I fell on my knees and placed my folded palms reverently at his feet.

My father was complaining animatedly to my grandmother in a weird mixture of normal talk and priestly talk. Sometimes he'd remember to refer to himself as *atma*, but at other times he'd speak like anyone off the street. He was saying, "But mother, *atma* is miserable, they only feed you once a day, and I'm hornier than ever! It's obviously not going to work, so why don't I just come home?"

My grandmother continued to pound vigorously at her betelnut.

"Anyway, *atma* thinks that it's time for more serious measures. I mean, calling in a professional exorcist."

At this, my grandmother looked up. "Perhaps you're right, holy one," she said. I could see that it galled her to have to address her wayward son-in-law in terms of such respect. "But can we afford it?"

"Phra Boddhisatphalo, *atma's* guru, is an astrologer on the side, and he's says that the stars for the movie theater are exceptionally bad. Well, *atma* was thinking, why not perform an act of merit while simultaneously ridding ourselves of a potential financial liability? I say sell out the half-share of the cinema and use the proceeds to hire a really competent exorcist. Besides," he added slyly, "with the rest of the cash I could probably obtain me one of those nieces of yours, the ones whose beauty your daughters are always bragging about."

"You despicable cad," my grandmother began, and then added, "holy one," to be on the safe side of the karmic balance.

"Honored father and grandmother," I ventured, "have you not considered the notion that Phii Lek's body might indeed be inhabited by an extraterrestrial being?"

"I fail to see the difference," my father said, "between a being from another planet and one from another spiritual plane. It is purely a matter of attitude. You and your brother, whose wits have been addled by exposure to too many American movies, think in terms of visitations from the stars; your grandmother and I, being older and wiser, know that 'alien' is merely another word for spirit. Earthly or unearthly, we are all spokes in the wheel of karma, no? Exorcism ought to work on both ."

I didn't like my father's new approach at all; I thought his drunkenness far more palatable than his piety. But of course this would have been an unconscionably disrespectful thing to say, so I merely *wai-ed* in obeisance and waited for the ordeal to end.

My grandmother said, "Well, son-in-law, I can see a certain progress in you after all." My father turned around and winked at me. "Very well," she said, sighing heavily, "perhaps your mentor can find us a decent exorcist. But none of those foreigners, mind you," she added pointedly as Mary entered the kitchen to fetch another tray of comestibles for the monks' feast.

* * *

The interview with the spirit doctor was set for the following week. By that time the wonder of my brother's possession had attracted tourists from a radius of some ten kilometers; his performances were so spectacular as to outdraw even the talking cinema in Ban Kraduk.

It turned out to be a Brahmin, tall, dark, white-robed, with a long white beard that trailed all the way down to the floor. He wore a necklace of bones—they looked suspiciously human—and several flower wreaths over his uncut, wispy hair; moreover he had an elaborate third eye painted in the middle of his forehead.

"*Narayana, Narayana*," he said, with the portentousness of a paunchy *deva* in one of those Indian historical movies. This, I realized, was a sham to impress the credulous populace, who were swarming around the stilts of our house. One or two children were peering from behind the horns of water buffaloes, and one was even peeping from a huge rainwater jar. The Brahmin had an accolyte just for the purpose of removing his sandals and splashing his feet from the foot-washing trough, an occupation of such ignominy that I was surprised even a boy would stoop to it. He surveyed my family (which had been suddenly expanded by visiting cousins, aunts, uncles, and several other grandmothers junior to my own) and inquired haughtily, "And which of you is the possessed one?"

"He can't even tell?" my grandmother whispered to me. Then she pointed at Phii Lek, who was crawling around the front porch moaning "*tachyon, tachyon*."

"Ah," said the exorcist. "A classic case of possession by a *phii krasue*. Dire measures are indicated, I'm afraid."

At the mention of the dreaded *phii krasue*, the entire family recoiled as a single entity. For the *phii krasue* is, as everyone knows, a spirit who looks like a normal enough creature in the daytime, but at night detaches its head from its body and, dragging its entrails behind it, propels itself forward by its tongue. It also lives on human excrement. It is, in short, one of the most loathsome and feared of spirits. The idea that we might have been harboring one in our very house sent chills of terror through me.

Presently I heard dissenting voices. "But a *phii krasue* can't act this way in the daytime!" one said. "Anyway, where's the trail of guts?" said another. "This fellow's obviously a quack ... never trust a Brahmin exorcist, I tell you." "Well, let's give him the benefit. See if he comes up with anything."

The Brahmin spirit doctor took a good look at us, clearly appraising our finances. "Can he be cured?" my Elder Mother asked him.

"Given your very secure monetary standing," the Brahmin said, I see no reason why not. You can take him inside now; I shall discuss the—ah, your merit-making donation—with the head of the household."

My grandmother came forward, her palms uplifted in supplication. "Fetch him a drink," she muttered to my mothers.

My mother said, "Does the *than mor phii* want a glass of water? Or would he prefer Coca-Cola?"

"A glass of Mekong whiskey," said the spirit doctor firmly. "Better yet, bring the whole bottle. We'll probably be haggling all night."

* * *

Since Phii Lek was no longer the center of attention, Mary and I obeyed the spirit doctor and brought him inside. He chose that moment to snap back into a state of relative sanity. We knew he had come to because he immediately began demanding chili peppers.

"All right," he said at last. "I've been authorized to tell you a few more things, since it seems to be the only hope."

"What about that monstrous charlatan out there?" Mary said. "He's only going to delay your plans, isn't he?"

"Not necessarily. I want you to insist that he perform the exorcism at the archaeological dig. Once there, I'll be able to home in on the device and get rid of the giant cockroach at the same time. You know, that exorcist wasn't far wrong when he said I'd been possessed by a *phii krasue*. Would you be interested in knowing what my alien overlords like for dinner?"

I take it they're scavengers?" Mary said.

"Exactly," said my brother. "But no more of this excremental subject. You have to convince that exorcist of yours. Unless the device is returned, there will be awful consequences. You see, the aliens were here once before, about 800 years ago. They planted a number of these devices as ... well, tachyon calibration beacons. Well, this one is going dangerously out of sync, and some of the aliens aren't ending up in the bodies they're were destined for. I mean, this psychic transference business is expensive, and the military ruler of nine star systems doesn't want to get thrust into the body of a leprous janitor from Milwaukee. That is precisely what happened last week, and the diplomatic consequences happen to be rippling through the entire galaxy at this very minute. Anyway, if the beacon is sent back post-haste for deactivation, guess who gets it?"

"You?" I said.

"Worse. They call it a preventative measure. They randomize the solar system."

"I think that's a euphemism for—" Mary began.

"That's right, Beloved Younger Siblings! No more planet Earth."

"Can they really do that?" I said.

"They do it all the time." My brother reverted for a moment to cockroach-like behavior, then jerked back into a human pose with great effort. "They might not, though. All the xenobiologists, primitive cult fetishists, and so on are up in arms. So it might happen today ... it might happen in a couple of years ... it might never happen. Who knows? But galactic central thinks that no world, no matter how puny or insignificant, should be randomized without due process. But ... I don't think we should risk it, do you?"

"Maybe not," I said. The theory that my brother had contracted one of those American mental diseases, like schizophrenia, was becoming more and more

Dragon's Fin Soup

attractive to me. But I had to do what he said. To be on the safe side.

Mary and I left Phii Lek and went out to the porch, where the spirit doctor had consumed half the whiskey and they had lit the anti-mosquito tapers, whose smoke perfumed the dense night air.

"Excuse me, honored grandmother," I said, trying to sound as unassuming as I could, "but Phii Lek says he wants the exorcism done at Mary's archaeological dig."

"Ha!" the exorcist said. "One must always do the opposite of what a possessed person said, for the evil spirit in him strives always to delude us!" His sentiments were expressed with such resounding ferocity that there was a burst of applause from the crowd downstairs. "Besides," he added, "there's probably a whole army of *phii krasue* out there, just waiting to swallow us up. It's a trap, I tell you! This possession is merely the vanguard of a wholesale demonic invasion!"

I looked despairingly at Mary. "Now what'll we do?" I said. "Sit around waiting for the earth to disappear?"

It was Mary who came to the rescue ... and I realized how much she had absorbed by quietly observing us and taking all those notes. She said, speaking in a Thai far more heavily accented than she normally used, "But please, honored spirit doctor, the field study group would be most interested in seeing a real live exorcism!"

The spirit doctor looked decidedly uncertain at being addressed in Thai by a *farang*. I could tell the questions racing through his mind: what status should the woman be accorded? She wasn't related to any of these people, nor was her social position immediately obvious. How could he respond without accidentally using the wrong pronoun, and giving her too much or little status—and perhaps rendering himself the laughingstock of these potential clients?

Taking advantage of his confusion, Mary pursued relentlessly. "Or does the honored spirit doctor perhaps *klua phii*?"

"Of course I'm not afraid of spirits!" the exorcist said.

"Then why would a few extra ones bother the honored spirit doctor?" Mary contrived to speak in so unprepossessing an accent that it was impossible to tell whether her polite words were ingenuous or insulting.

"Bah!" said the spirit doctor. "A few *phii krasue* are nothing. It's just a matter of convenience, that's all …"

"I'm sure that the foundation that's sponsoring our field research here would be more than happy to make a small donation toward ameliorating the inconvenience …"

"Since you put it that way …" the exorcist said, defeated.

"Hmpf!" my grandmother said, triumphantly yanking the half-bottle of whiskey away and sending my mother back to the kitchen with it. "These *farangs* might be some use after all. They're as ugly as elephants, of course—and albino elephants at that—but who knows? One day their race may yet amount to something."

* * *

Dragon's Fin Soup

The whole street opera of an exorcism was in full swing by the time my brother, Mary, and I pulled parked her official Landrover about a half hour's walk away from the site. It had taken a week to make the preparations, with my brother's moments of lucidity getting briefer and his eschatological claims wilder each time.

By the time we had trudged through fields of young rice, squishing knee-deep in mud, several hundred people had gathered to watch. A good 100 or so were relatives of mine. Mary introduced me to some colleagues of hers, professors and suchlike, and they eyed me with curiosity as I fumbled around in their intractable language.

Four broken pagodas were silhouetted in the sunset. A water buffalo nuzzled at the pediment of an enormous stone Buddha, to whom I instinctively raised my palms in respect. Here and there, erupting from the brilliant green of the fields of young rice, were fragments of fortifications and walls topped with complex friezes that depicted grim, barbaric gods and garlanded, singing *apsaras*. A row of trunkless stucco elephants guarded a gateway to another paddy field.

Every part of the ruined city had been girded round with a *saisin*, a sacred rope that had been strung up along the walls and along the stumps of the elephant trunks and through the stone portals and finally into the folded palms of the spirit doctor himself, who sat, in the lotus position, on a woven rush mat, surrounded by a cloud of incense.

"You're late," he said angrily as we hastened to seat ourselves within the protected circle. "Get inside, inside. Or do you want to be swallowed up by spirits?"

If I had thought Phii Lek's actions bizarre before, his performance now shifted into an even more hyperbolic gear. He groaned. He danced about, his body coiling and uncoiling like a serpent.

I heard my grandmother cry out, "*Ui ta then*! Nuns dropping in the basement!" It was the strongest language I'd ever heard her use.

Mary clutched my hand. Some of my relatives stared disapprovingly at the impropriety, but I decided that they were just jealous.

"And now we'll see which it is to be," Mary said. "Science fiction or fantasy."

"He's mumbling himself into a trance now," I said, pointing to the exorcist, who had closed his eyes and from whose lips a strange buzzing issued.

"Are you sure he's not snoring?" one of my mothers said maliciously.

"What tranquillity! What perfect *samadhi*!" my other mother said admiringly, for the spirit doctor hadn't moved a muscle in some ten minutes.

Phii Lek's contortions became positively unnerving. He darted about the sacred circle, now and then flapping his arms as though to fly. Suddenly a bellow—like the cry of an angry water buffalo—burst from his lips. He flapped again and again—and then rose into the air!

"Be still, I command thee!" the exorcist's voice thundered, and he waved a rattle at my levitating brother and made mysterious passes. I tell thee, be still!"

A ray of light shot upward from the earth, dazzlingly bright. The pagodas were lit up eerily. The ground opened up under Phii Lek as he hovered. There he was, brilliantly lit up in the pillar of radiance, with

Dragon's Fin Soup

an iridescent aura around him whose outlines vaguely resembled an enormous cockroach...

The crowd was going wild now. They clamored, they cheered; some of the children were disobeying the sacred cord and having to be restrained by their elders. My brother was sitting, in lotus position, in the middle of the air with his palms folded, looking just like a postcard of the Emerald Buddha in Bangkok.

The flaming apparition that had been my brother descended into the pit. We all rushed to the edge. The light from the abyss burned our eyes; we were blinded. Mary took advantage of the confusion to embrace me tightly; I was too overwhelmed to castigate her.

We waited.

The earth rumbled.

At last a figure crawled out. He was covered in mud and filth. He was clutching something under his arm ... something very much like a Ming spittoon.

"Phii Lek!" I cried out, overcome with relief that he was still alive.

"The tachyon calibrator—" he gasped, holding aloft the spittoon and waving it dramatically in the air. "You must get it to ..."

He fainted, still clasping the alien device firmly to his bosom.

The light shifted ... the ghostly, rainbow-fringed giant cockroach seemed to drift slowly across the field, toward the unmoving figure of the exorcist ... it danced grotesquely above his head, and he began to twitch and foam at the mouth ...

"I'll be dead!" my grandmother shouted. "The spirit is transferring itself into the body of the exorcist!"

In a moment the exorcist too fainted, and the sacred cord fell from his hands. The circle was broken. Whatever was done was done.

I rushed to the side of my brother, still lying prone by the side of the abyss.

"Wake up!" I said, shaking him. "Please wake up!"

He got up and grinned. Applause broke out. The exorcist, too, seemed to be recovering from his ordeal.

"And now," my brother said, holding out the alien artifact, "I can return this thing to the person who was sent to fetch it."

A small, white, palpitating hand was stretched forward to receive it. I turned to see who it was. "Oh, no," I said softly.

For it was Mary who had taken the artifact … and Mary who was now gyrating about the paddy field in a most unfeminine, most cockroach-like manner.

* * *

Later that night, Phii Lek and I sat on the floor of our room, waiting for Mary to snap out of her extraterrestrial seizure so we could find out what had happened.

Toward dawn the alien gave her her first break. "I can talk now," she said, suddenly, calmly.

"Do you need chilies?" I said.

"I think a good hamburger would be more my style," she said.

"We could probably fake it," my brother said, "if you don't mind having it on rice instead of a bun."

"Well," she said, when my brother had finished clattering about the kitchen fixing this unorthodox meal, and she was sitting cross-legged on my bedding munching furiously, "I suppose I should tell you what I'm allowed to tell you."

"Take your time," I said, not meaning it.

"Okay. Well, as you know, the exorcist is a total fake, a charlatan, a mountebank. But he does enter a passable state of *samadhi,* and apparently this was close enough to the psychic null state necessary for psychic transference to enable a mind-swap to occur over a short distance. His blank mind was a sort of catalyst, if you will, through which, under the influence of the tachyon calibrator, I could leave Phii Lek's mind and enter Mary's."

"So you'll be taking the spittoon back to America?" I said.

"Right on schedule. And it's not a spittoon. That happens to be a very clever disguise."

"So ..." It suddenly occurred to me that she would soon be leaving. I was irritated at that. I didn't know why. I should have been pleased, because, after all, I had essentially traded her for my brother, and family always comes first.

"Look," she said, noticing my unease, "do you think ... maybe ... one last time?" She caressed my arm.

"But you're a giant cockroach!" I said.

She kissed me.

"You've been bragging to your friends all month about 'arriving' in America, she said. "How'd you like to 'arrive' on another planet?"

* * *

In the middle of the act I became aware that someone else was there with us. I mean, I was used to the way Mary moved, the delicious abandon with which she made her whole body shudder. I thought, "The alien's here too! Well, I'm really going to show it how a Thai can drive. Here we go!"

The next morning, I said, "How was it?"

She said, "It was a fascinating activity, but frankly I prefer mitosis."

Fiddling for water buffaloes.

* * *

In a day or so I saw her off; I went back to the antique store; I found my grandmother hard at work in her antique faking studio. A perfect Ming spittoon lay beside her where she squatted. She saw me, spat out her betelnut, and motioned me to sit.

"Why, grandmother," I said, "That's a perfect copy of whatever it was the alien took to America."

"Look again, my grandson," she said, and chuckled to herself as she rocked back and forth kneading clay.

I picked it up. The morning light shone on it through the window. I had an inkling that …no. Surely not. "You didn't!" I said.

She didn't answer.

"Grandmother …"

No answer.

"But the solar system is at stake!" I blurted out. "If they find out that they've got the wrong tachyon callibrator …"

"Maybe, maybe not," said my grandmother. "The way I think is this: it's obviously very important to

Dragon's Fin Soup

someone, and anything that valuable is worth faking. You say these interstellar diplomats will be arguing the question for years, perhaps. Well, as the years go by, the price will undoubtedly go up."

"But Khun Yaa, how can you possibly play games with the destiny of the entire human race like this?"

"Oh, come, come. I'm just an old woman looking out for her family. The movie house has been sold, and we've lost maybe 50,000 baht on the exorcism and the feast. Besides, your father will insist on another wife, I'm afraid, and after all this brouhaha_I can't blame him. We'll be out 100,000 baht by the time we're through. I have a perfect right to some kind of recompense. Hopefully, by the time they come looking for this thing, we'll be able to get enough for it to open a whole antique factory ... who knows, move to Bangkok ... buy up Channel Seven so your brother can dub movies to his heart's content."

"But couldn't the alien tell?" I said.

"Of course not. How many experts on disguised tachyon callibrators do you think there are, anyway?" My grandmother paused to turn the electric fan so that it blew exclusively on herself. The air-conditioning, as usual, was off. "Anyway, *manus tang dao* are only another kind of foreigner, and anyone can tell you that all foreigners are suckers."

I heard the bell ring in the front.

"Go on!" she said. "There's a customer!"

"But what if—" I got up with some trepidation. At the partition I hesitated.

"Courage!" she whispered. "Be a *luk phuchai*!"

I remembered that I had the family honor to think of. Boldly, I marched out to meet the next customer.

The Last Time I Died in Venice

He beckoned to me in the dying sun.

Venice? What a joke. The Venice of the East. Some antediluvian travel brochures still call it that, but the canals were filled in before I was born, and now a skein of highways and overpasses covers the city like a threadworn yarmulke. Instead of the *vaporetto*, there's fleets of neon-colored taxis; if you fancy a gondola, hop on the back of a brimstone-belching motorcycle taxi and weave like a maniac through harrowing streets; here you don't sit sipping a capuccino on the Lido, gazing at the hazy sea, but instead, nursing that selfsame capuccino, perched on the eighth level of an endless shopping mall, staring, glazed, at the consuming throng.

The name of that coffee nook is, ironically, The Rialto ...

The second day of my thirty-ninth trip to Bangkok. A computer conference, this time, coupled with an Interpol sting of a RISC-chip pirating consortium; not even time for a massage yet. But I had to make time for my old friend Bob Halliday, who is to me as Virgil was to Dante. Bob knows everything, from the arcane declensions of Finnish irregular nouns to the dialectic nuances of Malaysian shadow puppets. He is very humble about it all, though one does detect a certain smugness.

The Rialto, situated as it was in one of the four catty-corner shopping malls that loom over the infamous Brahma shrine in the busiest intersection of Bangkok, was as good a place as any to watch the chaos go by. It had a Venetian motif; there was a mural of the Piazza San Marco, in front of which a toothless crone pounded green papaya and chili right next to the espresso machines.

I was born within a stone's throw of here, but I try not to think about it when I'm debugging search-and-replace algorithms in Jacuzzi County, California. I belong here, in the embrace of a beautiful, dying woman.

"We can't stay too long, Chai," Bob said. "If you sit here for more than 15 minutes, you're bound to run into someone you want to avoid." In a city of seven million, there are only a few players, and each has his own turf. "Look: there's Khunying Ingsuwan, the gossip columnist for *Siam Daily Times*—she's got her notebook out and peering at us like an interrupted mink." We both laughed. "And over there, for example—don't turn your head—is Dr. Phetch. 'Phetch 'n' Carry', we call him at the *Post*. He owns the virtual whorehouse concession; pays a pretty penny for it in protection, I understand."

"Protection?" I said. "From what?"

"Prostitution is still illegal here in the sex capital of the world …"

Dragon's Fin Soup

"But surely it's different, fucking a computer … victimless crime and all that …"

Bob laughed. "Bangkok," he said, "is not like other cities. The part is the whole. The illusion is the reality. Look around and you'll see all the trappings of the twenty-first century—the buildings shaped like giant robots, the shopping malls with built-in roller coasters, and the cellular faxes spitting out onto the upholstery of every chauffeur-driven Mercedes that's jammed into the alley—but just below the surface there's—well, a kind of churning emptiness."

"You mean, the diseased blood beneath the skin of a beautiful woman … all that crap," I said.

Bob merely laughed, and said, "There's a sleazy dive across the river I've gotta take you to—they make a *khao man gai* that'll have you coming in your Calvins."

From the stereo section of a department store came the continuous cussing of Snoop Doggy Dog; the endless fucks and bitches sounded curiously innocent here; they had no power to shock; it was just background music. Bob knows many things, though his ostensible job description is as food critic for the *Bangkok Post*. His girth betrays his occupation. His Thai friends call him Elephant, a nickname he bears proudly.

I took a good look at the cadaverous Dr. Phetch. He was sipping a capuccino, working on a green papaya salad and a laptop. He turned to me and smiled. That, in Thailand, can be the kiss of death.

"Shit!" said Bob. "He's noticed you."

Dr. Phetch was slowly working his way through the maze of little tables. At every marble-topped table, he was accosted by someone: an overripe matron in diamonds and silk, a man in a yellow suit with a cellular phone in each hand, a Japanese businessman with a Louis Vuitton briefcase. He paused at each table, long enough to show his attentiveness, briefly enough to show his arrogance; but he was clearly coming our way, and there was no way to extricate ourselves without making tomorrow's gossip column.

"Khun Chai, isn't it?" he said, or rather growled, that tiger-on-the-prowl sort of growl. "You're one of those LA Thais," he said, long-haired, denim-clad, disrespectful. And," he added, "you're investigating me."

"No he isn't," Bob said, but the protestations of a food critic were of no interest to him; it wouldn't have done for him even to notice Bob's existence.

"We are small potatoes, Khun Chai. You should leave us alone."

"My company just wants to get a sense of who's copying our look and feel," I said. "If you really are small potatoes, they won't do anything. But we never expected our code to be used for something so depraved as ... you know." That was a barefaced lie. Sex was the one use we were counting on to keep expanding our user base.

"Have you ever desired something, Khun Chai ... something that tantalizes you ... something that never quite seems to arrive within your grasp ... that drives you insane with unfulfillment?

"No," I said.

He raised an eyebrow. "Nothing at all? I am a little surprised. You see, we are not without our own investigators. It should not surprise you that the observer is himself observed. There is something you yearn for. That's why you keep coming back. And once we find out what it is—"

Dragon's Fin Soup

"No," I said again, but couldn't look at him, because I had just seen, with my peripheral vision, just what he was talking about. A shadow, a glance, a blurry movement, a creature from a half-forgotten dream. She beckoned to me in the dying sun, only there was no sun, only the flickering neon of a malfunctioning McDonalds sign.

"Then why," he said, "are you in Bangkok?" And thrust a business card into my half-drained capuccino.

* * *

"Something," said Bob, "is haunting you, Chai."

We had fled the shopping mall. We were in a *tuk-tuk*, weaving through the pollution at breakneck speed—the traffic, unaccountably, had abated. Bob lent me only half an ear; mostly he was typing furiously on his laptop, which he'd plugged into his cellular modem; now and then he paused, nodded, typed again.

"That's true," I said, "but I don't really know what it is … a sense of rootlessness, maybe."

The business card read:

Misled by morality? Limited by laws?
All you desire can be virtually yours.

There was a phone number.

"Lend me your phone," I said.

Dying, she beckoned to me in the sun –

I blinked again. The *tuk-tuk* rounded a corner, wheezing and farting, and we were somewhere in Silom. She beckoned to me, her arms outstretched, a jasmine garland in one hand, the oily sunlight glancing off her nut-brown flesh, and—

"Can't," said Bob.

"And then when I come here I always see things," I said. "Things that I know aren't really there. Shroom flashbacks maybe. I keep thinking there's someone, you know, calling out to me. A woman. A dying woman."

"How Freudian. Is it your mother? I know a good exorcist."

"Fuck you," I said. I don't have a mother. I'm an R&R brat. But I was brought up by many Thai women, interchangeable; my dad had very predictable tastes. "Give me that phone."

"Wait," said Bob. "I'm deeply ensconced in this *Finnegans Wake* IRC. It's amazing. There's this monk in Hungary who has compiled eight thousand glosses on the first chapter, and he's going to upload it all to his web page."

I glanced over at his laptop screen. It was scrolling insanely—not a word of English, or Thai for that matter. "Bob—"

He tapped a few more keystrokes and told the driver to let us off. "The *khao man gai* place," he said, "is down that alley a ways."

Silom was still an oven, even though the sun was setting. The vendors of fake Rolexes, fake software, and fake designer clothes were all erecting their stands, and the barkers were already shuffling about, looking to entice tourists into live shows; I took Bob's phone in one hand and followed him as he skillfully infiltrated the throng. Bangkok doesn't smell like any other city—there's not that heady melange of exhaust fumes and jasmine, vomit and mangoes, incense and stale fish. The neon was starting to come on. Bankers, hustlers, shamans, and lottery ticket vendors conferred under the garish teal, electric green, bubble-gum pink.

"It can't hurt to call them," I said. "It's virtual. It's fictional. None of it is true."

"And what," he said, "is truth?"

"Don't crucify me," I said.

"I wash my hands of the whole thing," He paused as though he expected a laughtrack to click on.

"A Pilate for a new sitcom," I said.

"*Touché*. But you'll regret it. Dr. Phetch, I am sure, has your number. Don't let him hack your soul."

Soon we were wolfing down chicken and rice in a shithole perched above an, open sewer, and I was reading my Visa card number to an operator at the virtual whorehouse.

* * *

Dying, she beckons to me in the setting sun—

I've sampled most of the unsavory delights Bangkok has to offer: safely of course, ever so safely, always with my American-made condoms. Didn't really set foot here until I was full grown—well, maybe when I was little—but I thought I knew Thai women—all those stepmothers. They cook a lot. They're very smothering. They drive you to school and they drive to the supermarket and they go to the temple in North Hollywood on Sundays and eat barbecued pork, and they refuse to speak English and they lie in bed watching television until your Dad comes home to fuck them.

My real mother's dead, I've heard. When she got sick, Dad shipped her back to the brothel. Maybe Bob was right. Maybe the woman who haunted me was part of some kind of sick Oedipal fantasy.

I think of her, in the sunset, dying, beckoning to me. She used to wear a Brahma amulet around her neck. Brahma is good for business. I played with it when I suckled. Thai women will breast-feed long after Dr. Spock tells you to stop.

"I'm going to be thirty soon," I told Bob, "and even though I've had a shitload of sexual encounters, I've still never loved anyone."

"That's the Thai in you," Bob said. "Christians have love. Love thy neighbor, love this, love that. Buddhists have compassion. It puts a completely different spin on existence. Of course, Buddhists don't really believe in existence, either."

We ate in silence. For a moment, the waitress reminded me of someone. I considered tipping her, but of course I didn't. Mustn't give them ideas.

* * *

The first thing they do at the virtual whorehouse is ask you a lot of questions. You say the first thing that comes into your head. They ply you with stiff drinks and there's a masseuse working over your feet the whole time; that's so you'll relax and spit out your true nature. Another woman in an Armani suit, very butch, keys your answers into a mega-profile that supposedly helps the computer to select the right, ah, scenario.

They didn't tell me any of this. But I recognized the questions. I recognized the program. It was sort of a second-generation Minsky AI thing. I wrote part of the code myself.

I also had to look at images that flashed by on a monitor while a potentiometer measured my penile tension. Shades of scientology. The girl who took down

Dragon's Fin Soup

the figures giggled now and then, and sucked on the juice of a coconut. Bob had run off to interview some big director passing through town—I don't know who, maybe Polanski.

The whole thing was transpiring in the basement of a nudie bar. The room was quite Spartan; its only decoration was a 'Thailand, the Golden Paradise' poster. In a wall niche was a statue of Nang Kwak, the goddess that draws in customers, one hand beckoning, the other daintily pressed against her hip.

Respond to the following words:
leather
jockstrap
breasts
big
mother
death.

* * *

"Have you visited us before, Khun Chai?" said the young woman who was zipping me into the suit. The clothes went back on over the second skin. Zippers are good. In classical Thai dance, they sew you into the clothes; one of my stepmothers told me that. The bodily fluids stay in.

"Why do you ask?"

"It seems, your sexual odyssey is on the house. You know important people, big people maybe, yes?"

So they were going to entertain me into ignoring their intellectual property peccadilloes. "Tell Dr. Phetch," I said, "that this better be good."

"It will be."

There was no huge contraption to strap on … no glorified dentist's chair. They just laid me down on a couch. The goggles went on. I was blind.

"Any special request? People from your country usually go for one of the pedo fantasies."

"No. Just play back what the computer says to play back."

I flexed my fingers. Hardly felt a thing. This dermoplast was good shit. Like a full body condom with a million nerve-endings sewn into its lining. I hadn't realized it was quite this snug. Like nothing at all.

"Time for your tailor-made trip," said the hostess.

Everything went black for a moment.

* * *

So I come to, and I'm in the same room, with the same vile disco music jangling upstairs. Something's changed. Is it the lighting? It's got to be video, it can't be reality. The colors are too vibrant, the audio too perfectly EQ'd. And then there's the fact that the walls are shimmering, that the geckoes are running too swiftly along the gray concrete. I blink again and the walls dissolve.

I'm moving slowly down a corridor. Not a corridor but a narrow alley … one of the tiny *sois* that interlace the city. Crowded. They've done that Bangkok smell just right, but sharpened it with a tinge of … I don't know, some sexual pheromone maybe. I'm drifting down the alley. I can't tell if the drifting sensation is from something that was in my drink or if it's part of the virtual reality experience. The alley narrows and until finally there's only room for one …

Dragon's Fin Soup

my footsteps echo ... I hear voices whispering ... there's a lot of mist ... and I see the open doorways ... I pause outside each one for the merest moment, sensing that the proffered diversions are not for me ... here a naked dwarf, twisting her own nipples with two pairs of pliers ... here a Rapunzel draped in her own hair ... a choirboy with a see-through surplice ... I'm curious about these delights, but not aroused. The corridor narrows some more. The pheromonal odor is more powerful now. It seems to be sweating out of the very stucco. Go ahead. Look in every doorway. Sirens entice me. A three-hundred-pound ebony woman with a slave collar and strange tribal scars. Go on, try it. It's safe in here. You can do anything. Anything at all because it's not real.

Deeper, deeper into the labyrinth.
She beckons to me in the dying sun—

How? It's the last doorway. It's the woman who has haunted my dreams. She's not beautiful; not at first. Her cheeks are hollow, her eyes listless, her jaundice-colored skin sags against a tattered sarong that's held up by a chain of silver links; she too stretches her arms out to me, calls me by name: Chai, Chai, Chai.

"Who are you?" I say softly.

"You don't have to ask," she says in Thai—Thai with a lilting provincial quality to it; she's a peasant woman; perhaps she's not as old as she looks; they wear out quickly, these upcountry girls. "I been standing here, waiting for you, all your life long." She is beautiful after all. She wears a Brahma amulet around her neck.

"You're my mother?" I blurt out.

"Mother, sister, maiden, crone, it no matter; I'm the thing inside you long long time; your mind make me flesh."

In the back of my mind I'm thinking, Jesus, this is convincing, they've spiked the program somehow, done a shitload of fancy crunching, maybe called in the Taiwanese. How it managed to pluck this image from my one-word answers to a questionnaire ... then reconstitute it out of the stored characteristics of a thousand women ... the verisimilitude of it's bowling me over, but I've got to keep my cool.

"I can't make love to you," I say. "Not if you're —"

She smiles. "Who else you make love to," she says, "if not me?"

"But you're dying—" The contagion is inside her. Didn't they ship her back to the whorehouse to die? Isn't she long gone, burned to a crisp in a funeral pyre, her ashes in an urn somewhere? Is that what my secret desire really is ... to die from the embrace of a dying woman?

Sadly, she shakes her head. "Inside you, I never die. Come home to me now, my son."

I guess it's a little too real for me. I stumble back. Go into one of the other rooms ... not even sure which one now ... I think it's that black earth goddess, who envelops me in her folds and wiggles me to sleep.

* * *

Had breakfast with Bob—he actually came to my hotel—because he was on his way to the *Post* to deliver his review of the *khao man gai*. Couldn't upload it because his hard drive crashed. The hotel has a great

Dragon's Fin Soup

river view, Temple of Dawn and everything, from one side of the top story dining room, but the other side overlooks a slum. To the left, you can imagine Somerset Maugham on a rattan chair, checking out the waiters' butts; to the right, it's Sally Struthers saving the children. They're building a big wall around the eyesore, having it painted, actually, with murals that give a sort of history of European art: there's Michelangelo's *Adam and Eve* being driven from paradise, for instance, and, oh, a colorized *Guernica.*

"Bangkok is just a big old movie set," Bob said, gazing glumly at the construction work. "They move the walls around, hey, presto, it's somewhere else. It's a chameleon of a city; it can imitate any other city. It's a virus of a city, copying other cities' DNA, insinuating itself into their genes."

"So you think I should have fucked her," I asked Bob, who was carefully lining up the dried shrimp, shortest to tallest, before dunking them in his rice soup.

"You said it, not me," Bob said.

I mean, you're saying that because it's all an illusion anyway, I might as well play out the Oedipal scenario, because that way, who knows, I might work through the trauma of my deprived childhood?"

"Sigmund couldn't have put it better," said Bob, "but I really don't know why you're asking me these things ... you seem to have decided already."

"Dr. Phetch is actually addressing the delegates today," I said. "He's going to offer some kind of rationale for his intellectual piracy."

Far below, I thought I saw the phantom woman by the river's edge. She was less dreamlike than she'd ever been before. I watched her for a while; it seemed to me that she was catching the water bus to Chinatown.

Almost too mundane to be a figment of my tortured inner life.

"She won't get out of my waking life," I said, "so maybe you're right, maybe I should, you know, get it over with."

"The hero slays the dragon-earth-mother and sets himself free so he can love the princess," Bob said.

"That's Jung, not Freud."

"Don't I know it!"

I fixed Bob's hard drive over a capuccino, and used it to send an email to the virtual whorehouse.

* * *

The landscape is more twisted than before. I'm moving more swiftly, too; I know the doors I don't want to look into. Not the pouting beauties with their heaving breasts. Not the dainty little half women with their chocolate smiles. I move further and further into the labyrinth. She's always just out of reach, in the shadow of a coconut tree, hidden behind the awning-flap of a souvenir stall. Children run underfoot, touting their lottery tickets and their souls. The smells are so intense I can hardly breathe. Sweat hangs in the air. The perfume of a decaying jasmine garland rises from a heap of garbage. I think I see a severed human hand.

Finally. the dingy room, the sunset, the window with the blood-red light striped noirishly by the Venetian blinds ...

"Come home to me, my son, my son."

She bares her breast to me. She is obviously dying. Her dugs process no milk. She touches my

Dragon's Fin Soup

head—that most profane of touchings and pulls me forward until my lips touch her bosom.

I fumble in my pants for a condom.

"Why you want be safe?" she whispers. "This not real, this fantasy, this a dream."

I can't help myself. I start to unwrap it anyway. Old habits die hard and all that. It's not a satisfactory coupling. I can feel the contagion boiling inside her, but I cannot bring myself to let it touch me.

But the contagion is the core of my unfulfilled longing ...

* * *

"Maybe that's what you really want," Bob said. This time, the eatery was the basement of a department store; you could trade in your little coupons for everything from pig's feet to a frankfurter.

Dr. Phetch was seriously under investigation now, and my own little observations about pilfered pieces of code were minor compared to what Interpol had on him; the Thai papers were full of his leering mug, but I couldn't read Thai well enough to know how far up shit creek he'd paddled.

"That's my forbidden fantasy? To have sex with my mother, catch AIDS, and die?"

I couldn't believe I'd actually said it. I hadn't said it to my therapist. I hadn't said it to my minister, in the year that I flirted with fundamentalism. I hadn't said it in confession, the year I converted to Catholicism.

"What other dime store analyses have you got to offer me?" I said. I was furious. I was shaking. Beads of sweat were dripping off my face into my bowl of blood-red, pungent *yentafo*. "Maybe you think I'm all guilted up because you think I think I somehow caused my mom to go away and I think I ought to pay for it?"

"I'm not the dime store analyst," Bob said calmly. "You're doing a pretty good job of it all by yourself."

* * *

That night, I actually do it. A mere 3,000 baht a pop on the old company credit card, why not? The labyrinth seems more and more endless ... the alleys branch off, twist, turn, like dividing viruses. There's an improvised quality about the streets, the buildings, the noodle stands; they're taking them up, putting them down, shuffling them, shifting them. Only the neon-tinged smog never changes. Only the fact that it's all too real, too clear, convinces me that this is a cybernetic simulacrum of the truth, illusion idealized.

And suddenly I come upon her, in a doorway, in a tattered sarong, in a shaft of teal-pink light that strobes over her tarnished features. Her eyes are my eyes and her lips my lips. She says to me, in a quiet voice that carries above the screeching of broken mufflers, "You're coming home to me at last, my son."

"But you're dead," I say.

"Not until you make me dead," she says. "Do you love me?"

She's not just my earthly mother, but she's the city that mothered me and spat me out. She's the darkness past forgetting, "I don't want to love you," I say softly, "But—"

"Then I will love you," she says, "the way only the dead can love,"

I toy with the Brahma amulet around her neck. I have a desperate need to suckle. She is beautiful after

Dragon's Fin Soup

all, though her breasts are speckled with tiny lesions. She enfolds me, and the world goes dark.

* * *

When I woke up, the tourist police were everywhere. Smashed computers all over the floors. Women in handcuffs. One of them—

This had to still be part of the illusion.

She stood between two policemen, haggard, the torn sarong tightly bound over her sagging breasts. She looked at me, stony-eyed. I said, "But you're not real."

She said, "What is reality?"

"But you told me lies ... you called me your son ... you let me indulge the darkest longings in myself ..."

She smiled sadly. Then she said to me in Thai, "You people think you're better than us because you left all this shit behind, you sit around in your American castles and look down on us like we're peasants."

"No I don't," I said.

"You wouldn't come back here if you didn't know you can still buy what you can't buy anywhere else. You can still buy love here, and you can still buy death."

They took her away. Later, I toured the labyrinth. The fog machines. The artificial alleyways that twisted and turned on casters, turning a few hundred square meters into a subterranean city, the odor generators, the cubicles where sat the women of our fantasies. The virtual world was a sham. The only computer output was the user profile, generated from those one-word answers by a program almost as antiquated as Eliza.

Why not? I thought bitterly. If you can fake a Rolex, a Super Nintendo cartridge, a Polo tennis shirt to perfection, why not go a step further and fake fakeness itself? Why bother with software when the cost of labor is so much lower? Dr. Phetch, I thought, is going to walk the plank for this.

I thought of the dying woman, and I began to wonder ...

* * *

She beckons to me, dying, in the setting sun ...

Today Bob comes to visit me in the hospital. My insurance cut me off, so I shipped myself to Bangkok to die. Dr. Phetch has become a cabinet minister, and nobody talks about the virtual whorehouse anymore, only about the possibilities of this technology for pilot training.

Bob brings me a new delicacy he has uncovered in the Northeast—a special kind of *laab* made with duck's heads and ground locusts. "I hope it's kept," he says. "I threw it in the fridge as soon as I got home, but you know, that five-hour traffic jam on the way back from the airport ..." He pauses. Looks at the display of orchids elegantly filling my window, masking my view of the pile-drivers as they put up another fifty-story condo. Reads the card. "Dr. Phetch sent you flowers?"

"Least he can do," I gasp, "considering he killed me."

"I brought you someone else, too," he says. A strange little woman totters in behind Bob. "She's a shamaness. She gets possessed by the god Brahma sometimes. Maybe she can help you ..."

"It's gotta be better for me than this AZT," I say.

Dragon's Fin Soup

The shamaness sits herself at the edge of my bed, in the lotus position, closes her eyes, and methodically begins putting herself in a trance. She wears a Brahma amulet around her neck, but otherwise there is no similarity.

"I should have known better," I say to Bob. "This is my own fucking fault. It was all too real to be virtual. I should have known better."

Bob smiles sadly in between mouthfuls. Crunching a duck's head in your teeth and spitting out the debris is an art form that still dazzles me. He lets me ramble on.

"Jesus," I say, "I'm actually gonna die."

He pats my hand.

"I should have known better. You were telling me all along, weren't you? You're the one who's always been saying, in this town, there's no distinction between the real world and the world of illusion. It's the only place in the world where all truths are true at the same time."

"Yeah," Bob says, "Bangkok is the north pole of existence; no matter which way you turn, it's all south."

Suddenly, the old woman begins to speak, in an eerie parody of a familiar voice: "Finally, you come home to me now, my son, my son."

And it's the truth.

Dragons Fin Soup Glossary

Ai hia—"you lizard"; an unspeakable obscenity
Bok choi—Chinese cabbage-like vegetable
Buat phra—to take holy orders
Cha shu bao—buns with pork filling
Cheongsam—the national dress for Thai women
Chiuchow—a region and dialect in China
Chok muay—boxing
Deva—Hindu "heavenly being or shining one" that lives on a higher spiritual plain
Farang—a slightly pejorative term for a white person
Gaeng kiow wan—green curry
Gaeng massaman—a curry made from chicken and potatoes that originated in the south of Thailand
Heng—"dry in taste"
Jongkabaen—a complex, formal brocaded trouser-like garment
Katoey—a transvestite or male homosexual of the passive variety

Khan—a vessel for scooping up water and aspersing oneself
Khao man gai—chicken with a special rice cooked in stock from the boiling chicken

Khao song—a medium or clairvoyant who tries to communicate with the dead like in a séance

Khii laad—to shit oneself

Khun—a respectful title: "your grace"

Khun mae—a respectful title for one's mother

Khun mae yai—a respectful title for a man's mother-in-law

Khun pii—"honored older sibling (or cousin)"

Khun por—a respectful title for one's father

Khun yaa—respectful title: "mother of my father"

Klua phii—"scared of ghosts"

Laab—a spicy dish from northeastern Thailand consisting of chopped meat chilies and onion

Luang poh—an respected elderly monk (check spelling)

Luk phuchai—"brave boy"

Mayom—a tree bearing fruit similar to a Western gooseberry

Naem sod—a salty and slightly fermented Thai pork sausage

Nagas—mythical serpents

Panung—a simple sarong-like skirt worn by women

Phakomaah—a homespun cloth wrapped about the legs

Phasin—a traditional Thai skirt, often made of richly embroidered silk

Phii—any sort of spirit, often malevolent

Pii—a shortened version of *khun pii*

Phnom mue—a humble gesture of reverence

Pinai—a Thai quadruple-reed soprano oboe
Plataphien—fish-like
Pohngkham—"protector"
Puangmalai—a garland of threaded flowers
Ramwong—a folk dance
Ranaat—a type of xylophone
Roti—a doughy dessert of Indian origin
Sadhu—an expression of reverence
Samadhi—a state of profound meditative concentration
Sangkha—any order or community of Buddhist monks
Shanti—peace, peacefulness
Soi—a narrow street leading off a large main road
Tambon—a district of a town or village
Taphon—a double-sided Thai drum
Thaokae—a term of respect for a Chinese businessman
Thephanoms—celestial beings
Vinyaan—soul or spirit
Wai—a respectful gesture, pressing the palms together

Yentafo—noodles in a vinegary, bright-red soup stock

S. P. Somtow
A Brief Biography

Once referred to by the *International Herald Tribune* as "the most well-known expatriate Thai in the world," Somtow Sucharitkul is no longer an expatriate, since he has returned to Thailand after five decades of wandering the world. He is best known as an award-winning novelist and a composer of operas.

Born in Bangkok, Somtow grew up in Europe and was educated at Eton and Cambridge. His first career was in music and in the 1970s he acquired a reputation as a revolutionary composer, the first to combine Thai and Western instruments in radical new sonorities. Conditions in the arts in the region at the time proved so traumatic for the young composer that he suffered a major burnout, emigrated to the United States, and reinvented himself as a novelist.

His earliest novels were in the science fiction field but he soon began to cross into other genres. In his 1984 novel Vampire Junction, he injected a new literary inventiveness into the horror genre, in the words of Robert Bloch, author of Psycho, "skillfully combining the styles of Stephen King, William Burroughs, and the author of the Revelation to John." Vampire Junction was voted one of the forty all-time greatest horror books by the Horror Writers' Association, joining established classics like Frankenstein and Dracula.

In the 1990s Somtow became increasingly identified as a uniquely Asian writer with novels such as the semi-autobiographical Jasmine Nights. He won the World Fantasy Award, the highest accolade given in the world of fantastic literature, for his novella The Bird Catcher. His fifty-three books have sold about two million copies world-wide.

After becoming a Buddhist monk for a period in 2001, Somtow decided to refocus his attention on the country of his birth, founding Bangkok's first international opera company and returning to music, where he again reinvented himself, this time as a neo-Asian neo-Romantic composer. The Norwegian government commissioned his song cycle Songs Before Dawn for the 100th Anniversary of the Nobel Peace Prize, and he composed at the request of the government of Thailand his Requiem: In Memoriam 9/11 which was dedicated to the victims of the 9/11 tragedy.

According to London's Opera magazine, "in just five years, Somtow has made Bangkok into the operatic hub of Southeast Asia." His operas on Thai themes, Madana, Mae Naak, and Ayodhya, have been well received by international critics. His most recent opera, The Silent Prince, was premiered in 2010 in Houston, and a fifth opera, Dan no Ura, will premiere in Thailand in the 2013 season. His sixth opera, Midsummer, will premiere in the UK in 2014.

He is increasingly in demand as a conductor specializing in opera and in the late-romantic composers like Mahler. His repertoire runs the entire gamut from Monteverdi to Wagner. His work has been especially lauded for its stylistic authenticity and its lyricism. The orchestra he founded in Bangkok, the Siam Philharmonic, is mounting the first complete Mahler cycle in the region.

He is the first recipient of Thailand's "Distinguished Silpathorn" award, given for an artist who has made and continues to make a major impact on the region's culture, from Thailand's Ministry of Culture.

Books by S. P. Somtow:

General Fiction

The Shattered Horse
Jasmine Nights
Forgetting Places
The Other City of Angels (Bluebeard's Castle)
The Stone Buddha's Tears

Dark Fantasy

The Timmy Valentine Series:
Vampire Junction
Valentine
Vanitas

Moon Dance
Darker Angels
The Vampire's Beautiful Daughter

Science Fiction

Starship & Haiku
Mallworld
The Ultimate Mallworld

Chronicles of the High Inquest:
Light on the Sound
The Darkling Wind
The Throne of Madness
Utopia Hunters
Chroniques de l'Inquisition - Volume 1 (omnibus)
Chroniques de l'Inquisition - Volume 2 (omnibus)

The Aquiliad Series:
Aquila in the New World
Aquila and the iron Horse
Aquila and the Sphinx

Fantasy

The Riverrun Trilogy:
Riverrun
Armorica
Yestern
The Riverrun Trilogy (omnibus)

The Fallen Country
Wizard's Apprentice

Media Tie-in

The Alien Swordmaster
Symphony of Terrror
The Crow - Temple of Night
Star Trek: Do Comets Dream?

Chapbooks

Fiddling for Waterbuffaloes
I Wake from a Dream of a Drowned Star City
A Lap Dance with the Lobster Lady

Libretti

Mae Naak
Ayodhya
Madana
The Silent Prince
Dan no Ura
Helena Citronova

Collections

My Cold Mad Father
Fire from the Wine Dark Sea
Chui Chai (Thai)
Nova (Thai)
The Pavilion of Frozen Women
Dragon's Fin Soup
Tagging the Moon

Face of Death (Thai)
Other Edens
S.P. Somtow's The Great Tales (Thai)
Other Edens

Essays, Poetry and Miscellanies

Opus Fifty
A Certain Slant of "I"
Sonnets about Serial Killers
Opera East
Victory in Vienna
Nirvana Express

Printed in Dunstable, United Kingdom